First Rains of Autumn

by Aubrey Diem

A novel of love and war in the Alps

To Ingrid
Thanks for all
your help and
support. with love -
Aubrey

Published by Media International, Waterloo, Ontario, Canada

Matterhorn from Zermatt

FIRST RAINS OF AUTUMN

A novel of love and war in the Alps

By Aubrey Diem

Media International
Copyright 1985/1992 by Aubrey Diem

PRINTED BY ALJON PRINT-CRAFT LIMITED
KITCHENER, ONTARIO CANADA

Canadian Cataloguing in Publication Data

Diem, Aubrey
    First rains of autumn + Enrico's War

The first title was prev. publ.: Waterloo, Ont.:
The author, 1985.
ISBN 0-9692291-5-1

1. World War, 1939-1945 - Fiction. 2. Loewenthal,
Enrico. 3. World War, 1939-1945 - Personal
narratives, Italian. 4 World War, 1939-1945 -
Personal narratives, Jewish. 5. World War, 1939-1945 -
Underground movements - Italy. I. Loewenthal, Enrico.
Enrico's war. II. Title.

PS8557.I45F57 1992   C813'.54   C92-0955620-9
PR9199.3.D53F57 1992

Copyright 1992 by Aubrey Diem

This novel is dedicated to the men and women who fought against the Fascist and Nazi terror in World War II, and especially to those who fought and died in the Valle d'Aosta, Italy.

The second writing is in memory of Primo Levi

"In a vivid insight, a flash of black lightning, he saw that all life was parallel: that evolution was not vertical, ascending to a perfection, but horizontal. Time was the great fallacy; existence was without history, was always now, was always this being caught in the same fiendish machine. All those painted screens erected by man to shut out reality--history, religion, duty, social position, all were illusions, mere opium fantasies."
FOWLES, **The French Lieutenant's Woman,** Little, Brown and Company, 1969.

Aubrey Diem

Aubrey Diem was born in Detroit, Michigan in 1931. He was educated there from elementary school to Wayne University. Later his graduate studies were completed at Clark University (MA) and the University of Michigan (PhD). Starting in 1954, he began travelling in Europe, and since has spent over 38 years exploring and observing Western and Eastern Europe, the Middle East, the Soviet Union, Japan, Mexico, and Canada. Much of that time has been spent hiking, climbing, skiing, and biking in the Alps. When in Europe he lives in the Alps in Zinal, Switzerland. He has guided students and professors throughout Eastern and Western Europe and in the spring of 1992 conducted a six weeks field course in Germany where he visited the major physical and economic regions of the united country.

In 1960, he moved to Waterloo, Ontario, Canada and began teaching geography at the University of Waterloo. Specializing in the Geography of Europe, world economic change, and environmental problems, especially of mountain regions, his articles and books have been published in England, Germany, Switzerland, Japan, the United States, and Canada. As well, he has exhibited his photos in Canada and Switzerland and has published them in England, France, Germany, Switzerland, Japan, the United States, and Canada.

Six books have resulted from his travels and research. The first, after a year spent in the Alps, was a photographic essay entitled **Val d'Anniviers**; then the text, **Western Europe: A Geographical Analysis** was published in 1979; **The Mont Blanc-Pennine Region** was written to coincide with the International Geographical Congress that took place in Paris in 1984; **First Rains of Autumn: a novel of love and war in the Alps** came out in December of 1985 and was rewritten in 1992; **Switzerland: Land, People, Economy** was published in the spring of 1986 to coincide with the conference on The Swiss Presence in Canada, held at the University of Waterloo. A chapter on Southern Europe and a section of France appeared in 1989 in George Hoffman's **Europe in the 1990's: A Geographic Analysis.** **The New Germany: Land, People, Economy** was published in 1991 after the author was present at the opening of the Berlin Wall. Entries on the "Alps" and the "Rhône Valley" appeared in the **Encyclopaedia Brittanica** in 1991 and "Switzerland" was published in 1993.

The ideas that resulted in his novel, **First Rains of Autumn**, emerged during the autumn of 1954, when he was doing field research for his Master's thesis in geography on the Valle d'Aosta, Italy. They have been supplemented with the works of Primo Levi and the translation of **Enrico's War**, a true account of an Italian partisan hero. Both men were linked to the Valle d'Aosta. Levy was imprisoned there before being sent to Auschwitz and the young Enrico Loewenthal was one of the commanders that liberated the city of Aosta.

Arch of Augusta, Aosta

CONTENTS

MAPS

ix

Introduction

In 1954, I, a young geography student, first set foot on European soil to write a master's thesis about the French speaking Valle d'Aosta in northwest Italy. My advisor at Clark University, Samuel Van Valkenburg, had grown up in Europe and wanted to know what was evolving in this remote corner of the Alps. Western Europe was then in a transitional phase. The continent had not yet fully recovered from the effects of World War II; however, the immediate horror of the devastation, famine, and killing had faded.

During my research, I came across writings and photos about the resistance of the locals after the Germans occupied the valley. Though my task was to complete my thesis, I thought of writing a novel about those terrifying days in 1944-45, and even jotted down the first few paragraphs. In 1954, I did not have enough experience to create a novel; however, years later I started to write about the incidents that ultimately were published as the **First Rains of Autumn: a novel of love and war in the Alps**.

After **First Rains** came out I read the writings of Primo Levi, the Jewish Italian chemist, who to escape the Nazis, had joined the partisans. He and his comrades were betrayed by Fascists and he was captured in a mountain cabin and jailed in Aosta. From there he was sent to Auschwitz and miraculously survived the Holocaust. Later, Levi wrote eloquent, powerful and incisive books about his experiences. He explained how the Dora Baltea river in the valley of Aosta got its name in the chapter on "Gold" in **The Periodic Table**. In 1987, Levi committed suicide at his home in Torino. His writings today, are as significant as ever in a world where the resilient viruses of Fascism and Nazism have erupted again, not only in a reunited Germany, but also in the democratic nations of Europe and North

America.

Levi's suicide affected me deeply. After reading his books, I realized we both had survived Auschwitz. He was there and survived; I grew up in the United States and survived. If I would have been born in Galicia, where my parents had grown up, no doubt, as a child, I would have perished in the gas chambers of Auschwitz.

I was struck by the similarity of the characters that I had created in **First Rains,** with some of the Italians that Levi had written about. They were young, impressionable human beings, who loved nature and the mountains, and were just beginning to discover themselves when their lives were overtaken by the cataclysmic events of the Second World War. I decided to rewrite my novel, dedicate it to Levi, and to use quotations from his books before each chapter. They work remarkably well, anticipating the action to come and providing an authentic counterpoint to the themes of the novel's narration. A last quotation in the epilogue, from an article in **The New York Times**, by Elie Wiesel on the perceived banality of the holocaust and the suicide of Levi, is a fitting and poignant tribute to the Italian author.

In this edition of **First Rains**, I have also included a short memoir: **Enrico's War: the true story of a partisan hero.** The diary provides a coda to **First Rains.** Enrico Loewenthal was about the same age as Primo Levi when he left his family and joined the partisans. His amazing true story, that of a young Jewish Italian, who miraculously survived the savage, brutal fighting and the extreme physical conditions of winter in the Alps, is an inspiration for all who believe in democratic ideals and the dignity of human beings. Loewenthal did more than just survive, he was among the Partisan commanders who liberated Aosta from the Fascists and Nazis and he was put in charge of areas, such as the Valpelline, that I have written about.

I came across his dairy, after receiving a letter from a Jewish Italian family living in Pittsburg. They had been sent **First Rains** by a relative who had bought the novel in Zermatt. The family had known Primo Levi in Torino, when he was a young man, and had fled Italy before the Fascists could arrest them. Their daughter, Vera Auretto, has ably translated **Enrico's War** from Italian to English.

Thus, the circle of events that have resulted in the publication of **First Rains** and **Enrico's War** have come to a close. I wish the readers a stimulating and enlightening read about events that are little known outside of northwest Italy, but which, nevertheless, are crucial to an insight and understanding of both the history of the Second World War and of the complexities of human behaviour.

Aubrey Diem
Zinal, Switzerland
09-01-92

EUROPE
Valle D'Aosta

DEUTSCH-
LAND

FRANCE

SUISSE

ÖSTER-
REICH

Valle D'Aosta

Torino

Genova

YUGOSLAVIA

ITALIA

Corse

Roma

Sardegna

Sicilia

0   250   500 km

Prologue

The Valle d'Aosta is almost completely enclosed by Western Europe's highest mountains. Mont Blanc, Monte Rosa, and the Matterhorn thrust their distinctive summits over 4500 meters into the north Italian sky. The main river of Aosta, the Dora Baltea, is nourished by a glittering diadem of alpine glaciers. Their moraines have left a distinctive topography above the farthest villages in the high lateral valleys.

The Valley has been an important Alpine routeway from Celtic times to the present. Invaders, pilgrims, travelers, and tourists have made their way over the Grand and Petit St. Bernard Passes, maintaining communications between the north and west of Europe and those lands south of the great Alpine arc.

Though inhabited since prehistoric times, the modern development of the site of Aosta began with the Romans. About 11 B.C., Augustus Caesar founded the city of Augusta Praetoria (Aosta) near the junction of the two St. Bernard Passes. At its height, the Roman city contained 15,000 to 20,000 inhabitants. The basic Roman street plan of Aosta has survived to the present and the city's Roman wall and triumphal arch of Augustus have become favoured tourist attractions.

Roman domination, lasting more than 400 years, gave way to the unstable period of barbarian invaders. Burgundians, Lombards, and Franks intermittently ruled the Valley until Aosta became part of the House of Savoy in 1032. From this date until 1691, when Aosta was invaded by France, the unique character of *Valtôtaine* political and social institutions developed along democratic lines quite rare for that period and in certain ways remarkable even when compared to present democratic institutions. For six hundred peaceful years, Aosta was the only possession of the House of Savoy, which was considered a separate political unit with its local aristocracy and its own representative institutions. Aosta's neutrality was violated with the French invasions. First in 1691, then in 1704, and again toward the end of the eighteenth century, French armies swept through the Valley. With Napoleon's victory at Marengo, Aosta became part of France until 1814, when it was returned to the House of Savoy.

After Italian unification in 1861, France was given all of Savoy west of the Alpine divide, leaving Aosta within the newly established state, with its linkage towards Torino and the Po Plain. A process of Italianization began that continues to the present.

Immigrants came to Aosta from the rest of Italy and intermarried with the local population. In 1879, the Italian government suppressed the teaching of French in the secondary schools. Although French was still taught along with Italian in the elementary schools, it was reduced to one hour a day in 1911. Family tradition, an active clergy, and French newspapers preserved the use of French until the Fascists prohibited the language entirely.

After World War I, the *Valdôtaines*, attempting to further their own self-determination, reacted strongly against continued efforts to alter the traditional character of the population. In 1919, a *ligue Valdôtaine pour la langue Française* was formed and a memorandum calling for the teaching and use of the French language and the gradual lessening of central administrative authority was presented to the head of the Italian delegation at the Versailles Peace Conference. This document can be considered the first draft of the autonomist movement in Aosta, and although it was received sympathetically, no action was taken to support its principals.

The coming of Fascism killed all hopes of strengthening the local culture. The Fascists ignored the fact that the Aostans, since unification, had been loyal subjects of the Italian monarchy and had fought nobly in the first World War. Mussolini banned the teaching and public use of French. The names of the streets, villages, and towns were changed into Italian. Thus, St. Vincent became San Vincenzo della Fonte, and Près St. Didier became San Desiderio Terme. All regional publications were burned, suppressed, or confiscated. Emigration to France, that had been a source of wealth to the Valley was stopped. Furthermore, disregarding the traditional water rights of the communes, the Fascists built hydroelectric stations with little consideration for the damage they would do in diverting water from pastures and irrigation systems. Thus, Fascist repression turned the Aostans away from Italy; they thought of themselves as aliens in their own land.

In 1921, a steel plant that utilized nearby deposits of iron ore, limestone, and anthracite began production in the city of Aosta. The old families of the Valley were opposed to its construction because they feared the onslaught of workers from outside the region. The factory, taken over by the Fascists in 1926, employed 6,000 to 7,000 workers during peak production and the anxieties of the *Valdôtaines* were borne out as labourers from Piemonte and as far south as Calabria and Sicilia settled in Aosta. The result was a predominance of Italians in the city of Aosta and the other industrial towns of the main valley, whereas the peasantry in the side valleys were the guardians of *Valdôtaine* culture.

To gain tighter control over the area and dilute the *Valdôtaine* influence, Mussolini created the Province of Aosta in 1926, combining 73 Aostan communes with the 113 communes of Ivrea beyond the Alps to the south.

3

Fascist officials from outside, many of whom were incompetent, were sent to administer the local government. During these oppressive years, *la jeune vallée d'Aoste*, an organization pledged to defend *Valdôtaine* tradition, preserve the use of French, and revive old customs and folklore, was founded. Lasting more than 20 years, the organization strove to make the future Valle d'Aosta autonomous and to provide a framework for *Valdôtaine* resistance to Fascism.

After Mussolini fell from power in 1943, underground activities began in earnest. Many inhabitants took to the mountains to escape the Nazis and their Fascist collaborators and formed in the first months of 1944, a powerful partisan unit that eventually made contact with the French *Maquis* west of the Petit St. Bernard. They were strong enough to establish themselves in the remoter side valleys of the Val Tournanche and the Val di Cogne for several months. Harassed, the Germans retaliated by shooting hostages and burning 22 villages. Near the end of the war, the partisans were continually supplied by Allied air drop, while engaging in guerilla skirmishes and helping downed Allied airmen and soldiers freed from Italian prisons escape to Switzerland....

Steel Mill, Aosta

CHAPTER I
Aosta 09-44

"In the cell I was welcomed by the solitude, the freezing, pure breath of the mountains which came through the small window, and the anguish of tomorrow. I listened - in the silence of curfew one could hear the murmur of the Dora, lost friend, and all friends were lost, and youth and joy, and perhaps life: it flowed close by but indifferent, dragging along the gold in its womb of melted ice. I felt gripped by a painful envy for my ambiguous companion, who would soon return to his precarious but monstrously free life, to his inexhaustible trickle of gold, and an endless series of days."
LEVI, **The Periodic Table, 1984.**

Cirrus clouds swept in from the western sky. They slowly thickened masking the sun behind a silver veil and diffusing its brilliance into a pale yellow glow. With an effort the peasant straightened, wiped his hands on his sweat-stained jacket, looked over to his wife rhythmically spreading manure onto the dry earth, and noticed the clouds. Touching the visor of his felt cap, he thought, the first rains of autumn would soon begin.

Something disturbed him. Not that he was unfamiliar with the roar of aircraft on their way to Torino and Milano. In fact, as the summer days grew shorter, planes were flying over his farmhouse day and night. But the engine sound from this one was different from the others and he knew that it was in trouble. Tilting his head, he shielded his eyes from the remaining glare of the sun and searched the sky in the direction of the noise. He focused on a curving dark dot plunging through the air and watched with astonishment as a parachute snapped open checking the fall of the flyer. He noticed that it was drifting towards the river that came down from the Alps.

"Guardà! Guardà!", the peasant shouted to his wife, his arm pointing in the direction of the floating white canopy. He ran and told her to hitch the oxen to the wagon and drive the 10 kilometers north to Pont St. Martin. At the Café Sport she should tell Carlo that an exhausted pigeon had landed on their farm. Then she should buy three bottles of Martini and Rossi and come directly home. The stocky woman, clad in a black woolen skirt and matching stockings, turned towards the stable. Her husband ran to the farmhouse, came out with his shotgun, whistled for his brown hunting dog, and headed through the maize field in the direction of the Dora Baltea.

The dog, barking excitedly, led the way. As the peasant cautiously walked across the rough ground, he spotted the parachute draped as a shroud over the straw coloured symmetrical rows of maize. At the end of the traces, surrounded by broken and bent stalks, was the still form of the pilot, dressed in baggy flying pants, warm boots, and a sheepskin lined jacket.

One leg was twisted grotesquely under the other.

"Màmma mia! He must have injured himself badly when he hit the hardened earth. I must be careful not to hurt him."

The injured man groaned and painfully looked up into the weathered face of the peasant. He gasped a few words, but except for "American", the farmer did not understand what he said.

The Germans will be searching for him, he thought.

"Don't be afraid, you'll stay here till nighttime, then we'll move you."

The exhausted aviator sank to the arid ground, enveloped by a haze of dust.

8

Twilight dissolved into evening. By now the clouds had blocked out the sky and the wind from the southeast was beginning to blow strongly. The peasant had made him as comfortable as possible but the face of the young man reflected the intense ache that was pulsating through his left hip and leg.

The sound of a motor car filtered through the rush of the wind and he made out the running lights of the vehicle as it came slowly toward his farm. It was Carlo's grey Lancia! The car stopped by the farmhouse as the peasant emerged from the maize field. He recognized the familiar goateed face of Carlo but did not know the two men who were with him. All three were dressed in heavy corduroy suits. The two younger ones wore berets; Carlo had on a Borsolino. All were shod in the cleated brown boots that were so necessary in the region.

"Ciào Carlo, come with me! An American aviator is lying near the river. He's badly hurt and we'll have to carry him to the car."

The men moved swiftly through the withered stalks and found the injured man conscious but unable to lie still because of the pain. The peasant had brought some twine and two stakes that he used for supporting his vines. He tied the stakes to the twisted leg forming a crude splint. Then as gently as possible the Italians lifted him off the ground and placed him on the parachute. Each grabbed a corner and together they started in the direction of the farm, trying to absorb the shocks of the hammock-like sling.

The wind rustled through the dry stalks. Carlo spoke quietly.

"We must head north into the mountains. I can find a temporary place of refuge for the American in Aosta. Then I'll contact Dr. Orlando who is sympathetic to our cause. He can set the poor boy's leg and put it in a proper cast.

Let's hope he'll walk again in three or four months."

Placing the injured man onto the back seat of the small *Aprilia* was an exacting task. One of the men, already inside, guided the twisted leg into the car, while the others supported the airman and slowly directed his body. The flying boot caught for a moment on the interior door handle bringing forth a yelp of pain from the weary American. Finally, he was positioned on the seat, supported as well as possible by the man who had guided his leg. Carlo got into the driver's seat, and the third man closed the back doors and slid into the front seat beside the driver.

The farmer appeared with a bottle of Bardolino, neatly uncorked it, and thrust it through the rear window.

"Drink some *Americano*, you'll feel much better afterwards."

Before he started the motor, Carlo rolled down his window, looked into the weathered face of the farmer, noticed the day's grey stubble on his chin and told him,

"Hide the parachute where it won't be found. Perhaps your wife can use it to make some clothes. Many thanks for your help, we'll not forget."

The peasant clasped Carlo's hand with both of his and shook it firmly.

"Arrivedérci, buona fortuna. Ciào."

"Ciào. Ciào."

As the car pulled away from the farm, the first drops of rain spattered in the dirt around his high leather boots.

"I must go inside and wait for my wife. Then we'll have some cheese and hot soup."

Carlo could make out the dark forms of Renaldo and the American in the rear-view mirror. He turned to Lucien in the passenger seat.

"With luck we should be in Aosta within an hour. I'd like to drive faster but visibility is poor and the rain has made the road as slick as black ice."

He peered through the streaked windshield, trying to follow the curving highway north of Pont St. Martin. The names of the villages, illuminated from the Lancia's headlights, stood out on the rusting sign boards. Donnaz..., Bard..., Verres.... A rabbit froze on the road, eyes shining like agates, and then scampered off into the underbrush. The auto sped northward towards the the Alps, their steep mysterious slopes barely visible in the deepening rain-swept night. Some moments later the sleek Lancia entered the Valle d'Aosta.

Carlo glanced at the faint green glow of the instrument panel. All appeared in order. He flexed his fingers around the leather-covered steering wheel, guiding the swift machine as it clung to the uneven surface of the wet highway, knifing through bands of mist and fog.

The driver remembered his high school teacher, Signore Bondaz, telling the class that under the House of Savoy, Aosta was at peace for over six hundred years, a privileged region that had evolved a unique Alpine democracy. Now their way of life had been corrupted and drowned by the Fascists.

He spoke loudly to the men over the whine of the motor.

"God damm that fat bastard for trying to Italianize our Valley; a Fascist prick who had to be rescued by the bloody Nazis. Two thousand years of culture can't be wiped out in two decades. You know the Romans marched on this road over the Grand St. Bernard to Switzerland."

He jabbed his right arm toward the window, just missing Lucien's nose.

"Here Napoleon passed the castle of Bard on his way to fight the Austrians at Marengo. Mussolini is only a papier-mâché Caesar, a puppet who thinks we can be forever humiliated in our own valley. We'll fight him and his Nazi

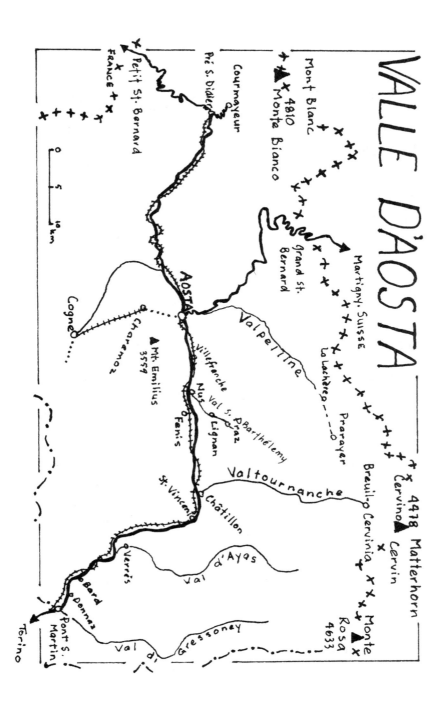

barbarians and win, dammit!"

The Lancia turned west at St. Vincent and climbed deeper into the mountains towards Chatillon. The name brought back visions of the winter before the war at Cervina. Carlo's family had ridden the train from Pont St. Martin to Chatillon and an old bus had brought them up the Val Tournanche to the small village at the base of the Cervino.

What a marvelous weekend it had been. His parents had taken him and his sister skiing for the first time that season. On Sunday they had gone up to the Testa Grigia with the *téléphérique,* skied into Switzerland and looked down to Zermatt, 2000 meters below; forty kilometers farther on was the haze of the Rhône Valley. Regardless of where they had been that day, Carlo had turned again and again to gaze at the Cervino, its glaciated peak thrusting boldly into the cloudless January blue above the Italian and Swiss villages. By the time the family had made their way back to Cervina all were exhausted. He recalled the small hotel where they had stayed and the long evening sitting around the table singing songs of the mountains. What had happened to those days of happiness and pleasure?

The American dozed fitfully in the back seat. The wine had worked well. Occasionally a car passing in the opposite direction would help to highlight the poplar trees that lined the road. After they passed through Nus, Carlo told Renaldo and Lucien that they were going directly in Aosta to the *Auberge de la Jeunesse* across from the cathedral of Saint Orso.

"There's room for all of us, but first I must get the key from the old priest. Tomorrow morning I'll find Dr. Orlando and tell him about the American."

The car slowed, crossed a bridge, and followed the main road through the Triumphal Arch. It continued a hundred

13

Peasant, Valle d'Aosta

meters past a bar and shoe store before turning right near the Roman wall. The ancient cathedral was across from a giant linden tree on the narrow side street. They had arrived at the hostel.

Soon after dawn, Carlo quickly dressed and made his way to the Via Saint Anselme. He was glad to be out of the primitive hostel and escape from the acrid smell of the latrine. The rain had stopped sometime during the night but the mountains that surrounded the city were still obscured by the morning fog. Carlo passed through the Roman gate and headed towards the central square where the weekly market was being set up. He walked hurriedly to number 19 Via de Tillier, climbed a flight of stairs, saw the plaque of Dr. Orlando over a door, and entered into the corridor. The Doctor was already in his office, working alone at a large wooden desk, surrounded by a microscope, some bottles containing pills and coloured liquids, antique blue and white apothecary jars, and an impressive fluoroscope. A single bulb illuminated the bare plaster walls that were broken only by the Doctor's framed diploma. Carlo took off his hat.

"Buon giòrno, Dottore."

"Buon giòrno, Carlo."

"Va béne?"

"Si Dotore."

Carlo began to tell the middle-aged man about the American flyer. When he finally finished, Dr. Orlando took off his steel-rimmed glasses and told him to return to the hostel by the back streets.

"Be careful Carlo. The Germans are waiting for us. They've already filled the jail in Aosta with a group of Partisans that were caught by Fascist militia men in the valleys west of Torino. I'll see you back at the hostel within the hour."

Carlo made his way downstairs. Aosta was awakening.

The shutters that protected the shop windows had been rolled up, revealing the meagre selection of goods inside; the kiosks were displaying the days editions of *La Stampa* and *Corriere della Sera*; and the main square was thronged with shoppers searching for an unlikely bargain at the market stalls. Grey-green uniformed German soldiers patrolled the piazza. The morning sun had burned off the fog. Glancing toward Mont Emilius, Carlo noticed the freshly fallen snow on its upper flanks and thought of the coming winter.

"Your American is a lucky boy. The break is not too severe, one bone of the lower leg and some badly stretched ligaments. Taking him to the hospital or to my office is out of the question. I'll set the leg and put on a cast here. At least two to three months must pass before he'll walk again."

Drugged by a shot of morphine, the American, his short blond hair damp with sweat, offered little resistance when his leg was set. Lucien had brought in a bucket of water from the fountain by the Romanesque *campanilé* of the cathedral. Dr. Orlando filled the syringe and then cleaned it by squirting the water against the wall. There was a burst of laughter from the men. He then dipped the plaster bandages in the icy water and smartly wrapped them around the broken leg, moving slowly from ankle to hip. As the cast built up in thickness the Doctor told Carlo of his plans.

"The place I have in mind is a mountain hotel in Prarayer at the head of the Valpelline. It's secure, can only be reached on foot, and will be completely cut off from the main valley of Aosta once the snow falls. One last consideration, when the American is healthy and strong again, he should need only one or two days to climb over

16

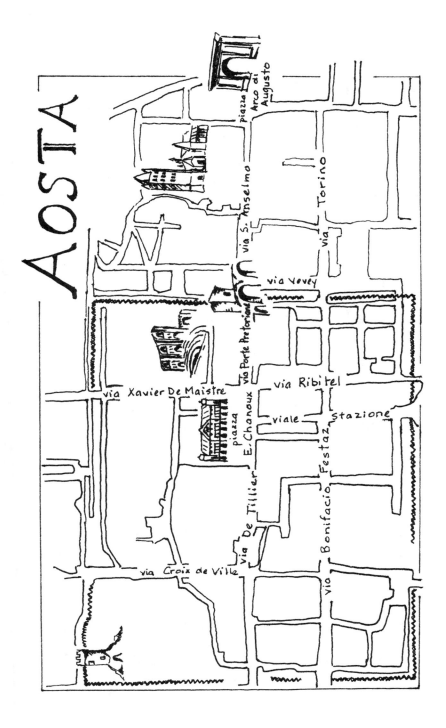

the mountains to Zermatt in Switzerland."

"You should have no trouble driving into the Valpelline. The German patrols rarely go there because the road is a dead end. Instead they block the upper part of the Grand St. Bernard to intercept anyone trying to escape to the Valais. Stay the night in Oyace at the Auberge Mochettaz and leave early the next morning for la Lechère. You'll have to go the rest of the way on foot so you'll need a stretcher. I'll arrange for you to pick one up at the emergency entrance of the hospital at 9:30 tonight."

"How will we be able to put such a long object inside the Lancia?"

"The intern who'll bring you the stretcher will also have my ski rack. Strap the stretcher to the rack and there will be no problems."

Washing the plaster off his hands, the Doctor assured the men that they would be given a warm welcome in the Valpelline.

"The peasants who live there are true *Valdôtaines*. Many made their way centuries ago over the glaciers from the Valais in Switzerland. They love and respect the mountains. They hate the Nazis and their Fascist lackeys."

The night was clear and black. Carlo was ready to head north toward the Valpelline. He was pleased that so far everything had gone smoothly. He had said goodbye to the priest while Lucien had fetched the Lancia from a parking place near the Arch of Augustus. They were able to move the American into the car with little difficulty. As promised, the stretcher and ski rack were waiting for them at the hospital. The young intern also handed Carlo an envelope containing a large-scale map of the Valpelline and letters of introduction to the patron of the Auberge Mochettaz and to Madame Colombo at the Hotel Tête Blanche in Prarayer. Before they left, the intern had given another shot of

18

morphine to the flyer. He told Carlo that a pair of crutches were wrapped inside the stretcher.

Across from the hospital, the road to the Grand St. Bernard Pass climbed steeply into the mountains. After travelling four kilometers the Lancia turned off to the right and headed down into the Valpelline. Twisting and turning, the machine rocked from one side of the road to the other, bouncing on the long neglected surface. Then, climbing steadily, the car passed the village of Valpelline. To the right Carlo could barely make out the deep cleft eroded by the Buthier river. On the left the mountains came down precipitously to the edge of the road. He braked and dodged some rocks on the highway that had fallen from above. A quick shifting of gears marked a series of narrow switchbacks that brought the *Aprilia* up to the hamlet of Oyace. Around the last bend, he saw the Auberge Mochettaz.

The village church bells tolled 11 o'clock as Carlo entered the Auberge. Monsieur Milloz, the patron, an ancient grolla in his hand, was sitting at a worn wooden table drinking red wine. He was in his late thirties, a strong well-formed man whose lined face reflected a life spent in the out of doors. Carlo walked over to the table and after a perfunctory *"bonsoir"*, gave the *patron* Dr. Orlando's letter.

After reading it, Monsieur Milloz told them, "Bring in the American at once! We'll put him in the room next to the kitchen. You and your friends can sleep upstairs on the *couchettes*."

After the injured man had been carefully placed in bed, Carlo, Lucien, and Renaldo gathered around Monsieur Milloz's table. Wine, Fontina, and apricots were placed before them. The patron spoke.

"I'll serve breakfast at seven. You should leave by seven-thirty for la Lechère. The car must be brought back immediately to Oyace so that we can park it in a secluded

19

Market, Aosta

spot. The other two can carry the flyer to the Hotel Tête Blanche, spend the day there and return by evening. On your way back you might meet some German soldiers. Some of them come here on their off days to walk and mountain climb. They rarely stay overnight, but occasionally stop somewhere for a meal or drinks. I've often spoken with them." He laughed, "They come from Bayern or the Tirol. Our enemies also enjoy the solitude and splendor of our mountains."

He took a sip of wine to wash down the cheese and studied his visitors. "Nevertheless, we try to know where the Germans are and what they are doing. There is an ancient watch tower in Oyace not far from the Auberge from where we can observe the valley. All unusual movement is immediately reported to me. That's why I was still awake when your car stopped here. Madame Colombo already knows that she might have visitors tomorrow. After you leave the American with her, we'll try to make certain that the Germans won't arrive unannounced at the Tête Blanche."

Monsieur Milloz swallowed the last of the wine, wiped his mouth with the back of his hand and got up from the table.

"I'm going to bed, *bonne nuit*."

"Bonne nuit monsieur."

The three men climbed upstairs, took off their rumpled clothes and snuggled under the blankets of the *couchette*. For the first time since they had set out from Pont St. Martin for the "exhausted pigeon", Carlo felt relaxed. The wine, cheese, and fruit had satisfied his hunger. Above him in the *couchette*, Lucien and Renaldo, having drained a bottle between them, tossed in their sleep mumbling unintelligible words of patois. Despite the stress of the last two days, the two young men had worked well together. Tomorrow would test them further. Renaldo would bring the Lancia back from la Lechère, while he and Lucien would carry the American to Prarayer.

Renaldo moved behind the wheel of the *Aprilia,* adjusted the seat and mirror, pulled out the choke and started the motor. The engine turned over a few times, then caught fire. He adjusted his beret and turned to his friends, shouting over the noise of the idling machine.

"I'll see you both back in Oyace. Be careful with the American, the effects of the morphine are wearing off."

Carlo responded,"We'll start back by five o'clock, and without the burden of the boy, we should be in Oyace by seven-thirty. Check the car and fill it with petrol. I want to leave for Pont St. Martin when we return. If anyone should ask what you're doing, tell them that you're with friends for some days of walking and climbing and that you had to make a minor repair to the car."

"Ci védiamo."

"Ciào."

Though the morning air was still cool, carrying the stretcher over the rough mountain path was arduous work, and dark patches of perspiration quickly spread across the coarse woolen shirts of both men. The American, more alert than at anytime since they had found him, was quietly staring at the mountains. Carlo glanced at his youthful face and sensed that his pain was still severe.

As they made their way higher up the valley, the groves of *mélèzes* thinned out and irregular grassland became more abundant. They were approaching 2000 meters. The early sun glistened off the hanging glaciers that were festooned on the sculptured peaks. Waterfalls poured off the precipitous valley sides.

The morning waned and the Buthier increased in volume, fed by the slowly melting ice masses. They picked their way carefully over the uneven terrain, walking past patches of melting snow that had remained from the fall of two nights ago. Carlo noticed a neglected hut that was used for shelter when the cows were driven to and from the *alpages* above Prarayer.

The pace of the two Italians slowed when they caught sight of the roof of the hotel emerging in the distance. Despite the chafing of their caloused hands and strain on their arms and necks from carrying the unwieldy stretcher, they did not stop until they came to the yellow weathered facade of the Hotel Tête Blanche. The men put down their burden, stretched their arms and opened and closed their fists. Slowly, the feeling came back to their hands.

As they walked up towards the entrance, Madame Colombo, wearing a dark brown sweater and skirt, her sandy hair framing her face, came outside.

"Bonjour messieurs, I can see that you have had a hard climb this morning."

Carlo reached into his shirt pocket, brought forth the letter that had become soaked during the walk, and gave it to the dignified woman.

She read the message and responded to the men,

"So this is where Dr. Orlando wants the young man to spend his convalescence. I was preparing to close the hotel and return to Aosta for the winter, but now I will stay here. Five months isolated in the high mountains can be very dangerous; however, there are compensations provided for by nature. Fortunately, the hotel is provisioned for an emergency and there is plenty of hay in the barn for the cows. For the present, the flyer can stay in one of the rooms upstairs. When it becomes colder, he will have to move down to the kitchen."

After a lunch of bread and *prosciutto*, Carlo and Lucien sunned themselves on the terrace protected by the south side of the hotel. Madame Colombo had gone into the kitchen to prepare a meal for the American. Carlo was impressed by the genuine elegance and inner strength of the woman. He wiped the crumbs off his jacket and turned to his friend,

"She can't be more than twenty-five, yet she seems to have the maturity of a grandmother. Her body is athletic, well proportioned, and strong. I wonder what she's doing here?"

Lucien glanced around, "You saw the ring on her finger. Perhaps her husband is in the army. These days, life is difficult for all of us."

The afternoon passed lazily. The men, tired from their climb, dozed on the terrace. When they were ready to leave for Oyace, they thanked Madame Colombo for her hospitality, gave her a warm embrace, and kissed her cheeks.

"Buona fortúna, take care of the *Americano."*

She walked a short distance with Carlo and Lucien, then watched as they made their way briskly down the valley. Illuminated autumn seeds like fireflys floated past their dark bodies that were outlined by the setting sun.

When the men were no longer visible, she picked up the stretcher and crutches that had been left near the door and entered the Tête Blanche.

Partisans, Valle d'Aosta

CHAPTER II
Prarayer, 11-44

"Each of us did his or her work day by day, slackly, without believing in it, as happens to someone who knows he is not working for his own future. We went to the theatre and concerts, which sometimes were interrupted halfway through because the air-raid siren would start shrieking: and this seemed to us a ridiculous and gratifying incident; the Allies were masters of the sky, perhaps in the end they would win and Fascism would end - but it was their business, they were rich and powerful, they had the airplane carriers and the Liberators. But not us, 'they' had declared us 'different,' and different we would be; we took sides but kept out of the stupid and cruel Aryan games, discussing the plays of O'Neill and Thornton Wilder, climbing the Grigne slopes, falling a bit in love with each other, inventing intellectual games, and singing the lovely songs Silvio had learned from some of his Waldensian friends. As to what was happening during those same months in all of Europe occupied by the Germans, in Ann Frank's house in Amsterdam, in the pit of Babi Yar near Kiev, in the ghetto of Warsaw, in Salonika, Paris, and Lidice; as to this pestilence which was about to submerge us no precise information had reached us, only vague and sinister hints dropped by soldiers returning from Greece or from the rear areas of the Russian front, and which we tended to censor. Our ignorance allowed us to live, as when you are in the mountains and your rope is frayed and about to break, but you don't know it and feel safe."
LEVI, **The Periodic Table, 1984.**

Andy pulled the brown blankets over his body, looked at the bare wooden walls of his room, and tried to make himself comfortable on the hard bed. The hotel was furnished simply. There was no electricity. Kerosene lamps provided light and a

27

wood-burning stove radiated heat in the kitchen. He washed in the icy water that spurted from the single tap in the *lavabo*.

He had been at the Tête Blanche for over three weeks. The intense pain in his left leg had eased somewhat, but when he moved around on his crutches, a dull throbbing reminded him that he had suffered a serious injury.

Madame Colombo had taken care of him the first week when he was confined to bed. She brought his meals on a carved wooden tray: coffee with hot milk, and a roll in the morning; and pasta, polenta, cheese, fruit, and wine for midday and evening.

After breakfast, she would bathe him. When he was finished with the evening meal, she would arrive with two small glasses of grappa. They would sip the clear potent liquid and talk to each other in French. Andy had studied it at college and had spoken French when he had skied in Québec. At first, he could only express himself in simple phrases; however, as the weeks went by, he was both surprised and pleased at the improvement in his comprehension and fluency.

The weather had been perfect. For days on end, the sky was without clouds. On the south side of the hotel, the sun still provided considerable warmth. As soon as he was able to use the crutches, he spent a good deal of time outside enjoying the weather.

Content, on a faded chaise longue, with the fur collar of his bomber jacket snug against his neck, Andy surveyed the high peaks, and looked down the glaciated valley towards the *mélèze* forest, that as the days shortened, turned from deep green, to light gold, and finally to pale grey.

One morning, he saw two chamois grazing near some large boulders. Only now, since leaving New Hampshire to join the air force, had he again time to contemplate and gain spiritual strength from nature.

Madame Colombo had told him that good autumn weather

was normal in the high Alps.

"While we are enjoying the fresh clear air and the final warmth of the sun before winter, the people living in Torino and Milano are scurrying to work in the damp cold fog that blankets the Po Valley for weeks on end."

Thinking about the sun in the cool dark of the room, Andy felt warm and cozy. He fell asleep almost at once, lulled by the muffled roar of falling water.

During breakfast the next morning, Madame Colombo asked Andy to call her by her first name.

"We have lived under the same roof for nearly four weeks and we will be together for the rest of the winter. Please call me Angela."

She filled their cups with more coffee and began to speak about the events that led to the formation of the resistance movement in the Valle d'Aosta.

"I am sure that you have wondered who brought you to the Valpelline? When Mussolini's government fell a year ago, the *Valdôtaine* people hoped that the war would be over and that twenty years of Fascist oppression would finally end. The troops in the local Alpine regiments wanted to lay down their arms and disband, but within a week, they knew that peace would not come without a struggle.

"The hard-core Fascists, many of whom were sent from outside the Valley, tried to rally support for the Nazis. Soon, truck loads of German troops were rolling north from Torino and occupying strategic positions in the towns of the main valley.

"When the news broke of the German occupation, many *Alpini* fled into the high valleys, taking with them guns and ammunition. Others went back to their villages, hid their weapons, and waited.

After a short sip of the bitter expresso Andy asked, "Were

there many battles?"

"The first few skirmishes were hit and run affairs. When the winter ended, the raids became more frequent and more violent. Bands of partisans, under cover of darkness, would surprise a German strongpoint, capturing supplies of grenades, mortars, and machine guns. They would blow up the rail-line to Torino, ambush a freight-train, and seize more weapons.

"Because the Valle d'Aosta is cut-off from the rest of Italy by the mountains, the partisans could check German reinforcements from the Po Valley by blocking the only road at such places as the narrows below the castle of Bard. By the end of the summer, the arsenals of the various resistance groups had become well stocked.

"After the assaults, the bands would retreat into the high valleys. The Germans could not follow the attackers. Their tanks and armoured cars were too clumsy to negotiate the steep narrow mountain roads. Later, their battle-hardened Alpine troops pursued the partisans. They rarely captured our men, who were like chamois on the rugged rocky slopes, always one step ahead of their hunters."

Andy looked at the intense face of Angela and the aura of strength about her. He knew there was something about this strong-featured woman that intrigued him. While at college his experience with the opposite sex had been limited to the usual fraternity-sorority parties. He realized that he was much more emotionally and physically attracted to this intelligent woman.

Glancing at the young American, Angela continued.

"Because they could not capture our men, the Germans looted chalets, burned villages, slaughtered the animals, and took civilian hostages. Once, after an officer had been killed, eleven innocent peasants were rounded up, driven to a field near Fenis, and machine gunned by the murderous Nazis. All night and the next morning their bodies lay where they had fallen, a hideous warning to the gathering crowds that their fate could be the same.

"After each German reprisal, more and more young men would leave their villages to join the resistance bands in the mountains. What began as a few separate groups, quickly swelled into a powerful force that numbered in the thousands."

"Because of their isolation in the different side valleys, communication among the resistance leaders was difficult. Nevertheless, as the spring days grew longer, the partisans began to coordinate their clandestine activities."

Andy finished his coffee and Angela moved to refill his cup from the aluminium expresso pot.

"In May, our cause suffered a severe blow. Emile Chanoux, one of our most brilliant leaders, a man of great moral and physical courage, was surprised by the Nazis in his home in Aosta. They imprisoned and tortured him.

"Before he died, his captors allowed his wife a brief visit. He told her, *'Dzi pas predza* Celeste,' 'I have not spoken Celeste.'

"We are not sure whether he was betrayed. There are always those willing to sell their souls for the right price.

"His loss strengthened the resistance. He has become our symbol for freedom, a martyr for our cause. His murder will be avenged."

Angela's eyes filled with tears. She continued to speak, but more slowly.

"Throughout the summer, contacts were established with our allies. English and American undercover agents met with our leaders. French Maquis units supplied us with food and ammunition over the Petit St. Bernard Pass. And the Valaisans aided our boys when they sought temporary refuge in Switzerland.

"Already, we have helped a number of downed airmen to escape over the Col de Téodule from Breuil to Zermatt, and we have smuggled Italian Jews into Switzerland by the same route.

31

"When you are well again, you too will go over the mountains to freedom."

She looked up at the wooden ceiling of the dining room, paused for a moment, then turned to the flyer and quietly said,

"Now you must excuse me, for I have to attend to the cows."

A week later snow began to fall. Because of the protecting mountains, there was no wind. The loose flakes piled up evenly and soon over a meter had buried the terrace.

Andy had experienced many winter storms in New England, the violent and dangerous 'northeasters' that had howled inland from the Atlantic, uprooting trees, snapping power lines, and burying roads and buildings under enormous drifts. This one, however, was different.

Outside, there was a persistent and peaceful build-up of snow. One day blended into another, with eight hours of soft grey light being replaced by sixteen hours of darkness.

Each morning and evening, Angela cleared a narrow path from the front door of the hotel down to the barn. Andy would look forward to the moment she finished the shovelling and returned to the hotel, cheeks flushed, yellow hair matted, and thick sweater and long skirt covered by large wet flakes.

One evening, while the snow was still falling, Angela suggested drinking an aperitif before supper. The kerosene lamp had been lit, spreading a soft amber glow in the kitchen. Heat poured forth from the cast iron stove. She took down a bottle of sweet vermouth from the cupboard and poured two glasses half full of the deep brown liquid.

"Chin chin Andy."

"Chin chin Angela."

Andy admired her resolved visage.

"Angela, how did you come to the Tête Blanche?"

"I was born and grew up some kilometers east of here in the

Valle di Saint Barthélemy. I never saw my father, he was killed in the first World War at Gorizia, fighting against the Austro-Hungarian Army. Because of the stupidity of General Cadorna, hundreds of thousands of Italians died in the Carso, and for what reason? Twenty years after the war, we became allied with these same Austrians. My family tried to find out where my father was buried, but it was no use. Like so many on both sides, he was probably blown into a thousand pieces during an artillery bombardment. All we know is that he was killed on October 21, 1915 at the age of 34. Hemingway wrote about this horrible time in 'Farewell to Arms'. The book was well known in Italy before the war and I had to read it in high school.

"I met my husband Benoit while walking over to the Valpelline. This hotel was owned by his family. He was a mountain guide and much older than I, a very tough and brave man. Many times he had to search for injured skiers or lost climbers, regardless of the weather. After our marriage, I came to live and work here. I have been married for over five years, but have been with my husband for only a few months."

"Where is he now?"

"I do not know whether he is alive or dead. Like most of the young men in the Valley, he was conscripted into Mussolini's army and sent to Abyssinia. He fought well, but his heart was not in what he was ordered to do.

"A man cannot take much pride in killing half-naked peasants who fight back with spears and rocks; he was not happy burning mountain villages that were similar to his own. But what choice did he have?

"After war broke out in 1940, my husband was transferred to Greece and later to Yugoslavia. The last letter I received was from North Africa where he was fighting against the English. All I can hope for is that he has been taken prisoner."

Angela paused and looked out of the kitchen window into the emptiness of the night. A stream of snow flakes caught the light from the lamp. When she spoke again, her face appeared angry.

"War is senseless, a *divertiménto* blessed by the church and started by spoiled nobility, hypocritical politicians, and bored generals. Did you know that during the First World War, Jews, Protestants, Catholics, and Moslems on both sides, all believing in their own God, fought and murdered one another?

"If you really want to know what war is all about you must look at Guernica."

Puzzled, Andy asked her,

"What is Guernica?"

"In July of 1937, my mother and I went to Paris to attend the funeral of an uncle. It was the first time that I had ever been out of Italy. He and many other *Valdôtaines* went there in search of a better life. During hard times, the money that they sent home helped us to survive. We caught the night train from Bourg St. Maurice on the French side of the Petit St. Bernard and arrived at the Gare de l'Est in the early morning. We walked out of the station carrying our bags and I looked up at the massive clock tower on the facade of this ornate building. Then we took the Metro to Clichy where my uncle had lived.

"After his funeral, my cousin showed me the city and took me to a fantastic International Exhibition. In the Spanish Pavillion, a modern building such as I had never seen before, was an enormous black and white painting by the Spanish artist Picasso. He had been outraged by the bombing of the Basque city of Guernica by Fascist and Nazi planes just a few months before and painted his impressions of the event: fallen warriors, maimed children, suffering women, and terrified animals. I had looked at many books of photographs of the First World War but somehow Picasso has better captured war's true vision. You can't photograph or write about war the way it emerges from his painting like a sudden, violent, and destructive thunderstorm."

The quiet energy of this imposing woman allowed her to go on.

"The *Valdôtaines* are peaceful human beings, our history is proof of that. We do not need the terrors of war to compensate for the dullness of everyday life, or the lure of far away places to replace the chaotic cities that most people live in. We do not covet what our neighbours have. Our life in Aosta is rewarding enough.

"Of course life is not perfect. We are not rich in material goods, but we are wealthy in culture. The fair of Saint Orso, where our best wood carvers, painters, and artisans show their wares, has been held every winter for nearly 2000 years.

"The mountains have always provided for us. We live simply, but as you have noticed we eat well. We do not have to seek out danger. There are rock slides, floods, snowstorms, and avalanches. We are constantly struggling against nature, but our way of life is a natural one.

"If our relatives in the next village are killed in an avalanche, we accept it as God's will. We do not have to fabricate artificial thrills by bombing, looting, and raping. We need only to walk in the mountains caring for our cows, look at the sky, watch the moving clouds, adjust to the changing seasons, and ski in the winter.

"We are part of the mountains."

Andy studied the appealing face of the woman.

"Do you think that life will be better when the war is over?"

"In some ways, of course. The Germans will leave and our men will come home. But I am not too optimistic about the future.

"I do not believe that it matters one bit who is in Roma: Fascist, Communist, Socialist, or Christian Democrat. For us, the results will be the same. Already they have drowned our forests and pastures in the high valleys by building enormous dams. Our irrigation canals have been destroyed. Most of the

35

electricity flows south to the factories in Torino and Milano. What remains for our use is very expensive."

Angela took a long sip of vermouth, reached for the bottle and refilled Andy's glass.

"The ugly steel mill in Aosta throws up foul smoke and vile fumes that pollute the pure mountain air. It provides employment, but not for the *Valdôtaines*. We were not born to be mill hands. So many of our people, as I have told you, have had to leave to find work in France and in Switzerland. The uneducated labourers come from Fruili, Piemonte, Calabria, and Sicilia. Their behavior is alien to our way of life.

"The families, who have become rich from our electricity, iron ore, and coal, vacation in the Valley to experience the splendor and tranquillity of the mountains. But they treat us like servants and leave us their garbage. They feel nothing but contempt for our language and our values. We despise them. Our true relations are with the people of Bourg St. Maurice and Martigny, not those of Torino or Roma."

Andy interrupted,

"But don't you believe in progress?"

"I am afraid that after the war is over *Valdôtaine* culture and tradition will never be the same. There has been talk of building a tunnel to Switzerland under the Grand St. Bernard and one under the Mont Blanc to France. Before the war, engineers already surveyed the Valpelline for a dam site. Perhaps we will become more prosperous as a result of all this 'progress', but I fear that we will pay the price for our material gains by the loss of our heritage and the desecration of our beautiful valley. So-called progress can be a Faustian pack with the Devil."

She turned toward the American.

"Andy, the vermouth has loosened my tongue. I have talked enough about myself and the Valle d'Aosta. Now you must tell me about life in America."

36

The request took the aviator by surprise. He turned toward the kerosene lamp, focused on the moving flame for a few moments, and then began to talk.

"The town where I grew up isn't far from the Connecticut River that rises in the highlands of New Hampshire. Nearby is Mount Sunapee, where I learned to ski. My life has also been lived close to nature."

"Are your mountains like the Alps?"

Andy thought a moment,

"No, they're not as high or as rugged, and have no glaciers, but they also isolate one region from another, and when the weather is bad, they can be dangerous for hikers or skiers." Many people have been killed on Mt. Washington, the highest in the northeast."

"What is the weather like in New Hampshire?"

He looked at the snow piling up on the windowsill and laughed.

"The climate can be extreme, but there are always good periods during the year. The summer can be hot and fine. Then I spend my free time camping, fishing, and swimming in the mountain lakes. In the autumn the temperature drops quickly and the leaves on the trees turn to red, orange, and yellow, a last burst of spectacular colour before the grey landscape of November descends. Winters are very cold but the weather can change quickly. One day temperatures can be minus 30 degrees Celsius with winds of over 75 kilometers per hour. The next day temperatures can be above freezing and it can rain. We soon learn how to ski in deep powder or on glare ice."

"How long have people lived in your mountains? In Aosta we trace our origins to the Salassi, a Celtic tribe that encamped here before the Romans."

"The Natives hunted and fished for thousands of years before the white settlers arrived. During the 18th century my relatives built their farms in the valleys, cleared the forests, and

37

planted their crops in the rocky soil. You see, Angela, the climate and land have made the New Englanders tough and fiercely independent people."

"And what do your parents do?"

"My father drives a truck for the post office and my mother takes care of our small house. They live in a straightforward, rather simple manner. I remember my father often telling me, 'Don't hide your thoughts Andy; speak the truth even though someone's feelings may be hurt.' I'm sure that's why my friends and teachers thought that I was too forward and outspoken. I can tell you that I got into plenty of trouble for that."

"Before you joined the Air Force, what did you do?"

"When I finished high school my parents wanted me to go to the University of New Hampshire. I was accepted and studied biology and geography. During the summers I took odd jobs to help pay my expenses. One year, I worked in a small factory on a grinding machine, and once I was a camp counsellor."

"I enjoyed university but my real love was skiing. My brother gave me my first pair of skis for my fourth birthday. When I grew older I began to compete in school races. When I was sitting on the deck of the Tête Blanche, looking at the mountains, I realized that life had had its fullest meaning and my senses where at their peak when I was skiing through a course and trying to get as close to the slalom gates as possible. I was alone. If I skied poorly or fell, I had no one else to blame. If I won the race, it was my victory!"

His cheeks became flushed.

"I raced to win, but I also learned how to become a gracious loser."

"At the Tête Blanche, I've had a lot of time to think about myself. I went to university and yet you seem to know so much more about the world and your life appears to be so much richer than mine. I studied about the First World War in a European history course, but I know very little about life and politics in Europe. When I heard you speak about the culture and history of Aosta, I realized how the forces of history have influenced your life."

Angela sneered, her upper lip raised a bit.

"America is too isolated. In Europe we've been killing and raping for thousands of years. Our men have gone off to war and millions have never returned. The idealism of childhood does not last very long under those conditions."

"True, my friends and I grew up sheltered from what was going on across the Atlantic. Once we heard Hitler on the short wave, but nobody could understand what he was saying. He sounded so funny and we all made jokes about him afterwards."

There was a sparkle in her hazel eyes.

"What did you do for amusement?"

"Our lives were pretty uneventful, but there were times when we had a helluva lot of fun. We would meet every weekend during the winter at ski resorts such as Stowe, Cannon Mountain, and Mount Sunapee. I looked forward to seeing my friends, listening to Louis Armstrong and Billie Holiday on records, drinking beer, and skiing and racing together. A strong comradery developed among the boys and girls from the different New England universities. Many were the children of Austrian and Bavarian immigrants who had fled the Nazis and settled in New Hampshire before the War. They introduced skiing to the White Mountains."

"In the evenings they would tell me about the ski races held in St. Anton, Davos, and Kitzbühl. Those places were only dots on a map, but they fired my imagination and the more I heard about them the more I wanted someday to go there and ski. We were the first generation of young Americans to come to love the mountains. We were truly ski pioneers."

Angela caught the excitement in Andy's eyes.

"Our unsuspecting way of life was shattered by the War. I remember the Sunday that the Japanese bombed Pearl Harbour. My brother was home on furlough from the army. We were talking about the coming winter, when the first snowfall would occur, and whether the ski meets would be held. After dinner, he went to Bez'es drugstore to buy some cigarettes, while we tuned in to the 6:00 o'clock news."

"The announcer was excited. He talked about an American lumber ship being sunk in the Pacific and then read a bulletin describing the Japanese attack. I don't know why, but my mother told my father and me not to tell my brother when he returned. The front door opened and we all knew that he had heard the news. Without saying anything he went upstairs to pack his duffel bag so that he could catch the last bus to Manchester."

"Soon afterwards, I left university and enlisted in the Air Force. After training to be a pilot, I flew to England and in the autumn of 1942, took part in the invasion of Morocco and Algeria. Later, the war shifted to Sicily and to the mainland. I was on a mission over Torino to bomb the FIAT plant when my B-24 was hit by flak. I told the crew to parachute and then tried to fly towards Switzerland. But the damage to three of the plane's motors was too great and I had to jump as well." He shrugged his shoulders. "You know the rest of the story."

The empty vermouth bottle caught the light from the kerosene lamp. Both young people were drained from the intensity of the night's conversation. Angela looked at Andy and saw the American as an innocent coming of age. She wondered if he ever thought that his bombs were killing old men, loving women, and helpless children. Before she went to her room, she walked over to him, kissed him on the cheek, placed her hand over his, and said quietly,

"We are good friends, Andy."

He understood.

After six days and six nights the snow stopped falling. Angela spent the morning clearing the terrace, shovelling the light powder into great mounds that formed the border of the deck. Excited by the snowfall and warmed by the hard work, she barged into the hotel, disappeared into her room, and emerged a few minutes later dressed in comfortable dark ski pants and a hip length anorak.

"I am going for a walk on my skis, Andy, and will return in about an hour. The snow still has not settled so the going will be tough, but I need exercise after the week's confinement."

When she returned, the sky was clearing, but not without a struggle. One by one the great peaks emerged above the stratus. An exposure of blue would be covered by the shifting clouds. Finally, the mountains were revealed and the sky turned an emerald colour. As the evening progressed, the drama of nature continued to unfold. After the sun had set, the white tops of the glaciated massifs turned to brilliant gold that was edged against a purple black screen.

Then the curtain of the oncoming night fell.

CHAPTER III
Valle di St. Barthélemy, 12-44

We were cold and hungry, we were the most disarmed partisans in the Piedmont, and probably also the most unprepared. We thought we were safe because we had not yet moved out of our refuge buried under three feet of snow: but somebody betrayed us, and on the dawn of December 13, 1943, we woke surrounded by the Fascist Republic: they were three hundred and we eleven, equipped with a tommy gun without bullets and a few pistols. Eight of us managed to escape and scattered among the mountains; three of us did not get away: the militiamen captured Aldo, Guido, and myself, still half asleep. As they came in I managed to hide in the stove's ashes the revolver I kept under my pillow, and which in any case I was not sure I knew how to use: it was tiny, all inlaid with mother of pearl, the kind used in movies by ladies desperately intent on committing suicide. Aldo, who was a doctor, stood up, stoically lit a cigarette, and said: "Too bad for my chromosomes."
LEVI, **The Periodic Table**, 1984.

Andy did not sleep well. He could tell that his leg was healing. For the first time since he had been picked up by the partisans he was uneasy and restless. The vision of Angela walking on skis triggered thoughts about the wintery months ahead.
"I must get into shape after my cast comes off so I'll be able to ski as soon as possible."
He dreamt about New England. Images of the headwall at Tuckerman's Ravine, the snow covered New Hampshire forests, and races at Stowe clicked through his mind. The night passed slowly, its deep silence disturbed by the thunder of avalanches that smashed down the mountainsides after the six-day snowfall.
After breakfast, wearing a pair of high altitude glasses that

43

Angela had given him, Andy went out on the terrace. He placed his crutches carefully on the snow-packed deck and settled into the chaise longue. Although it was already ten o'clock, the sun was just emerging over the high crests to the east. The air was much colder than anything he had experienced at the Tête Blanche. The brilliance of the morning light startled him. There were no clouds. An intense blue sky and stark white mountain panorama had replaced the dull monochromatic atmosphere of the previous week. Christmas was only a few days away. What a glorious place to celebrate the holiday. He could hardly believe that men were killing each other outside the confines of this beautiful valley.

Searching the high peaks, he could see where the avalanches had scarred the smoothness of the snow-covered slopes. He was attracted by some motion to the southwest and watched in astonishment as first one fine line and then another was traced on the mountainside. The skiers, enveloped by plumes of snow, were almost invisible in the deep powder. They broke from their high traverse into long graceful arcing turns and quickly dropped towards the valley floor.

"Angela, come outside! Skiers are heading towards the Tête Blanche!"

Andy could make out ten separate tracks. Then one by one the tracks merged into a low traverse and the skiers aimed for the hotel.

She ran from the kitchen.

"Get inside, quickly!"

Startled, the American began to move toward the door as fast as he could work his crutches.

The skiers were soldiers, uniforms thickly coated with loose powder and menacing guns slung across their shoulders.

Angela shouted, "Wait! They are our men."

The leader, after taking his skis off and placing them against the railing of the terrace walked slowly towards Andy.

"Buon giórno Americano. Cóme Sta?"

It was Carlo. Angela embraced him and kissed his cheeks. Tears glistened on both of their faces. Carlo looked exhausted. He had a rough beard, there were fine lines at the corners of his eyes. His clothes were steaming from the heat of his body in the cold morning air.

Angela opened the hotel door, "Come in all of you, there is enough room and food."

The haggard soldiers stuck their skis into the deep snow, took their boots off and carried them into the warm kitchen. Andy followed and soon the room smelled of stale body odour and wet wool. The men slumped on the benches and sprawled on the floor. They hardly moved; however, their eyes were alive with excitement.

Angela disappeared in the kitchen and soon everyone had a mug of hot coffee, hard rolls, and some peach jam.

Carlo was standing near her.

"How's the *Americano?*"

He is doing fine, the cast should be removed in a week or two."

Carlo sipped from his cup, "Does he cause any trouble?"

"Not at all. We get along well."

Angela surveyed the chaotic scene in the hotel and asked, "What are you doing, coming here to the hotel?"

Carlo was biting into his roll, "We were forced to seek a place of refuge."

"What happened?"

He sat down on a chair and started to tell her the events of the past days.

"For almost a week, ever since the snow began to fall, we've been fighting the Germans.

"A month ago I received a message that instructed me to take my climbing equipment and go to Courmayeur. The train ride from Pont St. Martin to the end of the line at Près St. Didier was uneventful, just a few peasants smoking their pipes and sharing the hard wooden benches in the third class compartment. The weather was perfect and I passed the time by gazing out the window at the yellowing vineyards and the glaciers of Monte Bianco.

"The bus at Près St. Didier had broken down, so I walked up the slope to Courmayeur, admiring the mountain ash that had been planted along the roadside. The air was warm and the contrasting colours of autumn were at their peak. There were thick clusters of red berries hanging from the wiry branches of the trees. They were set against a deep blue sky and the white of the mountain tops."

After Carlo reached Courmayeur, he made his way along a narrow street past the Alpine Museum to the Albergo Dente di Gigante. There he met a number of resistance leaders from the remote valleys. That night they were told about a military operation, that if successful, would shut down the steel works in Aosta for many months.

Carlo tilted his chair against the wall of the kitchen and took a deep breath.

"You know, the factory is supplied with iron ore from the mine in the mountains at Cogne south of Aosta. Because it's at a high altitude, the ore comes down to Cogne by *téléphérique* and then is transferred to a narrow gauge electric train that carries it to Charemoz above Aosta. From there another *téléphérique* transports the ore in buckets down the mountain to the steel mill.

"The leader of the group, a tough coal miner from La Thuile, told us that we were to simultaneously destroy the téléphérique in Cogne, blow up the rail-line and tunnel between Cogne and Charemoz, and demolish the second *téléphérique* between Charemoz and Aosta. We would need three separate groups of about a dozen men each to do the job. After a long discussion,

46

we decided to set the time of the attack for the night of December 16th, as close to midnight as possible."

Carlo's men were to cut the second *téléphérique*. That in itself was not too difficult. However, their escape route was the most dangerous because they had to come down from Charemoz, cross the main valley and head up the Valle di St. Barthélemy towards Cervinia. The meeting ended at three in the morning. He went to his room and collapsed into bed. The next day Carlo took the train back to Pont St. Martin. He had two weeks to organize his group, brief them about the mission, and gather their equipment together.

"In ones and twos we left for our rendezvous in the Castle of Fenis some kilometers to the west of Aosta."

"Have you been there Angela?"

"Oh yes. I went once with my school. I remember the inner courtyard with the steps leading up to the wooden balconies. The beautiful frescos gave life to the grey stone of the castle."

"So you liked St. George killing the dragon. I had plenty of time to look at him during the two days that we stayed at the castle."

"The caretaker put us up in one of the hidden rooms, and except for the cold, the experience was rather romantic. We cleaned and checked our guns and I handed out explosives that would be used to destroy the *téléphérique* towers. The castle had been a perfect place to cache arms and dynamite that the resistance had captured from the Germans."

One afternoon, Carlo walked to Aosta where he observed the *téléphérique* as it crossed the stoney flood plain of the Dora Baltea. Every twenty seconds a bucket of iron ore was emptied at the edge of the factory.

"The last day in Fenis, I climbed one of the castle's turrets and looked up the valley towards the smoke of the city. The stench of the steel mill permeated the mountain air. I could

47

easily imagine myself as a knight during the Middle Ages, waiting to go into battle. Except for the paved road and single track of the railroad, nothing much had changed since the 14th century."

Carlo stopped for a moment and noticed that his men, scattered about the kitchen, like trees swept from the mountainside by an avalanche, had fallen asleep from exhaustion. He looked at the pensive expression on Angela's face and continued his story.

"When we left late on the afternoon of December 16th, visibility was poor. A cold rain was falling and the outline of the mountains was fading in the dusk. The rucksacks, loaded with explosives, ammunition, and provisions were low on our backs. We moved steadily along a narrow path that would take us up the mountain to the *téléphérique* in three hours."

Because they could not risk walking in the main valley, they moved along the lower flanks of the mountains on a route that followed the contour of the slope. From time to time the group would come to a small isolated hamlet of two or three *racards*, but for the most part, the path, covered with rust-coloured needles, led through the *méléze* forest.

When it was completely dark, Carlo switched on a small climber's light that he wore over his hat. It belonged to one of the mountain guides in his band. He had painted the lens blue so that only enough light was given off to faintly illuminate the path. Closely behind were his twelve companions, the noises from their boots and moving bodies muffled by the rain running off the branches of the trees.

By nine-thirty, they had climbed over a thousand meters, and had arrived at an *alpage*. If it had been daytime, the partisans would have been able to see the Monte Bianco directly ahead and the Cervino at their backs.

"Far below, somewhere in the black silence that fell away from my right side, was the braided bed of the Dora Baltea, the river that some families still exploited for gold. Ahead, lay the *téléphérique*. I could hear the steady rhythm of the ore buckets as they passed over the supporting steel pylons. The miserable weather was a blessing. No one would be patrolling the towers on such a cold and wet night."

Carlo asked for another cup of coffee.

"We grouped together where the pylons were but a few hundred meters apart. From the faint glow of my light, I could make out the sweating faces of the men. Some wore berets, others had on the prized brimmed hat of the *Alpinisti*, and a number had the hoods of their anoraks drawn about them for protection from the rain."

He told Rinaldo and Lucien to take four men and place explosives around the base of the upper tower, then worked rapidly with the remaining group, most of whom were boys just out of high school, to mine the lower tower. They were careful to make certain that all of the wires were properly connected. Then the explosives were covered with ground sheets to keep them as dry as possible.

By the time they were finished, another hour had gone by. They huddled together like penguins in a blizzard and waited in the drenching rain. The last sixty minutes passed swiftly for Carlo. He was concentrating on the escape route down the mountain to the bridge at Villefranche. There the men would cross the Dora Baltea and head up the other side to the Valle di St. Barthélemy. Carlo was counting on the turmoil that would occur after the explosions in Cogne and along the narrow-gauge railway to help them get away. Each partisan band would head in separate directions to confuse the Germans.

"At midnight, I forced the plunger of the detonator. A few moments passed before a brilliant orange flash blinded me. Almost simultaneously, the tower farther up the mountain was outlined by the second explosion. Ore buckets came crashing to the wet earth, cables whipped along the grass, and pylons collapsed. For a stunned instant I stood in the darkness, white, yellow, and orange streaks stabbing my eyes. Then I called to the men and we began to move down the mountain into the emptiness of the night. I remember how hot my body was and how cold the icy rain felt as it spattered in my face and dripped through my beard."

Andy moved closer to Carlo to try and understand what he was saying, but he couldn't make out the words of the young soldier as he talked to Angela in staccato phrases of French, Italian, and patois.

"We arrived at the bridge within two hours. The rain-swollen river was running high, covering our noise. There was no time for diversions. A small group of Germans were guarding the crossing. They must have known that the *téléphérique* had been blown up. We crept as close to the bridge as possible and then opened fire with machine guns and grenades. The attack lasted five minutes, an outburst of stress and emotion against the cursed Nazis!"

The Italians ran across the bridge past the torn and bloody bodies of the enemy and charged up the mountain slope toward St. Barthélemy. German reinforcements would search after them. Despite their fatigue and the slippery footing they forced themselves to climb the steep pitch. To avoid capture they had to remain above their pursuers. The partisans had been moving for over nine hours in bad weather and in total darkness. So far their luck had been good.

Carlo shifted on his chair.

"Above Villefranche, we came to a small road that led to Planavilla. Keeping to the left, we took the fork that followed the west flank of the valley for a number of kilometers before reaching the main road near the stone quarry."

As they worked their way higher, the air temperature dropped and heavy wet flakes of snow began to fall with the rain. The men moved as fast as possible on the rutty road; however, their pace was slowed by rocks, some as large as footballs, that because of the downpour were falling from the slopes above. At the village of Lignan they stopped. Here, Carlo had been told, would be a cache of skis in the cemetery by the church. Except for the sound of water running off its roof, there was total silence.

The remainder of the march was blurred by the weariness and cold that overwhelmed the soldiers' bodies. By the time they reached Praz, the morning light was filtering through the heavy snow. They ate some food, drank wine to ease their thirst, and then put on skis and climbing skins.

"The men were covered with snow and ice. One of the boys, it was Claudio, had taken off his beret and was placing a balaclava over his long wet blond hair. I'll never forget the strained expression on his face. Two hours later he was dead."

Carlo looked past Angela to the mountains beyond the kitchen window. Some seconds passed before he continued.

"The harsh roar of trucks shifting gears on the road below alerted us to the Germans. The falling snow hid their cumbersome vehicles behind a descending curtain of white. Fortunately, for us, they would have to follow on foot or skis because the road ended beyond Praz. Then we would be both above treeline, hunter, and hunted."

Carlo had the choice of heading east over the pass at Nebbia and making for the Val Tournanche, or continuing up the valley to over 2800 meters and coming down in the Valpelline. He planned to make his decision at Nebbia, but first, the partisans had to outdistance the Germans.

They started to ski single file, heading for the upper reaches of the valley, the hum of the climbing skins against the snow keeping time to their gliding bodies. Visibility was bad, a total whiteout. The heavy snowfall hadn't let up. They could only go higher and somehow outdistance the Germans. That would be difficult. The enemy was fresh, had the advantage of following

51

in a packed track, and outnumbered the Italians.

"Their dogs had found our tracks, but the deep snow prevented the animals from following. After two hours of pursuit, I could tell that they were gaining. We were facing experienced mountain troops, no doubt the best in Aosta. With our dark uniforms, we were but vague shadows moving through the falling snow. That didn't stop them from firing at us. A stray bullet hit Claudio in the back of the neck. He slumped into the snow without uttering a sound and almost disappeared in the loose powder, a widening red stain marking where his body lay. He was dead. We had to leave him."

Angela, tears flooding her eyes, turned away.

"We skied past a stone and timbered *alpage* barn and two lone *mélèze* that were enveloped within a grey fog. Here, the snow had been falling for over 15 hours and was nearly a meter deep. I could barely make out the pass at Nebbia and decided instead to head up the couloir that led to the Fenêtre de Tzan. This was our moment of gravest danger. We were funneled together on the steep face, frantically trying to climb through the deep snow. I prayed that an avalanche wouldn't bury us. I don't know how we were able to keep moving. My body was numb."

Two hundred meters below, the Germans, sensing the vulnerability of the partisans, started after them. Some of their men stopped and began to fire. Renaldo let out a cry and pitched into the snow, shot in the back. The rest of the Germans had closed the distance to 150 meters.

"Then I realized that an avalanche would be our only salvation. One of the older men in my band, Georgio, had fought in the First World War against the Austrians. He was in an *Alpinisti* regiment that was sent to the Ortler Mountains near the Stelvio Pass. Many times at the Café Sport, after two or three génépy, he had told me how both armies had set off avalanches with murderous effect. Tens of thousands of Italians

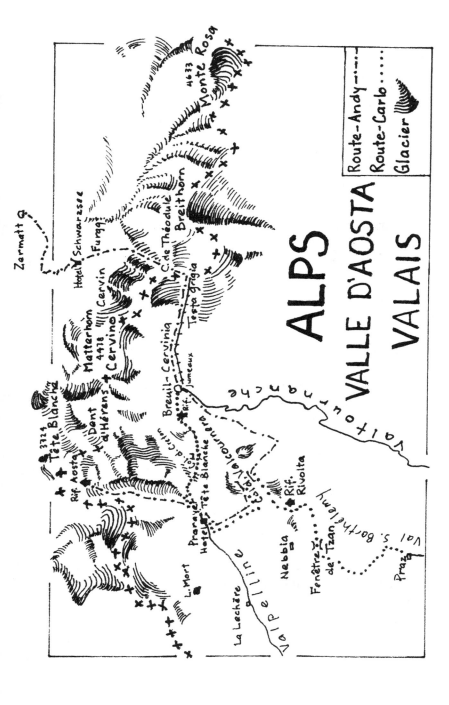

ALPS
VALLE D'AOSTA
VALAIS

Route–Andy
Route–Carlo
Glacier

Zarmatt

Hotel Schwarzsee
Funggl
Cervin
Cervino
Matterhorn
4478
Monte Rosa
4673
C. de Théodule
Breithorn
Testa Grigia
Breuil–Cervinia
Rif. Jumeaux

Tête Blanche
3724
Dent d'Hérens
Rif. Aosta

Col Crête
Hotel Tête Blanche
Pranayel
Malacoursena
Rif. Rivolta
Nebbia
Fenêtre de Tzan
Val S. Bartholomy
Praz

L. Mort
La Lechère
Valpelline
Valtournenche

and Austrians had been slaughtered, buried by the 'white death'." Carlo paused. Angela wiped her face with a serviette, then filled his cup with more coffee. After taking two sips of the steaming black liquid, he began to speak in a subdued tone. "We were just below the top of the pass. A thick cornice of snow marked the exposed upper slope. Martino, his eyes flashing anxiety, cut off a chunk and watched it fall harmlessly below. One by one, the men struggled through the opening and moved out of sight of the Germans. I was the last one through, my body chilled by the sudden gust blowing off the exposed arête."

The exhausted Italians were slumped on the windswept rocks taking a short respite. Snow completely covered their uniforms. Only their fear-ridden faces were visible. Carlo shouted at them to prepare their grenades. They waited until the Germans were only 75 meters below, then pitched them onto the cornice. A series of muffled explosions broke the wind-packed snow and sent it tumbling below. Slowly, the slope hit by the shattered cornice began to move. The faint cry of *Lawine!* was heard. Gathering speed the snow swept the couloir. The silence of the mountains was broken by the roar of the cascade. Then all was quiet.

"Peering over the edge, I could make out a faint white mound where the avalanche had come to rest. Some guns and skis were strewn on the surface. All of the Germans had been buried. For the moment, we were safe."

They couldn't stay long at the top of the pass. The cold was stiffening their arms and legs. After taking off the climbing skins, the men skied one by one down the other side toward the *Cabane de Tzan*. Five or six turns would have brought them to a long slope from where they would have been able to schuss the rest of the way. What should have been a simple run, took over an hour. They were cold, wet, and weak from fatigue. In the bottomless powder, the skiers couldn't control their legs.

First one and then another would fall. They lay trapped like animals, skis, poles, rifles, and rucksacks buried in the snow. The men had to help one another on to their skis. Fortunately, except for some strained muscles, no one was seriously injured.

"We stopped at the *cabane* for a break and ate the remainder of the salami we had packed and took long drinks from our wineskins. The cold of the interior of the stone hut permeated our bones, but at least we were sheltered from the fierce wind. The men wanted to sleep but the location of the *cabane*, below the pass, was too dangerous. Instead, I decided to head for the *Rifúgio Rivolta*. We would have to make a dangerous climb to over 2900 meters, but once inside we would command a view in all directions."

Carlo sipped more coffee. Andy was watching the changing expressions of his face; first pain, then exhaustion, and finally triumph.

"The next few hours were a nightmare. We were strung out in a long traverse, skiing slowly above the Basin of Tzan. Visibility was getting worse as the snow continued to rain from the sky. An avalanche could bury us at any moment. We were forcing our luck to the limit."

The final climb of 350 meters was steeper than the ascent of the Fenêtre de Tzan. At every step they floundered in the snow up to their waists. The partisans moved like robots, first one ski and then the other, half a meter at a time. Carlo lost track of the hour. The white scene before him was fast turning dark. His hands and feet were frozen. Finally, the men half climbed and half dragged themselves to the top of the pass. Off to the right, perched above a rocky ledge, almost invisible in the failing light, was the *rifúgio*. It was to be their home for the next five nights.

"The storm continued. Good, our tracks were buried beneath meters of new snow. Because the supply of wood was limited, we could make a fire for only a few hours each day. We kept warm by lying side by side on the *couchettes,* covered over with piles of blankets that were stored in the *rifúgio.*

"We rationed the remaining food, some bread, cheese, nuts, and dried fruit, that we had brought from Fenis. Each day faded into the next almost imperceptibly as the snow permeated the air. The men moved listlessly trying to fend off the incessant cold."

Carlo reached across the table for another roll. Crumbs scattered as he tore it in two. Then his story was concluded.

"Our destination was Cervina. For some weeks the partisans had been in control of the village and the *téléphérique* to the Testa Grigia. But there was still the risk that the Germans could cut us off before we reached our comrades. I decided that we must first come down to the Tête Blanche where we would be able to dry our clothing and replenish our food."

The last night in the *rifúgio* Carlo stepped outside. The snowfall had finally ended, the air was calm and the bitter cold tore at his face. The heaven was brilliant with stars; Orion dominated the winter sky, and to the south he could make out the warm glow of Jupiter. There was no God up there. Fate was in his own hands.

They started their descent to the Tête Blanche in the arctic dawn. A pale orange alpine glow lit up the surrounding peaks as the morning unfolded. The group skied in a northeast direction down the long slope that led from the top of the pass toward Cervinia. The snow had settled and visibility was exceptional and as they warmed up the partisans skied with greater confidence and skill. In ten minutes the men descended nearly 400 meters. To the left, Carlo could see the route toward the Col de Valcournera. One more climb and then they would be in the Valpelline.

After putting on the skins, the men started up at a steady pace. They passed an abandoned *alpage,* the remains of the barn sticking up through the drifted snow. Above the opening where the door had been was a weathered grey timber secured between the rocks of the wall. Carved into the wood were the Roman numerals **MCMXXIII**. Carlo's thoughts shifted to the short alpine summers at this altitude. How time played with one's mind. Looking at all the snow, it was hard for him to believe that cows, flowers, and insects were part of this barren landscape, and that families worked, played, and loved on these slopes.

They then skied by two frozen lakes on their left and continued climbing until the 3000 meter level of the pass. After taking off the skins, they drank some tea that had been prepared at the *rifúgio* and marveled at the awesome beauty of the mountain panorama.

Carlo cautioned the men to ski down about ten to fifteen meters apart for safety. They had made two or three turns in the hissing powder when he heard the crack of the avalanche. Looking back, he could see the last three men being overtaken by the speeding snow. Two had fallen, but their bodies were free. The third had disappeared, catching the full brunt of the moving mass.

"The rest of us began to climb back to the avalanche track. I looked around, all the men were there except for Mickey, Eugenio, and Georgio. We took fifteen minutes to get up to the slide. Mickey and Eugenio were dug out, their skis still on their feet. Georgio was not in sight. We climbed to where I had last seen him and began to probe the snow with the handles of our ski poles. Slowly, we moved down the slope, ten men strung across, hoping to find Georgio alive.

"Fifty meters from where I had spotted him, Albert struck a buried form. We dug frantically to free the trapped body. I knew when I saw him that he was dead, legs and arms twisted in an obscene manner, suffocated by the 'white death'. We took his gun and rucksack, then buried Georgio in the snow. We had lost the third member of our band, killed by the mountains that he had loved."

Carlos stopped talking and glanced about the room. The late afternoon sun filtered through the frosted kitchen windows. In twos and threes, the soldiers rose from where they had slept and made their way upstairs to the *couchettes*. When they returned, wrapped in coarse wool blankets, they transformed the kitchen, the only heated area in the hotel, into a combination bath and drying room.

Lines of climbing rope were strung across the room and wet uniforms were hung up to dry. Water was brought from the *lavabo* and warmed on the stove. They began to wash the week's accumulation of sweat and filth from their bruised bodies.

That night Angela served everyone a hot soup, thick with pasta, and coated with *Parmigiano* cheese. The soldiers ate ravenously and after supper, went back to the *couchettes*. Andy followed up the stairs and went to his room. Angela cleaned off the table and washed the dishes. She dodged around the uniforms hanging awkwardly on the lines and studied their mysterious trembling shadows projected on the wooden walls from the light of the kerosene lamp. Picking up the lamp and carrying it into her room, she thought, "Tomorrow is Christmas eve. We will have a party."

A fine snow had fallen during the night, partially covering the ski tracks of the soldiers. The weary men slept late, so Angela prepared a large breakfast that included sausage and Fontina cheese. She added boiling milk to the coffee, sprinkled in some cinnamon, and served *cappuccino* to the men. It was almost as good as they could order in the cafés of Aosta.

After finishing breakfast, Carlo spoke to her about his plans.

"We'll leave for Cervinia early Christmas morning. I don't think the Germans will be searching for us then. If you have any spare climbing picks, shovels, and rope, I'd like to have them. We'll head up the valley to the huts at Gordze, and then climb over the Glacier des Dames to the Col du Créton. I've done this route in late summer and it was tough enough. I only hope that the snow on the glacier has settled so that we'll be able to cross the crevasses without too much danger. From the col we'll ski along the slope of the mountains until the *Rifúgio Jumeaux* above Cervinia. If all looks well in the village, we can ski down before sunset. But if we have to, we can bivouac in the snow for one or two nights."

Angela nodded in agreement, excused herself, and went down to the cave to see if there was some good white wine to serve with the evening meal. She was going to prepare a fondue. There was enough stale bread and a good supply of cheese. But fondue without white wine was like a beautiful woman without a lover.

In one corner of the cave, the kerosene lamp illuminated a dust-covered wooden case lying on its side. As luck would have it, she discovered twelve bottles of Fendant *Les Murettes* 1937.

Before the war, her father-in-law had driven across the Grand St. Bernard to spend some days with a Swiss doctor and his young wife who had stayed a week at the Tête Blanche and climbed in the Valpelline. After visiting the ruins and church of Valere above Sion, where they saw the world's oldest playable organ, they walked in the steep vineyards and viewed the deep glacial trough of the Rhône Valley, not unlike that of the Valle d'Aosta. The couple had given him the wine as a token of appreciation for his hospitality.

Happily Angela thought, "The party will be a success!"

By four o'clock, dusk had obscured the mountains. The men came down from the *couchettes* looking brave and handsome in their uniforms. An aroma of bubbling cheese filled the kitchen. Angela had added some kirsch and with a wooden spoon was stirring the viscous substance in a large cast iron pot.

Everyone sat on benches around a long rectangular table. The dozen green bottles of Fendant, yellow sun and grey church and vineyards on their labels, added spots of colour to the worn taupe tabletop. Candles were flickering and Angela poured the liquid cheese into three smaller pots and placed them on fondue burners before the men.

Carlo uncorked some of the bottles, glasses were filled, and a toast proposed.

"To our fallen comrades, Claudio, Renaldo, and Georgio; may their deaths have not been in vain."

He tasted the cool wine and paused to savour its delicate bouquet.

He looked into Angela's eyes,

"*Salúte.*"

"*Salúte* Carlo." The men responded. Eyes filled with tears, they sipped the pale Fendant. Minutes passed and they started to eat the fondue, placing the hard bread on the long forks and dipping it into the steaming creamy cheese. They began to smile and laugh a little in the bittersweet ambiance of the kitchen.

Angela thought of past summer nights when climbers and hikers returned to the hotel from the day's outing to enjoy a simple meal and established friendships based on their common experiences in the mountains.

Albert, a handsome man with dark wavy hair in his early thirties, scraped some cheese from the bottom of the pot, tasted the salty crust of the fondue, and drank the rest of his Fendant.

In a soft voice, he began to sing songs of the Alps. Francesco joined in, then Roberto, and soon harmonious musical sounds filled the room.

One song followed another, the tempo shifting from adagio to vivace, then back to adagio.

Andy could only make out a few of the words; however, he

relaxed in an inner glow from the wine, overcome by the beauty of the yodeling and the a cappella melodies.

"*la violètta...*,"

"*la montàgna...*,"

"*un po piú lúngo...*,"

"*les fleurs des Alpes...*,"

Inhibition swept away by the drinking of the wine and the music, the soldiers, arms around each other's shoulders, wept unashamedly. One gripped Andy's hand. Angela, held tightly to his other arm. She kissed him on the lips and caressed him warmly.

The hour was late. Carlo stood up. The singing faded softly. He poured a last glass of wine, and held it in the air where it caught the light from the dying candles.

He saluted the men of the mountain.

"To the soldiers of the mountains who were buried under the avalanche. Before this terrible war, I skied and climbed with such men. Each autumn, they arrived with their families at the St. Vincent folk festival from the Tirol and Bayern to sing their mountain songs and dance the *Schuhplattler* silhouetted against the setting sun in the Valle d'Aosta.

"We had so much in common. We shared so much beauty. How can it be that on this eve before Christmas in 1944, we are forced to fight and destroy one another?"

The men murmured to each other.

Carlo nodded.

"To peace," he said.

There was silence. Then the soldiers, leaving the empty wine bottles strewn on the table, got up unsteadily from the benches, walked carefully out of the kitchen to bed down in the *couchettes*.

Tomorrow, they would have to ski to Cervinia.

CHAPTER IV
Prarayer, 1-45

"We chewed in silence, as attentive to the precious acidulous flavour as we would have been to a symphony. In the meantime, in the pipe opposite ours, a woman had taken refuge. She was young, bundled up in black rags, perhaps a Ukrainian belonging to the Todt Organization, which consisted of 'volunteer' (they had little or no choice) foreign labourers recruited for war work. She had a broad red face, glistening with rain, and she looked at us and laughed. She scratched herself with provocative indolence under her jacket, then undid her hair, combed it unhurriedly, and began braiding it again. In those days it rarely happened that one saw a woman close up, an experience both tender and savage that left you shattered." LEVI, **Moments of Reprieve, 1986.**

The next seven days passed quietly. On the morning of the soldier's departure, Angela had brought together the equipment Carlo had requested. He picked out an ice axe, looked at Grivel-Courmayeur stamped in the cold metal of the pick, and set it aside. She gave them enough provisions for three days and filled their wineskins from the cask in the cave. After putting on their boots, the men kissed Angela and went out on the terrace to collect their skis. Carlo reached for her hands and kissed her lips, then followed.
  "Arrivedérci. Arrivéderci."
  "Arrivéderci. Augúri."
  In a few moments, the skiers were reduced to slowly moving points on an endless field of snow. Angela watched them as they started to climb the upper valley of the Buthier. Then one by one, they moved out of sight.
  "I will not know until the spring whether or not they will reach Breuil safely," she thought.

For the rest of the week, Angela busied herself with the chores of the hotel. The cows would be milked and she would spend hours in the barn, keeping the fire stoked under the giant copper pot, making Fontina. Then she would return to the kitchen and bake some bread.

Andy felt uneasy. His leg was irritated and the itching was unbearable. He was anxious to remove the cast.

After supper, on the last night of the year, Angela asked him to come into her room that opened onto the kitchen. On the *armoire,* the steady flame of a candle softly illuminated the furnishings. She motioned to him to lie down on the dark wooden bed, as she reached for the saw that was propped against a pine chest. She had used it that afternoon to trim firewood.

Angling the blade on his cast, Angela moved swiftly from one cut to another. Then she began to tear off the pieces of dirty plaster. Within minutes, the rough pink flesh surrounding the thigh and calf bones was exposed. He tried, but couldn't bend his knee.

She went into the kitchen and returned with a crock of olive oil, then poured some of the cool, fragrant liquid onto her palms and began to gently massage the limb, moving her hands slowly from toes to thigh to stimulate the circulation. Eyes closed, Andy felt her strong fingers soothing the wasted muscles. and thought of how radiant she had looked the evening after the snowstorm when she had returned from skiing.

"You are going to need at least a month to get your leg back in shape."

Startled, Andy said, "I'll start exercising tomorrow, but I know what you mean, I've no strength in it at all."

She squeezed his thigh.

"Be careful and keep using your crutches, you could easily injure yourself again."

Angela continued the rhythmic movements with her oil-covered hands. She was sitting on the edge of the bed and had drawn the down comforter over his body, leaving his naked leg uncovered. Her fingers were massaging the flyer's groin when almost imperceptibly, she began to move her hands over his balls. She hesitated for an instant, but began again when she saw him open his eyes and smile. His hand reached for her other arm and he held it firmly.

Andy felt her move from his crotch to his cock, and he sensed its growing strength. He had never had a woman make love to him. The first time he had been with a girl, he was only fifteen. It had felt good, but it was an act lacking in affection, a little better than masturbation, and quickly over.

He was aware that what was happening was much more than that. The woman beside him was running her hands over his body with deep tender feelings. He meant something to her.

Andy drew Angela closer and responded to the heat of her body.

When they awoke, an orange light from the dying candle was flickering across the ceiling. Their steady breathing formed small puffs of vapour in the bitterly cold room. Under the comforter, they were secure in an oasis of warmth, aware that what had happened was a loving moment in a shattered world.

"I feel really close to you Angela. Does your marriage make any difference?"

"No Andy, what I did expressed my true feelings. At times we have no control over our actions. We experience anxiety, jealously, or hatred. There is a part of us that we never know until after the fact. My sexual passions poured out of my inner being. I am not sorry for I do not know if I will ever see my husband again. You are in my house now."

"But your religion forbids love like this."

"What do the persons who preach religion know. They want

to deny normal emotions. Can a dried-up old priest in the Vatican understand sexual sensations between a man and a woman? They tell us to love one another, yet they bless the soldiers who are going to commit murder. We are not supposed to prevent conception, but the rich limit their families. Only the uneducated and the poor peasants in the south produce many children."

Andy took her hand and felt her slender fingers.

"Are you afraid of having a child?"

There was no hesitation to her answer.

"We are cut off from the mad world and so our actions in the Tête Blanche are natural. I can think of worse things than to create life when so much of Europe is experiencing a nightmare of death and destruction."

Andy turned on his side and ran his fingers through her long golden hair and touched her eyebrows and soft lips. Feelings for this woman, who had been so kind, and had fed and cared for him, welled inside. He realized that he had truly made love for the first time. His hands stroked her full breasts, brushed her erect nipples, and softly scratched her red pubic hairs. She carefully rolled him on his back and moved on top of him and kissed him deeply. He held her firm buttocks and she began to move up and down with a steady motion. Andy felt his cock slide deep within her, like a pistol in its holster, and met each of her firm thrusts. Then the room filled with the sounds of love, and they were one and indivisible.

Angela slipped naked from beneath the comforter and as Andy watched, quickly dressed to ward off the intense cold. She stepped into the kitchen and stoked the fire in the cast iron stove. In half an hour she returned, carrying a cup of hot chocolate.

"*Bonne Année, Andy.*"

"Happy 1945, Angela."

She set the chocolate on the night table, embraced him, and softly kissed his lips and neck.

"How is your leg this morning?"

He laughed.

"Oh my leg! I wasn't thinking about it. I'm still dreaming about last night. A few more 'massages' like that and I'll be ready to climb the Cervin next week."

"I am going to make some Fontina. Would you like to come to the barn and see how it is done?"

"I'm ready, but first I want to hold you and kiss you, then we can start off the New Year by making cheese."

The room was slowly warming. Andy, thankful for the hot drink, sipped the chocolate carefully so as not to burn his mouth. Shivering, he pulled on his clothes and followed Angela through the kitchen to the stone barn at the side of the hotel. The path had been packed solidly and he was able to use his crutches on the snow with little difficulty. What a difference to walk without the weight of the plaster on his left leg!

He stooped through the low door into the subdued light of the barn. It had two floors and a small storage cellar. There was room for four cows and part of the barn was divided into a cheese-making room. The earthy odour of cows, hay, and manure contrasted to the sterility of the white world outside.

Angela, working swiftly and efficiently, changed into wooden clogs, fed the cows, cleaned the manure from the stalls, and shovelled it outside atop the winter's accumulation.

She warned the flyer, "Keep away, if this *merde* gets on your clothes, it will never come off."

He sized up the cows, "These are pretty tough looking beasts."

"You should see them fight in the annual competition at Nus. The one on the far right was crowned 'Queen of the Valley', the year before the war broke out."

"What do you mean", Andy asked, "How do they fight one

another?"

"They face off and then butt heads. The cow that turns away loses the match and the winner goes on to fight another round. The peasants drink liters of wine and bet enormous sums on the outcome. Then they turn their backs and piss in the fields." Angela giggled and said, "I hear that's good for the grass."

She put on a charcoal-coloured leather apron that was hanging on the wall of the barn, milked the cows and poured the steaming fluid into the copper pot that was hanging in the cheese room. More milk was added from a storage can, and branches and kindling were shoved underneath the caldron. Soon orange flames were licking against the soot-covered sides and illuminating the grey rock slabs that supported the roof. Smoke from the fire and vapour from the heated milk filtered out through chinks in the wall. Satisfied, she added something to the frothy contents and began stirring it with a wooden paddle.

"I have just put in the rennet and some bacteria. Take this and keep on stirring, it is good exercise."

He kept the paddle moving first in one direction and then in the other. After a few minutes, his arms were weary but he forced himself to continue. Slowly, the liquid began to solidify. Angela was ready with a wooden fork-like implement strung with wire. She deftly cut the coagulated milk into uniform particles about the size of rice grains, then took the paddle and continued to stir the cooking mass.

During the next hour, they took turns stirring. The aroma of the heated curds blended with the odours of the barn. From time to time, Angela took some from the pot and squeezed them in her hand. Finally, she expressed satisfaction with their texture.

Reaching for the coarse cheesecloth that was attached to a semi-circular wooden hoop, she skillfully drew it along the bottom of the pot. Releasing the hoop, she gathered the ends of the cloth and tied them together, strung a rope over the beam to the pot, attached it to the cheesecloth, and motioned Andy to help her lift the gathered curds out of the whey. She directed the dripping substance onto a nearby slate-covered table and deposited it into a round wooden form that was used to mould the cheese. Placing a lid over the form, she bore down on the curds until they were transformed into a semi-solid circular shape. Then she changed the original cloth for a finer one, took the cheese from the form and began turning it at regular intervals.

"I will have to come back two more times today to finish the work. Then the Fontina will be ready to age in the cellar."

After pouring the whey out of the copper pot, she cleaned it with icy water. Then, taking off her apron and clogs, she took Andy by the arm and they stepped out into the brilliant January light and returned to the hotel for lunch.

CHAPTER V
Mont Tremblant, 12-39, 1-40

"To see Sandro in the mountains reconciled you to the world and made you forget the nightmare weighing on Europe. This was his place, what he had been made for, like the marmots whose whistle and snout he imitated: in the mountains he became happy with a silent infectious happiness, like a light that is switched on. He aroused a new communion with the earth and sky, into which flowed my need for freedom, the plenitude of my strength, and a hunger to understand the things he had pushed me toward. We would come out at dawn, rubbing our eyes, through the small door of the Martinotti bivouac, and there all around us, barely touched by the sun, stood the white and brown mountains, new as if created during the night that had just ended and at the same time innumerably ancient. They were an island, an elsewhere."
LEVI, **The Periodic Table, 1984.**

The February sun was warming the snow. Reflecting off the south side of the Tête Blanche, the strengthening rays were slowly melting the high banks piled up near the wall. On the upper slopes, the delicate hexagonal crystals of powder that faced the sun were metamorphosing into rounded granules.

After the New Year, the weeks had drifted by. Andy would spend an hour each day pacing back and forth on the hotel's deck. His exercises and Angela's nightly massages had brought back the muscle tone and flexibility to his leg. One dreary afternoon she cut his hair, that by now had grown to his shoulders. In the ski-room he had found a decent fitting pair of boots and some wooden skis in a 210 centimeter length. The next day, he made a track around the hotel and circled it for thirty minutes. It was the first time in four winters that he had been on skis.

Were it not for the war, the visitor, wearing the uniform of the German Alpine Corps, might have thought that the young couple were taking a winter honeymoon. They had just finished a late breakfast and were doing the dishes when a noise startled them. Their eyes met in fear as the door opened and the soldier entered.

"Grüß Gott."

He took off his white anorak and walked towards the table.

"I have come on skis and am alone", he said in simple Italian.

Angela, regaining her composure, asked, "What do you want here? This is my hotel."

The man, short and dark, like so many who lived in the Alps, spoke calmly. He told them that he was from a valley, the Stubaital, south of the Inn River. Before the war, he had worked in a small foundry that hand-crafted ice axes and crampons that were sold in the sport shops of Innsbruck and München. In winter, he had been a ski instructor for tourists who came to the Stubaital from Wien. He was content with his work, but after the *Anschluß*, like so many young men from the valley, he had to join a mountain regiment. They had fought in Albania, Yugoslavia, and Greece, always coming to the rescue of the inept Italians.

After seeing action against the Americans and Canadians in the mountains around Salerno, his regiment was sent to Aosta.

Here he said, "The Italians are not so inept. They fight hard and well....against us."

Angela shot back, "Why did you come to the Tête Blanche?"

"I'm sick of this stupid war and want to see my wife and children in the Stubaital. I needed to be by myself, away from the barracks. On a hot day, late last summer, I walked the Valpelline and saw the building in the distant haze. It's only normal to want to see what it looks like under the winter snows. I'm reminded of home."

72

Angela measured some coffee beans from the wooden container above the stove.

"Sit down", she said. "Why are you really here?"

The soldier's brown eyes shifted nervously over the bare walls of the hotel. He waited until she had served him the coffee before answering.

"My family has lived in a valley like this one since the Middle Ages. We are the same religion though we speak a different language. The style of our chalets isn't like yours, but the life is the same. We wouldn't like to see strange soldiers in the Stubaital killing our friends and burning the villages. I want to be left out of this madness."

"There was a battle that took place with the partisans before Christmas. Many of our men were killed in an avalanche. The *Kommandant* is searching for those responsible. We've been trying to capture Cervinia, but because of the deep snows, we must wait until the spring".

Angela interjected, "What does that have to do with us?"

The soldier hesitated, then he said, "Our patrols will be coming here in a few days to check the hotel. We want to be sure that there are no partisans staying here."

He paused again, "That is all I can say."

Andy took Angela's hand and gripped it tightly.

The Austrian asked, "Do you have anything to eat?"

She brought out some cheese and a stale roll. The soldier took a few bites of the food and put the rest in the large pocket on the front of this anorak. Then he glanced at his watch.

"I must be going. It's not safe to be out after dark."

The two of them followed him through the front door of the hotel onto the deck. Shafts of sunlight filtered through the grey sky and played on the high mountains. He fixed his boots on the skis, placed the pole straps over each mitten, and looked at the couple.

"Thank you for your hospitality. Please be careful. I wish

73

you luck. If you come to Neustift in the Stubaital, ask for Joseph."

"*Auf Wiedersehen.*"

"*Arrivedérci.*"

Arm in arm, they watched the Austrian glide down the slope in front of the hotel. After ten minutes, they lost sight of him when he skied into the forest that led to Oyace.

At dawn, the following day, Andy set out for the *Rifúgio Aosta.* When the soldier from the Stubaital had left, Angela, after making another pot of coffee, had told the flyer how to get to the mountain hut.

"From Prarayer, the route is easy and within your skiing ability. It should take from three to four hours depending on how well your leg holds up and the state of the snow. I do not think that the Germans will search at that high elevation, they would be too exposed above the forest."

"The trail leads from the hotel up the Buthier to its source at the glacier. Keep high on the left side of the river. After 45 minutes to an hour, you will come out above the trees into a broad U-shaped valley. Head in the direction of the saddle between an isolated peak on the left, the Dents des Bouquetins, and a lower ridge on the right that leads to the Col de la Division. As you climb up the valley, you will make out the *rifúgio* on the right side of the glacier that comes down from the saddle. It is located on the moraine at 2781 meters."

She drew him a sketch map, using as a base the 1:50,000 sheets that were hanging on the wall of the dining room.

"When you return, if all is well, I will open the shutters on one of the the top floor windows. If there is still danger, all of the top windows will remain covered."

The rest of the day was spent preparing for the climb. Angela packed a rucksack with the usual bread, Fontina, dried

Cow Fight, Nus, Valle d'Aosta

fruit, and salami. She filled a wineskin with a dark Nebbiolo drawn from a *tonneau* in the hotel's cave. The skis were checked and Angela showed him how to attach the sealskins. The Kandahar bindings were similar to the ones he had used in New Hampshire. He adjusted them so that the cable permitted easy flexing of his boots.

The evening meal was pasta with dried mushrooms that Angela had soaked in water to bring out their flavour. She served it with melted butter, grated *parmigiano*, and a sprinkling of mountain sage.

They concentrated on eating and only spoke a few words to each other. After the kitchen was cleaned and the dishes washed, dried, and stacked in the cupboard, they went to bed so as to be able to get up early the next morning.

That night, the couple lay in bed as one. Andy had his right arm under Angela's head and his left arm between the softness of her breasts. He felt her long hair on his elbow, and her buttocks and thighs with his groin and legs. Their physical closeness brought forth deep feelings of love and affection. Both bodies radiated a warmth that the *duvet* trapped, shielding them from the frigid cold that gradually spread over the room.

At the first sign of daylight, Angela left the bed and prepared a large pot of strong tea. They slowly drank the steaming brew and she poured what was left into an aluminium gourd.

"You must drink a lot when you are climbing, otherwise you will become dehydrated and tire easily."

Andy took the rucksack and adjusted its straps to his body. He stepped out onto the terrace of the Tête Blanche, walked across the frosted deck, and set his skis on the snow. The sun was still below the eastern peaks and a silver sliver of a waning moon was visible in the southwest.

Angela embraced him and kissed his lips and mouth deeply. They clung to each other. After four months living together, they would soon be apart. Their eyes warned each other of the coming danger; Angela alone with the Germans, and Andy by himself in the high mountains.

He snapped the cables of the bindings forward and pushed off with his poles, schussing down the low hill in the direction of the upper valley. After 200 meters, he turned. The hotel could still be seen, the stark geometric pattern of its facade, broken on either side by the bare branches of *mélèzes*. The shuttered windows were clearly visible. Above the building, the still air of dawn had trapped a layer of blue haze, fed by the wood smoke that rose from the chimney.

Angela was watching him. He waved; she returned his gesture, took a long last look, then walked into the hotel.

Satisfied that all was well, Andy started to move with strong strides through the forest. The snow was firm and presented no difficulty. He was just getting up a smooth rhythm when he came to a level area that had been the run-out for a massive rock slide. Enormous crystalline boulders, that had crashed down the mountainside centuries ago, were strewn haphazardly across the meadow, their angular forms softened by a thick veneer of snow. Interspersed among them was a scattering of tall trees. As he studied the scene, he was again impressed by the primordial power of nature. Man, for all his pomposity, was puny by comparison. He took the climbing skins out of the rucksack and fixed them to his skis.

As he climbed, the meadow narrowed and gave way to a deep gorge. The clusters of naked brown *mélèzes* thinned out and soon he was moving in a landscape of almost total whiteness. At first, the view up the valley was blocked by the precipitous slope that he was traversing. Soon, however, the open basin that Angela had described, emerged.

At the head of the valley, he could make out the dark triangular shape of the Dents des Bouquetins, the saddle, and the ridge over which lay the Col de la Division. The *refúgio*, though, was still hidden in the morning shadows that covered the upper valley.

Andy had the impression that he could reach out and touch the surrounding mountains. However, distances in the Alps are deceiving and the hut was still two and one-half to three hours away.

The skis were working well, He slid them over the granular snow and they gripped tightly at each step. Though a light wind was blowing down the valley, the temperature was only a few degrees below zero. Already he was soaked with sweat from his climb. He stopped again, drank some tea, and took off his bomber jacket and arranged it under the flap of the rucksack. A woolen shirt and sweater that Angela had given him provided enough warmth.

As the sun arced higher in the sky, it illuminated a scene that was but a few thousand years removed from the ice age that had shaped the Alps. On the right side of the basin, a glacier, its séracs back lit by yellow rays, tumbled 500 meters to the valley floor. Beyond the ice, a frozen waterfall appeared cemented to the steep rock face. Directly ahead, a lateral moraine, grey stones exposed where the sun had melted the snow on its south-facing flank, led up the mountainside. Andy had to cross it before coming to another moraine that had been formed by the glacier coming down from the saddle. Far up on this one was the *Rifúgio Aosta*.

The final hour was a steady ascent up the crest of the second moraine. Andy's breathing was regular and slow, keeping time with the movement of the skis. He was perspiring profusely under the radiant heat from the noonday sun, hair matted down, and sun glasses coated with salty water that his body had given off during the sustained effort.

Andy reflected, "My muscles seem fine, but both feet are sore at the heels from the constant rubbing of the boots. I wonder what I'll feel like tomorrow morning."

The hut appeared more distinct with each painful step; his breathing became laboured because of the altitude and lack of conditioning. Just before the *rifúgio*, he stopped to gulp some more tea.

Finally, the flyer arrived at the shelter, took off his rucksack, stripped to the waist, and hung his shirt to dry on a protruding iron rod. He cleaned the snow off the steps, sat down, and unlaced his ski boots. Easing them off his feet, he slowly peeled back the thick wool socks. Both heels were covered with blood from the blisters that had broken during the last steep section of the climb. Fortunately, the pain was worse than the wound.

"Not bad," Andy thought, "for my first outing in four months."

As he pulled his lunch out of the rucksack, he could feel the warm rays of the sun radiating off the rust and grey-flecked stones of the south-facing wall.

The closeness of the mountains and the glacier ice reflecting the sun, contributed to the special atmosphere of the simple meal. He ate, chewing each morsel and thinking how intense the flavour of the food was in the fresh air. Except for an occasional falling rock, and the hum of the wind around the *rifúgio*, the silence was total.

Andy decided to stay outside the rest of the afternoon. He was comfortable sheltered by the wall. Besides, it was much warmer there than inside the stone building. He dozed. It wasn't a deep sleep, but he was unconscious of his immediate surroundings....

The drone of the B-24's four engines strengthened to a powerful roar. Andy adjusted his parachute, looked out of the vibrating cockpit window and waved to his mechanics. He caught a glimpse of Giro, the Golden Retriever mascot of the "Suicide Six" lopping along the concrete runway. They had brought him to Italy from England. The pilot closed the sliding window on the side of the plane and noticed the 16 painted bombs on the fuselage. Already, all those missions had melded as one. Would there be a 17th bomb stenciled on by tomorrow morning? He taxied out to the takeoff strip, following Bater in the No. 1 position. The "Suicide Six", carrying a full load of 2,000 pound bombs and extra fuel, slowly picked up speed, broke free from the ground and headed north.

After breakfast, the briefers had told the officers that there would be 36 bombers on this raid, all heading for the FIAT Mirafiori plant in Torino. They would probably encounter little opposition from German fighters but the flak could be heavy. This was one of the largest industrial concentrations in Italy still in German hands and the crumbling Third Reich desperately needed its output of armaments and trucks.

The flight path from Roma took them over the azure Mediterranean in the direction of Genova. Here, the formation of bombers crossed the narrow crescent of the Ligurian Alps and turned northwest towards Torino. Visibility during the three hour trip was unlimited and soon after they passed over the docks of Genova, Andy could make out the ragged edge of the Graien Alps. Thirty minutes later, the broad, tree-lined boulevards of Torino were below them. There was no difficulty in identifying FIAT. The factory area, an enormous complex of low buildings surrounded by the cultivated fields of the Po Valley, was to the southwest of the city within sight of the Alpine foothills.

Just as the B-24s started their bombing run the anti-aircraft gunners opened up. Vicious bursts of orange and black flak alienated the peaceful morning sky. The pilots struggled to keep the bucking aircraft on a steady course before the bombardiers took over. One of the planes in their unit was struck in the left wing and started losing fuel. Almost at the same moment, the "Suicide Six" took a hit in the right engine and fuselage.

Preston, the flight engineer, emptied a fire extinguisher at a blaze in the hold but couldn't contain the flames. He rushed forward to the cockpit, through a maze of ammunition belts and machine guns and told Andy that the situation was hopeless. The pilot shouted in the intercom to the bombardier, "Nick, jettison the bombs! We're bailing out."

"Shit", came the reply.

As the bombs slipped out of the B-24, it lurched higher in the polluted sky.

Walker had already bailed out of the rear turret, and Preston was frantically trying to get the rest of the crew out. With the hydraulic system failing, the smoke spreading, and the yawing plane beginning to go out of control, Andy broke radio silence and told Bater that he was ordering a bailout. One by one, those left of the nine man crew jumped from the crippled aircraft.

Andy steadied the "Suicide Six" as best he could. He unfastened his seatbelt, left the cockpit, and groped his way past the top turret through blinding smoke and twisted metal to the middle of the plane. He hesitated for a moment, took off his oxygen mask, and stepped out into space through a jagged hole that had been blasted by the flak. As the aviator tumbled clear of the B-24, it slowly turned on to its back and began a long, graceful arc into the rich earth of northern Italy.

He awakened shaking from the cold and immediately wondered where the members of his crew were? The wind had picked up and the sun was behind a band of clouds. Realizing that he was by the *rifúgio*, he put on his shirt, reached for the rucksack and opened the door. The interior was like a cold storage chamber with the stone walls covered by a fine film of frost. Some split *mélèze* logs were stacked in the corner for fuel. He busied himself making a fire in the stove, then went out to get some snow to melt for tea. After eating some cheese and bread, he covered himself with blankets and lay down on the *couchettes*.

Outside, the sun lowered over the western crests. Lengthening shadows covered the valley floor and started to climb up the north slopes. Brilliant yellow light still shone against the south-facing forest, but inexorably the shadows climbed ever higher. Darkness soon cloaked the trees and spread over the snow-covered high pastures and the exposed rock of the summits. The upper reaches of the mountains were coloured a radiant orange that dissolved into a pale pink. Gradually, like a dying ember, the alpine glow waned and was replaced by nocturnal purple.

Perhaps it was the altitude, the fact that he had already dozed during the afternoon, or the large amount of tea that he had consumed, but Andy hardly slept that night. Though he was under half a dozen blankets, the cold in the cabin still penetrated his body.

He chuckled to himself, "What a difference a *duvet* and a woman make."

"I hope that Angela can handle the visit from the Germans."

He thought again of the way she had cared for him. What a brave and unselfish woman. He envisioned the two of them together in the kitchen, eating the evening meal and drinking the richly coloured red wine of Piemonte. When the candles burned low, they retired to the intimacy of Angela's bed. There was no doubt in his mind that they were deeply in love, but, what would happen now?

Reflecting on the morning climb to the hut brought back memories of the trip that he had made to Mont Tremblant on New Year's in 1940. That was the last ski competition that he had entered before enlisting in the Air Force....

Andy and his friend Bob Sandler, a fellow geography student from Detroit, had decided to drive through the night of

82

December 30th so that they would arrive at Mont Tremblant in the morning. That would give them the day to check out the slope on the "Flying Mile" that would be the site of the annual New Year's day slalom.

They had left his house in Newport after supper, driving an old V-8 Buick four door sedan that Andy had borrowed from his brother. After stowing their ski gear and sleeping bags, they settled into the front seat for the long drive through the mountains to the Québec border.

The Buick reminded Andy of a Mafia car. It was an enormous black box, with a spare tire on each running board, and two chrome plated horns under the lights. Inside, it boasted a ride control lever, a radio, and a shade on the back window. His brother had told him that it burned quite a lot of oil, so they had picked up a five gallon can at Demer's Gas Station to last them for the trip.

The weather was blustery and bitter cold and there was some blowing snow, but the highways had been cleared and the car's lights, reflecting off the banks on both sides, provided good visibility. They could manage about 45 miles per hour on the winding and hilly roads that were so typical of the New England countryside.

Following the Connecticut Valley to White River Junction, they turned west on Vermont 14 to Barre. At Montpelier the boys stopped at a diner, had some coffee and mince pie, and went to the men's room. They tanked up at an open Esso station across the street and rolled out of town. Highway 2 took them past Burlington and onto Grand Isle. Here, the road was covered with bumps and pockmarked with potholes. Andy set the ride control to hard.

The strong winds coming off Lake Champlain buffeted the heavy car and whipped flurries of snow past the headlights in a steady stream, creating hypnotic driving conditions. The radio was their saviour as they picked up New York City and heard

83

QUÉBEC

Québec

(960)
Mt. Tremblant

St. Lawrence

Montréal

Ottawa

ONTARIO

NEW YORK

Burlington

(1339)
Mt. Mansfield
• Stowe

Montpelier

Barre

VERMONT

NEW HAMPSHIRE

Claremont

Sunapee
Newport

Manchester

NORTH
EASTERN
NORTH
AMERICA

MASSACHUSETTS

Boston

0   50   100 km

Hartford
CONNECTICUT

a jumping arrangement of "Sing, Sing, Sing", with Benny Goodman, Ziggy Elman, and Gene Krupa.

Andy, tapping his fingers on the gearshift knob, glanced at Bob slumped in the passenger seat.

"Thank God the finals are over."

Bob sat up.

"The Economic Geography exam was really stupid. All O'Brien wanted to know was where in the world are iron ore and coal found? As far as I'm concerned all you have to do is look it up in a book. Why bother going to all the trouble to memorize that trivia for the test and then forget it the next day."

The New Englander, absorbing the road shocks with his strong arms told Bob, "I think the profs are stuck in a rut. They've been testing and asking the same sort of questions since the Middle Ages."

"Do you remember when O'Brien showed us the photo of a fountain in a Paris park and asked whether we thought something like this should be in a textbook on the geography of Europe?"

Bob nodded, "I guess it wasn't scientific enough for him. He couldn't plot the effects of the fountain on the population using one of those little graphs that he loves so much."

Andy warned, "Watch out for him, if you get on his shit list, you're finished."

Bob laughed, "If I get a C in that course, I'll be happy."

The driver, with a reputation among the students as a map making expert, responded, "If you think O'Brien is tough, try taking cartography with Burnham. He looks at your lines under a microscope before marking your maps. I took it last year and passed with an A-. One thing I can do is draw a straight line."

The Detroiter thought about the men that had been his lecturers, "It's too bad that the department is so split up. Every prof wants to be a prima donna. Except for Rigbee, they don't

Train, Mont Tremblant, Québec

encourage original thinking. All they do is search for disciples. As long as you answer their test questions with the stuff that they've been preaching you're O.K."

Andy's reply was to the point, "That's their ego trip. It promises a kind of immortality. After all, if they didn't teach, what could they do?"

On the bridge crossing to the mainland they hit some black ice and skidded. Andy skilfully brought the car under control and headed for Rouses Point.

Passing the border, the Buick pulled up at a small house that served as Canadian customs and stopped near the flagpoles flying the red ensign and *fleur-de-lis*. Two sleepy men, wearing rumpled uniforms of His Majesty's Customs and Excise Department, came out to great them. The odour of stale tobacco permeated the car.

"Welcome to Québec boys, where ya born?"

"Newport."

"Detroit."

The one with the mustache asked, "What are youse doin here?"

Andy rolled the window down even further and explained that they were heading for Mont Tremblant to ski.

"Y'know we're fighting a war up here. What d' ya have to declare?"

"Nothing that I can think of."

The officers asked for the registration, looked over the car, and opened up the trunk. Satisfied that the boys were not smuggling in anything that could be sold on the black market, they motioned them to go on.

Andy looked at his watch and saw that it was past midnight. The gas gauge was nearing the quarter mark and a red light was warning that the oil was getting low. He got out of the car, opened up one side of the hood, and filled the crankcase with oil. At this time of night they would be lucky to find an open gas station in Montrèal. His hands were already numb as he slammed the door and started the motor; turning the car onto the highway, he drove north following the Richelieu Valley. The wind had died down and the moon broke through sporadically from behind the clouds. They made good time to St. Jean and then headed west across the snow blown flatlands of the St. Lawrence Valley to Montrèal.

Both boys were impressed by the skyline. From the south shore of the St. Lawrence they could make out the large cross on top of Mont Royal and the dark shapes of the downtown skyscrapers. They followed the signs to the Jacques Cartier Bridge and headed across the partially frozen river to the island that was the site of Canada's largest city. With temperatures close to minus 30 degrees, fog was forming over the open water. Below to the left, expanding clouds of steam were pouring forth from the stacks of the Molson Brewery.

Checking the map, Bob told Andy to look for Highway 11 North; it would take them through the city and towards the Laurentians. After some difficulty in finding their way, Andy turned on rue St. Denis and they were once again on the right route. Both boys were beginning to feel hungry, but there were few restaurants open at such a late hour.

Seeing some lights down one of the side streets, Andy swung the Buick off St. Denis and stopped at an all night bagel factory. Stepping out into the frigid air, the two Americans climbed over the mounds of frozen snow piled on the curb and entered the store. They were greeted by the warm aroma of freshly baking bagels. Two men, behind a plywood partition, were kneading the dough and placing the round doughnut-like objects into the wood burning ovens.

They bought a dozen, six plain and six salty, and sipped on some coffee that the bakers had just brewed.

The short dark one asked, "You guys from the States?"

They nodded affirmatively.

"When ya gona join us against the Nazi rats?"

Both shrugged their shoulders.

A few minutes later they thanked them for the coffee, said goodbye, and made their way back to the car.

Bob took over the driving and they went north past scores of silent greystone houses that had outside stairways coming down from the second floor to the sidewalk. He stopped to fill up at a Supertest station that stayed open 24 hours. Twenty minutes later, they drove across the Rivière des Prairies and were on the Ile Jésus. Here, the built up areas were clustered together, interspersed by vacant fields. The open country took over after they crossed back to the mainland and picked up the Boulevard des Laurentides.

Andy was asleep as Bob drove towards Shawbridge where the ancient mountains of the Laurentian Shield jutted out of the broad, fertile valley of the St. Lawrence. Because of the late time, nearly three-thirty in the morning, there was no traffic. They still had two and one half hours to go before reaching St. Jovite where the road branched off to Mont Tremblant.

The driver fiddled with the radio and picked up an all night music station with a French announcer that he could barely understand. He discovered that the Laurentians were more like rolling hills than the mountains that they had passed in Vermont. The highway meandered through the countryside, at times following a broad valley for a few miles and then climbing the rounded summits of the rocky outcrops. Frost heaves in the road rocked the Buick like a fishing trawler in choppy seas. Music crackled over the radio....

He had met Andy in the Geography workroom at Clark. They shared the same cubicle and the moment that he had heard that Andy was a ski racer they became friends. He certainly was different than the boys that he had grown up with in the Jewish neighbourhood of Detroit. Was it only last summer that he was still there driving a taxi at night to earn money to go to university? How time evaporates. He wondered if his mother would be able to handle his father, a man who squandered at the races and bowling alleys any money he made. Wayne had been a positive experience; he would never forget his professors, highly intelligent, opinionated men and women, who encouraged him to go on to graduate school.

That Friday evening was hot and humid, typical mid-summer weather for the Great Lakes. He parked his green and black Checkered Cab on a side street near the Paradise Theatre and walked up Woodward Avenue. Traffic from downtown was heavy, the yellow DSR streetcars rattled back and forth, and the sidewalks were filled with the weekend throngs. A block from the theatre he saw the glittering marquee announce: **DUKE ELLINGTON** and his band **DIRECT FROM THE COTTON CLUB IN HARLEM.** Special guest **BILLIE HOLIDAY-THE GREAT LADY DAY!** The line at the box office snaked around the block. He discovered his friends near the front and waved to them to buy him a ticket. Mayer, Eddie, Moishe, and George were there. They had been together since the fifth grade at McCulloch, antagonizing the Hebrew school teachers, playing baseball and basketball and walking Dexter Boulevard, looking for girls that never seemed to appear.

The crowd, dressed in smart, brightly coloured clothing slowly filed into the Paradise, their black and tan faces anticipating the evenings entertainment. Elegant woman and strong men had come from their east side ghetto to experience their music played by their own musicians. Bob and his friends found seats close to the stage along the left aisle. They were the only white faces in a crowd of close to a thousand, but no one seemed to notice or care. That night, the music was foremost on the minds of everyone.

Stuck to the thick humid air that penetrated the theatre, was the mixed smell of sweet perfume, pomade, and cigar and cigarette smoke. The crowd settled in their seats, the lights dimmed and an announcer dressed in a black tuxedo walked out on stage, cracked a few off colour jokes and settled the audience. Empty chairs and musical instruments were waiting for the band's entrance. Off to one side was the Duke's piano.

"Ladies and Gentlemen, the Paradise Theatre is proud to present Duke Ellington and his orchestra direct from Harlem's famous and fabulous Cotton Club."

A wave of applause greeted the distinguished Duke and his men. The famous band leader and song writer came forward. He had played at theatres, hotels, and dances all over the U.S., and had already toured Europe.

"Greetings to all you fine people living in the Motor City. I want to present the inspired musicians who are going to entertain you tonight. In alphabetical order, otherwise I have problems with their egos, Barney Bigard on clarinet and tenor sax, Lawrence Brown on trombone, Harry Carney, baritone sax, Sonny Greer on drums, Milt Hinton on bass, Johnny 'rabbit' Hodges on alto and soprano sax, Ray Nance on trumpet, and Rex Stewart and Cootie Williams, on trumpet."

One at a time the band members, dressed in white suits and bow ties, came forward, then sat in their chairs. The Duke looked around, waited until all were ready, raised his arms and the strains of an Ellington medley filled the packed hall. There was instant recognition and sharp applause for each of the memorable melodies and the solo players that were featured.

They started with "I've Got it Bad", then "In a Sentimental Mood", followed by "All Too Soon", "Mood Indigo", and "Satin Doll". The audience swayed rhythmically in their seats. By the time they came to "Take the A Train", the players were warmed up for something more than sweet music. The band pulled out all stops. First piano then brass set the theme followed by Bigard's sax solo and the drums and cymbals of Greer. Counterpoint from the trumpets of Williams and Nance

91

blared forth. The Duke's piano punctuated the music and Johnny Hodge's powerful soprano sax brought the diverse melodies back to the main theme. Duke soloed again and Stewart, with a muted whine of slurred notes from his trumpet, brought forth cries of "more more" from an excited crowd. Piano and tenor sax improvisations alternated beat for beat and note for note. The groaning trumpet of Williams joined in and by that time the audience was aroused, ecstatic, and dancing in the aisles, two thousand hands clapping out the beat. It was wild music from such a big band. A sax took control-the theme reappeared-a short drum solo punctuated the air-then full steam as all instruments crescendoed onto the theme--da da, da da da dadam--then the melody slowed and gently faded.... Yeah! Yeah!, whistles, stomping, and swelling applause resounded throughout the Paradise. It took ten minutes for the crowd to quiet down and get back to their seats. The musicians, wiping streams of perspiration from their faces and realizing that they had activated the primordial forces that were within the human psyche, were high.

Finally, the announcer came back on stage. "Ladies and Gentleman, we're in for a treat tonight. Fresh from her success with Count Basie and Artie Shaw, and with great records to her credit, I want to present to you all, the one and only "Lady Day", Billie Holiday."

The audience sat quietly as this gorgeous woman appeared from the wing. Her black hair was styled with a bouffant front and she was wearing a long pink dress with matching gloves that ended above her elbows. Barely recovered from "A Train", the crowd, struck by her beauty, gasped as she walked on stage and then started to applaud and whistle loudly.

The orchestra began to play softly and Billie began to sing in her distinctive, mellow, bluesy voice,

"Night and daaay you are the one,

Only yoou beneath the moon and under the sunnn,
Whether near to me or far,
Its no matter darling where you are,
Iah think of you night and daaay,
Day and night why is it soooh?
That this longin for you follows wherever I goooh,
In the rOARing traffic boom,
In the silence of my lonely room,
Iah think of you night and daaay,
Night and daaaaay under the hide of me,
Theres an oh such a hongry yernin burnin inside of meeee,
And its torment won't be truuue till you let me spend my
life mAking love to you,
Night and day night and daaay."

The Duke carried the melody with a short solo and Billie
finished strongly,

"Night and daay under the hide of me,
There's an oh such a hungry yearin burnin inside of me,
And its told me it won't be true till you let me spend my
life making love to youu,
Day and night night and daaay."

The audience, transformed by Billie's singing into a world
of nostalgia and fantasy, applauded vigorously.
She went right into her second song, Duke's solo piano
setting the mood.

"Away from the city--there was a scattering of applause--that
hurts in knots,
I'm standing alone by the desolate docks in the still and the
chill of the night,
I see the hurizon, the greaat unknown,

93

My heart has an ache its as heavy as stone,
Will the dawn coming on make it light?
Iah cover the waterfront--applause--
I'm watching the seeee,
Will the one I love be coming back to meeee?
Iah cover the waterfront in search of my love and I'm
covered by a starlit sky above,
Here am I patiently waitin, hoping and longing, oh how I
yearn,
Where are you? Have you forgotten? Will you remember?
Will you return?
Iah cover the waterfront, I'm watching the seea, Will the one
I love be coming back to meeeee, Will the one I love be
coming back to meeeee."

Acknowledging the strong applause, Billie came forward.
"Thank you very much, and now another little tune that I
recorded with Duke in New York. I do hope you like it."
When she started to sing Sophisticated Lady, there were
sobs from the women in the audience.

"They say into your early life romance came,
And in this heart of yours burned a flame,
A flame that flickered one day and died....away,
Then, with dissolusion deep in yah eyes,
You learned that fools in love soon grow wise,
The years have changed you somehow, Iah see you now,
Smoking, drinking, never thinking of tomorrow-nonchalant,
Diamonds shining, dancing, dining with some man in a
restaurant,
Is that all you really want?
No, sophisticated lady I know,
You miss the love you lost long ago,
And when nobody is nigh, you cry."

A solo muted sax prolonged the mood and melody of the song until Billie began to sing again....

Five deer crowding the highway forced Bob to slam on the brakes. He swerved to avoid the animals and felt a slight bump as they scampered into the bush. Stopping the Buick to see if it was damaged, he found only a tuft of fur stuck to the left side of the bumper.

A string of towns drifted by, Mt. Rolland...., St. Adèle...., and St. Agathe. Then they drove through a coniferous forest before coming to St. Jovite. Bob coasted through the sleeping town and followed the signs to Mont Tremblant Village. A faint orange glow in the east signaled the beginning of the last day of 1939.

Pulling up at the wooden railroad station, the Detroiter jumped out of the car and went inside searching for a toilet. A few moments later he returned just as a train was arriving. **Traverse du Chemin de Fer-Railway Crossing**, caught the powerful headlights of the automobile. Three bronze coloured cars of the morning Canadian Pacific passenger train were blocking the road. A few locals, hoods from their parkas drawn tightly around their heads, scurried out of the building and climbed aboard. The conductor slammed the doors shut and the train started to roll, chugging ahead amidst a billowing tongue of white steam that hung suspended in the still air of the icy dawn.

The driver shifted into first and the Buick bumped across the single track, passed the Hotel Mont Tremblant, and headed towards the mountain. As the sun was edging over the snow covered hills, he stopped at a small *auberge* that stood by the outlet of Lac Tremblant in view of the south side ski trails. The young men left the car and walked stiffly into the foyer. A sign over the desk announced *Bienvenue au Chalet des Chutes, Famille Arsenault.*

Holding a mug of coffee, the proprietress, a heavy set woman in her mid-30s, told them that for $4.50 a day they could have a room, with breakfast, picnic lunch, and supper. Fatigued, they decided to move in and try and get a few hours of sleep before skiing. They got up at ten-thirty, put on ski clothes and went down to the dining room. After a breakfast of Canadian bacon and pancakes with maple syrup, the Americans climbed into the car, skirted the frozen lake, and parked by the small habitant village that had been constructed at the base of the mountain.

Purchasing lift tickets, they rode the single chair that went up the left side of the "Flying Mile", the expert falline run down which the New Year's day slalom would be set. As they were slowly carried to the top of the mountain, Andy studied the trail and saw the steep pitches and the wooden ramps that had been built across the ice covered rock ledges. He knew that he would have to be in top form in order to finish among the first three.

The skiers spent the rest of the morning on the "Flying Mile" and "Standard". After stopping at a warm-up hut to eat their sandwiches and have a cup of hot chocolate, they took the upper T-bar and skied through the hardwood and coniferous forest down the easy "Nansen" run that led to the village.

Half way, Bob stopped to catch his breath and glanced at the trees. The spruce limbs, heavily laden with snow, folded in against their trunks like a closed umbrella. In contrast, the spreading branches of the sugar maples and yellow and white birches were a filigree of rime ice. The forest stood out starkly white against the ultramarine Québec sky.

He pointed his boards down the twisting trail and quickly picked up speed, absorbing the bumps with his knees. What a joy to be on skis again after the grind of the fall semester!

When the lifts closed at four o'clock, the men, their faces red and muscles satisfyingly spent, stopped at the Chalet des

Voyageurs for a drink. They checked out the bulletin board and saw that there would be a torchlight descent down the "Flying Mile" and a band from McGill as part of the New Year's eve festivities.

The heavy wooden tables scattered about the snug timbered interior were filling with the après ski crowd. There were members of the ski patrol and ski school in their distinctive jackets, smartly dressed young women and men, and a sprinkling of racers. The noise of their animated conversations filled the lodge. Andy was surprised that almost everyone spoke English, even those persons who appeared to be French Canadian. An attractive waitress came over and they ordered two beers.

The Americans stayed until six o'clock and then went back to the Chalet des Chutes. They peeled off their damp clothes, found the shower in the hall and went back to their room and slept for about an hour. Supper was a spicy *tourtière* and a bottle of red wine from Ontario, that tasted like grape juice. After the meal, Madame Arsenault mentioned that she would give them an old blanket to cover the motor.

"It's going down to 30 below tonight, and if you want to be able to drive to the mountain tomorrow morning for the race, you'll have to try and keep the engine from getting too cold. Otherwise, it won't start."

They drove back to Mont Tremblant, walked past the brightly lit windows of the pastel-coloured cottages and entered the Chalet des Voyageurs. Sitting down near the bandstand, they hailed the same waitress. Looking around, they saw that most of the tables were already occupied. At ten-thirty, everyone went out on the frozen deck to watch the torchlight descent. The December cold pierced their parkas and they jumped about to keep some circulation going.

One by one, at the top of the trail, the torches sprang to life, like cigarettes being lit in a darkened hall. A long snake-like configuration of moving orange lights began to wind slowly down the black mountainside towards the spectators. As the skiers arrived at the bottom, the lower half of the hill was bathed in a luminous incandescence that gradually disappeared as the torches flickered out.

The instructors and ski patrollers made their way past the crowd to a well deserved *Glühwein* in the "Voyageurs". The throng applauded their courageous performance, not only for the skill shown in skiing down the precipitous slope with a torch in one hand, but also because of the added challenge of descending in Arctic-like temperatures. Most of the well wishers had difficulty negotiating the "Mile" during the best of daylight conditions, let alone without proper illumination on the coldest night of the year.

There was a friendly spirit that night in the Chalet des Voyageurs. Burning logs in the stone fireplaces at either end of the lodge were giving off waves of heat. Locals and strangers, beer glasses in hand, mingled with one another, spoke about the next day's race, and questioned their new found friends about their plans. Many of the Canadians sensed that it would be their last New Year's eve in the Laurentians for some time. They were at war with Hitler's Germany. The future for them was an unpredictable one.

The Americans, most of whom had never been to Tremblant, were asking questions about who had built these beautiful buildings and created such a challenging ski area just 90 miles north of Montreal. They were rather surprised to find out that the developer was a millionaire's son from Philadelphia. Rumour had it that he didn't like Jews. Someone piped up, "No wonder he found such a warm welcome in this Province." Another loud voice exclaimed, "Mackenzie King is no Jew lover either."

Andy and Bob were talking to two girls, Heather and Sheila, who were students at McGill. Both lived in Westmount; they

98

told the boys that it was a wealthy English speaking area of Montreal that was surrounded by French Canadians. Sheila mentioned that, "Some of the stone houses on Mount Royal are almost as large as anything you find in the English countryside."

Heather, her burnished red hair catching the dim light coming from the wrought iron chandeliers, confessed, "Most of us hardly speak a word of French, there is no need. Besides, almost everyone can speak some English in Montreal."

Bob rather naively ventured to say, that except for the province of Québec, he didn't see much difference between Canada and the U.S.

Sheila interjected, "There's a difference alright. It might be difficult to put your finger on, but it's there. My family spends a lot of time in New York on business, so I have good friends in Manhattan. They're so sure of themselves. They believe that they can do anything."

"What a contrast to the people I know around here. They have little confidence. They're always making excuses. All I hear is how the Americans control everything in Canada. Yet, we few Canadians live in the second largest country in the world, a land with almost unlimited natural resources and opportunity."

Andy, who was a jazz trumpeter at college, with a liking for Bix Beiderbecke and Sidney Bechet, was watching the drummer set up. He turned to Sheila and joking said, "What you say might be true. Except for eskimos, mounties, and hockey, I really don't know much about your country. But one thing is for sure, your beer is a helluva lot better than ours. At least it has a taste and there's some alcohol in it."

He thrust the long necked bottle of "Export" towards her and gestured to drink.

Then Sheila, the dark haired girl with brown eyes and cheeks rosey from the day's outing, laughed at both the

Americans.

"Our beer should be good, we've made our real reputation with booze. Haven't you ever heard of Seagrams; its one of the biggest distilleries. When it comes to alcoholic beverages, we Canadians lose our inferiority complex, and take on the rest of the world."

The band started to play and the foursome made their way to the dance area. It was an eclectic set, with alternating strains of blues, jazz, and swing filling the lodge; the floor quickly became crowded with young dancers. Andy held Heather closely as they moved around the floor to a slow rendition of "Summertime". He felt her breasts and legs with his body and smelled the fragrance of her hair as she hummed softly to the melodious strains of the music. They then broke into a real sweat in the heated lodge jitterbugging to "Alexander's Ragtime Band". All four of the young skiers sat down to replenish their drinks when the trumpeter began a medley of Dixieland tunes.

Just before midnight, the band took a break. As the seconds ticked off, the crowd began to sing "Auld Lang Syne" in a warm nostalgic tone. After the last refrain, there was a moment of meditative silence. The Chalet erupted with shouts of "Happy New Year" and the sound of clinking glasses; the band struck up "When the Saints come Marching In", and the revelers began to chant the words.

They danced again and returned to the table to finish their drinks. At one o,clock, they exchanged addresses, shyly kissed each other good night, and said goodbye. They boys walked out into the crystal night and headed for the parking lot. Today, Andy had to race down the "Flying Mile."

Morning was clear and bitter cold. The small waterfall at the side of the *auberge* was bathed in dense fog. Bob scraped the night's accumulation of frost off the windshield. Andy removed the blanket from under the hood, sat down on the frozen seat and put the key in the ignition. He had a slight panic when the Buick wouldn't start; however, after ten minutes of harsh grinding sounds, it finally kicked over. He revved the motor until the cylinders were moving smoothly in sync.

At the mountain, he registered for the race and picked up his bib, Number 23. The course had been set down the middle section of the "Mile". Andy took the chair to the top of the hill, and skied down to where the race would begin. He sideslipped past the slalom poles and started to memorize the gates.

The top five were straight forward open ones that led over some undulating bumps on a moderately steep section of the hill. Then came a number of closed gates, some "hairpins" set at various angles, a "flush", an "H", and a final "enfilade". He would have to be in perfect control in every section to have a chance to win.

Starting time was set for ten, so Andy kept going up and down the hill, looking at the course and warming up his muscles. He stopped for a few moments, took off both skis, admired their fine wooden grain, and gave a final polish to the blue wax that he had applied after breakfast. The tiny screws holding his metal edges were flush with the running surface. As usual when he was waiting for a race to begin, he was tense and nervous. He had to urinate, but decided to wait until the first run was finished. The racers were lining up waiting for the start. Andy adjusted his plastic goggles, checked the long thongs on his boots to make sure that they were as tightly wrapped as possible, and flailed his arms to keep warm. He made sure that the bib with its stylized blue maple leaf and yellow Mont Tremblant script was secure and did a series of short hops on his skis to keep the blood circulating in his legs.

The first forerunner, started down, then the second. He could see that they were having problems with the second hairpin section. They skied out of sight just before they passed through the flush.

Five, four, three, two, one, go! The first racer pushed off. Every fifty seconds another followed. They were a colourful group with striped hats, dark ski pants and sweaters in hues of white, blue and red. Number 20 left the starting gate. Andy took off his parka and began to breathe deeply. He had on a white woolen sweater with a blue reindeer pattern across the shoulders, that his mother had knit for Christmas. Bob, at the side of the course, was waiting to bring down the parka after his run.

Andy moved into position, glanced below at the lake, and heard three, two, one, go! He pushed on his poles with powerful thrusts of his arms and skied with rounded turns through the open gates at the top of the course with little difficulty. He had to edge harder to make the closed ones, and checked while moving through the tight "hairpins". The "flush" was coming up. "Easy Andy, don't turn the skis too much.., let em run.., get that body around the poles..," he felt them slap against his arms.., pass the "H" and into the final gates.., lunge through the finish!

He made a sharp turn coming to an abrupt stop in a spray of snow. Muscles trembling, he skied over to the side and waited for Bob. It had been a good run. There was some trouble in the "flush" when he caught an edge in the ruts, but he had quickly recovered and only lost a few tenths of a second. He checked the times and found that he had 49.2 seconds, which, for the moment, was good enough for fourth place.

The other racers continued to come through the gates as Andy and Bob made their way to the Chalet des Voyageurs for lunch. Andy couldn't eat more than a few bites of his ham and cheese sandwich. He did, however, finish a pot of tea. After the final racer, the course would have to be reset, and the second run would begin at one-thirty. Heather and Sheila passed by, said hello, and then joined a group at another table. Andy tried to relax, but the pressure was building up. He knew he had a

102

chance to win.

They went out again at twelve-thirty and decided to ski to keep loose and warm. Coming down the "Mile", they checked the timesheets and saw that Andy had held fourth with just over a second between him and the leader. First was a Canadian, Fripp from Tremblant, followed by a Swiss, Gabriel who was instructing at Tremblant, and third was an American, Krueger from Vermont.

The skiers were preparing for the second run. Out of a first group of 55, only 32 were left. The rest had fallen or had missed a gate and had been disqualified. Andy would start in the fifth slot.

Again, he memorized the course. Watch out for the "hairpins". They came after a steep fall away section and could be easily missed. Then they went off to the left for a short distance before the "flush" began. The forerunners, young eager boys in their early teens, went through the gates. The racers lined up like nervous racehorses, spitting, and shuffling their skis. Number three started. The wind had picked up, clouds had covered the sun, and the light would be flat.

Off came the parka. Five, four, three, two, one, go! Andy polled furiously through the first open gate. He accelerated past the top section, swept by the closed gates, and attacked the "hairpins". He concentrated on the flags, red..., blue..., red..., blue..., red.... There was no time to think; it was all reflex action; movements were automatic; skis were an extension of the body, shifting swiftly from one edge to another. After the last gate, he skated hard across the finish line.

Exhausted, he leaned on his poles for support. The scorekeeper marked his time on a large blackboard: 48.5. For the moment, he was in first place. The agony of waiting for the others began.

Number 10 was the Swiss. He had a good run but lost precious moments when he almost skied out of the "flush":

49.5 was chalked up on the board. The skier from Vermont came down a few moments later. He was attacking all the way until he caught a tip three gates from the finish and piled up in the snow. The last racer that could beat him was Number 15, the Canadian from Tremblant. Andy could see him start and neatly pass through the open gates on the steep upper section. Then he was out of sight in the "hairpins". Some seconds later, he came over the brow of the "Mile" just before the finish, skiing aggressively and confidently. Andy watched him flash under the finish banner.

He looked for Bob, saw the girls near the scoreboard, and watched as the Canadian's time was posted: 49.3.

Andy thought, "He must have had some trouble through the 'hairpins'."

Because the course had become deeply rutted, the times recorded for the last group of racers were much slower.

Everyone was milling about the scoring shack. Andy pushed his way toward the board and saw his total of 97.7. The Canadian's was 98.0, and the Swiss instructor's was 98.5. He had won by 3/10s of a second!

Castle, Fenis, Valle d'Aosta

CHAPTER VI
Zermatt, 2-45

"Nobody checked up; along that whole line, and on the majority of European railroads, there was still plenty of other work to do; repairing tracks, removing rubble, putting the signals back into operation. The train traveled slowly, almost entirely at night; during the day it remained endlessly on sidings, roasting in the sun to allow other trains, with precedence, to go by. The passenger trains were few: these were convoys of freight cars carrying human beings, but packed in like freight; the hundreds of thousands of Italians, men and women, soldiers and civilians, employees and slaves, who had worked in the factories and the camps of the destroyed Third Reich. Mingled with them, less noisy, less numerous, anxious to avoid notice, other passengers were traveling, Germans swarming from occupied Germany to elude the Allies' justice; SS men; functionaries of the Gestapo and the party. Paradoxically, for them, as for the transient Jews, Italy was the land of least resistance, the best jumping-off place for more hospitable countries: South America, Syria, Egypt. Openly or in disguise, with documents or without, this varicolored tide headed south, towards the Brenner: the Brenner had become the narrow neck of a vast funnel. Through the Brenner you gained Italy, the land of the mild climate and notorious, open illegality; the affectionate mafioso land whose double reputation had reached even Norway and the Ukraine and the sealed ghettos of eastern Europe; the land of evaded prohibitions and anarchic forbearance, where every foreigner is welcomed like a brother."
LEVI, **If Not Now, When? 1985.**

Sometime during the night, the weather had changed. The *rifúgio* was buffeted by high winds and snow was falling. Just before dawn, Andy had to go outside to urinate. It was dangerous to venture more than a few meters from the shelter as visibility was zero. Once back inside, he set about trying to make the place as comfortable as possible. He had to keep warm and occupy his mind.

Unwrapping the candles that Angela had packed in the rucksack, he took one and started it burning with a precious match. Then he melted the bottoms of the others and fixed them to the table near the stove. After stoking the fire, the American brought some blankets to the table to cover himself while eating. Breakfast was stale bread and hard cheese, washed down with a pot of tea.

Andy looked over the interior. On the wall near the entrance, the climber's register was hanging on a chain. Thumbing back a few pages, he noticed the small number of inscriptions for the past few years; however, when he went back to the summer of 1939, the book was filled with names from Belgium, the Netherlands, Switzerland, and England. There was even one, Milan Matolin, from Prague, Czechoslovakia.

He was pleasantly surprised to discover some old copies of the **Illustrated London News**, among the pile of dog-eared magazines near the cupboard. Though dated from July and August of 1939, they were a welcome relief from the tedium of his surroundings.

IS WAR IMMINENT?
By Norman H. Drake
Tutor in Politics at Christ Church, Oxford

Are we faced with the possibility of another war only twenty-five years after the beginning of World War I? Enormous changes have occurred in Europe's political geography since that ominous day in August 1914, when the Central Powers and Allies locked in combat. To understand the aggressive nature of the Third Reich, we must go back to the early years of the twentieth century.

Germany's meteoric economic and military expansion brought the country into conflict with England, France, and Imperial Russia. She strengthened her alliance with Austria and thereby was drawn into the deteriorating political situation in the Balkans. Few individuals would have dared to predict that the assassination of an Austrian Archduke by an unknown Bosnian Serb at Sarajevo would ignite the most destructive conflict the world had ever seen. Germany supported Austrian demands on Serbia; Russia supported Serbia, and France and England backed Russia. When war broke out, the Germans, though engaged on two fronts, came within an ace of capturing Paris. The French, however, held fast on the Marne and by the end of September, the war in the west had stagnated. The protagonists confronted each other from a series of barbed-wire protected trenches that zig-zagged from the Channel across Flanders, the northern Paris Basin, and over the Vosges crests to the Swiss frontier.

A war of attrition had begun, which when ended four years later, cost Germany over 1.7 million soldiers dead and over 4.2 million wounded. Because the war was fought mainly on French soil, the outward signs of destruction in Germany were few; nevertheless, the wounds to the German psyche were deep. At one time, the military had almost achieved the goal of creating a Greater Germany that would have controlled the commerce and immense resources of all of continental Europe. With victory having been so near in 1917, how had Germany lost? Whatever the real answers to this question may have been, they were obscured by the economic and political upheavals that followed the Treaty of Versailles.

The peace settlement drastically revised the map of

Europe. The political units of Imperial Germany, the Austro-Hungarian Empire, Ottoman Turkey, and Imperial Russia ceased to exist.

Among the major territorial changes, Alsace and Lorraine were returned to France; the Sud Tirol was given to Italy; a reborn Poland with a 'free and secure access to the sea' was created; and Czechoslovakia and Yugoslavia were recognized as independent states. In addition, Germany's colonies were taken from her, and her armed forces were reduced to a level of impotence. Both the creation of Poland, with a corridor of territory separating East Prussia from Germany, and the recognition of Czechoslovakia, within whose frontiers lived large numbers of Germans, would provide cause for future German aggression.

Attempts to democratize Germany by adopting a new constitution were unsuccessful. The foundations of the Weimar Republic began to crack shortly after the signing of the treaty of peace in the Hall of Mirrors. Conservative elements in German society, who owned the heavy industries, large estates, and banks, neither accepted the treaty nor the Republic that signed the ratification.

The army, though it had sworn to support the new democratic regime and had made the final decision to sanction Versailles, could not be counted on to accept the treaty. The generals began to circumvent the military restrictions almost as soon as the ink was dry. The officer's corps managed to maintain the Army's Prussian tradition and to become the real centre of political power in the new Germany.

Continuing clashes with the Allies over the devaluation of German currency and the French occupation of the Ruhr provided rallying points for German resistance. Inflation, seriously affecting the middle and working classes, became catastrophic. By November 1923, four billion marks were needed to buy one dollar. Internal political tensions, assassinations, and riots brought the Republic to the brink of chaos. Though a semblance of order was restored and economic conditions improved greatly in the late '20s, German grievances were ripe for exploitation.

When the '29 depression plunged Germany into economic ruin, Adolf Hitler, a founder of the National Socialist Party, who had been jailed in 1923 for attempting to overthrow the Bavarian government in the infamous "Munich Beer Hall Putsch", capitalized on the unstable conditions. Helped by a small band of fanatical, ruthless men and playing on the weaknesses of the opposition parties and the prejudices of the German people, the electoral strength of the Nazi party grew.

In 1933, Hitler was asked by the aging and senile President Hindenburg to become Chancellor of Germany. On June 30, 1934, under orders from Hitler, hundreds of his fellow Nazis and potential rivals for power were executed. The reign of terror had begun.

Political analysts believe that the significance of the National Socialist movement is that it is aimed at securing the complete unification of the German people, both in outward institutions and in inner spiritual beliefs. The Nazis insist that they and they alone are the great movement of the mind and soul of the German people, and not just a new political party amongst others. They are seeking to transcend all the deep cleavages of tribe and class, of religious and political creeds amongst Germans, and to unite them in zealous trust behind the God-given infallible personality of *Der Führer*, Adolf Hitler.

We are seeing that whatever means are necessary to justify these aims are acceptable to the Nazis. Lies, brutal cruelty, breach of faith, bribery, blackmail, terror, and murder are being used against all of Hitler's enemies.

None have suffered more than the Jews. Stripped of their rights as German citizens by the Nuremberg laws, these once proud people, who have made such a significant contribution to the country's art, drama, music, and science, have been excluded from all aspects of normal life.

There is no denying the evil genius of the man. Between 1933 and 1939, he has transformed a nation, that had been brought to its knees by the Allies, and was racked by discord, into the supreme military power of Europe, closely allied with the Fascist dictatorship of Mussolini.

In 1936, the demilitarized Rhineland was occupied by German troops; two years later an independent Austria ceased to exist; and in 1938, Hitler, threatening war, occupied parts of Czechoslovakia and shortly thereafter took over the country. We have seen that the Allies failed to intervene militarily. Now, he is poised to strike at Poland. Certainly, the situation of the Allies is much weaker today than it was before the capitulation of Chamberlain and Daladier at Munich. We know from reliable sources that the Czechs would have fought behind formidable defenses in the mountains of Bohemia.

Further aggravating the present geopolitical situation, is the Soviet-German Non-Agression Pact that a stunned Western World learned was signed on August 21st. The last barrier to Hitler's grand design in the east has now been eliminated.

One thing is certain, if Hitler marches on Poland, England and France stand little chance in stopping the *Wehrmacht*. Poland is too far away and the country's terrain is too flat for meaningful Allied help. Nazi tanks will have little trouble in rolling over the horse-drawn artillery of the Polish army. The only possibility of relieving the pressure on Poland would be if French and English troops attacked Germany across the Rhine.

If Hitler marches east, are we in Britain prepared to fight?

The American studied the photos accompanying the article that traced Hitler's rise to power. He was stunned and deeply disturbed by what he saw: Hitler at a field hospital recovering from a gassing in 1916. The men that founded the Nazi Party in Salzburg in 1920. Swastikas unfurled by war veterans in Munich in January 1923. Hitler after the Munich *Putsch* reading a newspaper in Landsberg prison where he wrote **Mein Kampf**. Hitler standing in an open Mercedes, arm extended in the Nazi salute. Hitler shaking hands with the Papal-Nuncio. Goosestepping soldiers wearing leather boots that disappeared under their long coats. Hitler receiving flowers from flaxen haired young girls. Long lines of men carrying Nazi banners, marching through the medieval villages of Germany. Hitler in the Berlin stadium officially opening the summer Olympics of 1936. Entranced crowds of spellbound Germans listening to Hitler's hate filled speeches. Storm troopers rounding up Jews, destroying Jewish shops and burning synagogues on *Kristallnacht* in November 1938. Hitler's generals with Franco during the final siege of Madrid in 1939. The fanatical faces of Hitler and his sycophants.

Andy's concentration was broken when the door to the *rfiúgio* suddenly opened. Half the candles on the table were extinguished by the incoming gust of wind. Startled, he looked up. A skier, anorak covered with a thick layer of wet snow, entered the hut. It was Angela.

"My God! What are you doing here?"

He rushed towards the door, grabbed her in his arms, and kissed her moist lips.

Angela, her face reflecting an anxious state started her story at once.

"The Germans came just after you left yesterday, twenty-four

113

of them. They searched the hotel and told me that I had to leave today, otherwise they would burn it down. I told them that they could not threaten me, a woman whose husband fought for their Fascist glory all over Europe and North Africa. "What are you, I asked, *Einsatzkommandos*?"

The *Kommandant*, an arrogant officer, became very agitated. He insisted that there was no alternative and told me, *We are not Einsatzkommandos, we are elite mountain troops, but we must do our duty, nevertheless.*

Andy, with a quizzical look, asked, "What are *Einsatzkommandos*?"

Angela's reply shocked him.

"They are mobile killing units that operate on the front lines in Russia. Some of the Italian troops who were there told us horrible stories about them. Hundreds of thousands of Jews, Communists, Gypsies, and other undesirables who were captured were killed on the spot in cold blood by these mad exterminating teams. No one was spared.

"I forbade the Germans to stay in the Tête Blanche. The atmosphere was becoming tense. After a brief discussion with another officer, the *Kommandant* ordered his men to set up tents below the hotel. Now, they are waiting to see if anyone should try and enter. I decided to leave at four this morning to warn you."

He wondered aloud? "How did you manage in this horrible weather"?

"I have done this trip many times, and could do it in the dead of night if necessary. You must go to Breuil immediately."

"But how?"

"It is too dangerous to go over the glaciers here across the Col de la Division. If you were to fall into a crevasse that would be the end.

"You must come back with me and then go over the Col di Valcournera. That way is also perilous, but at least you have a chance. I have brought enough food. Get your things together, we must leave in a few minutes."

She walked over to Andy, who appeared distraught by the sudden turn of events, looked closely into his eyes, and held him tightly. He felt the contours of her desirable body beneath the ski clothing.

"Angela, please come with me."

"No, I cannot."

"But why?"

She looked to one side.

"I don't know how long this horrid war will continue. I must fight the Germans here. Besides, I cannot leave the cows. They would die. And perhaps..., yes perhaps, my husband will return after the war is over."

"But we love each other."

"Yes, if only for a few months, we have experienced a love that I have never felt before. We were blessed Andy, most people never experience love in a lifetime."

She looked at him with tears streaming down her reddened cheeks.

"Please always remember, a part of your love will remain with me until I die."

She stepped back and focused her hazel eyes on his face.

"Now we must prepare to go."

Angela set about making a pot of tea while the flyer gathered his clothes and packed the rucksack. Fifteen minutes later, they were ready to depart.

She told Andy, "Follow closely behind, you could easily lose your way in the white-out. There is not too much falling snow but the *föhn* is blowing without letup."

They went outside into the furious storm, fixed their bindings to the boots, and began to ski in wide arcs, using stem christies to control their speed down the steep side of the moraine. The snow surface was covered with small drifts that they plowed

115

through. Because of the constant strain, Andy felt the soreness in his weak leg. He realized how much his muscles had been taxed during the climb. His toes, pressing against the front of the boots, became cold and then numb.

As soon as they came off the moraine the terrain flattened. There was just enough slope so they could move along without too much effort. The passage through the broad U-shaped valley was completed speedily and they began to climb above the river where it had eroded the deep gorge. The two of them skied down through the trees and stopped to drink some tea. Though visibility was still bad, Andy could make out the faint outlines of the giant boulders that had plunged down the mountain during the landslide.

Angela veered to the left. The Buthier, a raging torrent during the hot summer months, had been reduced to a trickle. They crossed the snow covered river bed easily and were once again in the forest. Pausing, she motioned for him to come closer and began to speak in a whisper.

"In a few moments, we will be passing the Tête Blanche. It is about one hundred meters on our right, but because of the mist and falling snow, the Germans cannot see us. In ten minutes we will be at the beginning of the trail to the Valcournera. It is a long ascent. You must walk up the valley for two kilometers and then begin a steep climb. That will be the difficult section as you must go from 2300 to over 3000 meters.

"The Col is between two higher peaks, so if the visibility improves you should be able to make it out. If you have trouble, there are *alpage* huts where you can shelter. But if all goes well, you should try and arrive at Breuil before sunset. Because of the *föhn* there will most likely be cloud and snow when you go over the top; however, as you descend, the visibility should improve, but the wind will continue to blow. On the way down, ski by the lakes and then traverse up the

116

valley. With good fortune, you will see Breuil at the base of the Cervin."

She moved closer to the American, took hold of his mittens, and drew him towards her. They hugged in a tangle of skis and poles and almost burst out laughing. Realizing the presence of the enemy, they muffled their sounds and wrapped their arms around each other. As they kissed, thousands of intricate snowflakes fell on their bodies and turned to small droplets of water.

When they arrived at the divide, Andy skied to the left and Angela returned in the direction that they had come. She was going back to the hotel to lead the cows to Oyace.

Attaching the sealskins, he watched her vanish in the falling snow and felt a surge of anxiety flash through his chest and stomach. Hesitating a brief moment, he turned away and began a steady climb through groves of *mélèzes*, up the Valcournera. On both sides of the narrow cleft, the rocks came down precipitously to the valley floor. He could make out the first fifty meters and then they disappeared into the mist and cloud.

As his boots lifted, he felt the chafing of blistered heels against the inner leather. The pain faded as the aviator plodded ahead as if in a deep trance. Without warning, he heard a commotion and looked up to see four large chamois bounding away from a tree where they had been feeding on branches.

After a march of an hour and a half, he sensed that the head of the valley was approaching. The snow was still sprinkling down but visibility had improved. He searched the left side of the rocks to find the route up to the Col. Twice he thought he had discovered the way, only to be blocked by sheer cliffs. On the third attempt, he came across a wooden signpost that was almost buried by the snow: **Col di Valcournera 3 ore**.

He saw that he had to initiate a series of switchbacks in order to climb above the outcropping rock ledge and reach the trail that led to the Col. Starting the ascent with a series of zig-zags, Andy gained height and moved cautiously across the face. The ledge was coated with frozen streams that had flowed down from between cracks in the rocks. Their ice-encrusted forms were deceptively beautiful. The water had covered the narrow path during the late autumn, spreading out and freezing. As the ice was concealed with a dusting of snow, the skis could easily slip on the slick surface and he could slide over the precipice. After an hour of carefully testing each section with his ski poles, Andy at last came out above the cliffs. The trees became fewer and then, only one or two stunted ones could be seen poking out of the encompassing whiteness.

The steep trek to the Col had begun. The American kept going back and forth, back and forth, up the face of the mountain, making a kick turn every time he wanted to change direction. It was exactly the way he had climbed Hillman's Highway when he went skiing at Tuckerman's Ravine on Mount Washington. He moved upwards slowly but steadily.

The flyer's mind was tuned for the repetitive moment when he slid one ski alongside the other. He was painfully aware that the past, whether five seconds or five hundred years ago, was over, never to return. One could only think about the present and the uncertainties of the future. A man was extremely vulnerable alone in the high Alps. If anything went wrong, if he should injure his leg, lose his way, or break a ski, they would find him in the spring, frozen to death.

"What are mom and dad thinking? By now they must have heard that I'm missing in action. They know that as long as I'm alive, I'll never give up."

Blocking out the danger of the present, his imagination took over....

They decided to spend the day walking. Rain had fallen on and off for the past week and the sky was often overcast with

118

bands of mist floating by the hotel. After two days of sun, it appeared that the weather had stabilized. The young couple left at six in the morning in the soft light of early summer. Angela had packed a lunch the night before and filled the wineskins. Breakfast was a large cup of *café au lait* in which they dipped their crusty bread. The path led down the valley for three kilometers and then branched off to the right towards Lac Mort. Angela explained, "The lake, at 2843 meters, is one of the highest in the Valpelline and very beautiful."

They were wearing olive corduroy knickers, red high socks, and mountain boots with cleated rubber soles. Andy had never seen Angela looking so lovely. There was nothing artificial about her fair hair and lovely face or the confident way that she walked. She had been physically and spiritually nourished by living and working in the Alps.

The cool morning was ideal and they moved quickly in the direction of Oyace, surrounded by sounds of rushing water, cow bells, and barking dogs. The dew was glistening on the needles of the *mélèzes*. Life in the summer was bountiful; nature was generous for the people who chose to live here.

Before they started to climb, they took off their sweaters and kept on light cotton shirts. At first they were in the damp shade of the forest. Soon the sun came up over the southern edge of the valley and warmed the south-facing slopes. Waterfalls, fed by the melting winter snows, funneled down the mountain side. Andy followed Angela up the narrow path. He saw her muscular calves beneath her socks and her firm buttocks, and watched as she moved gracefully over the steep terrain. The heat intensified and they began to perspire heavily.

The forest disappeared below and they found themselves on an exposed rocky pitch that had been grazed by sheep and cows. Multi-coloured alpine flowers were scattered everywhere. There were myriads of species; Angela pointed out the white crocuses, alpine roses, orchids, asters, and violets.

119

They looked up to see a bearded man coming towards them. He wore dirty cotton pants, a denim shirt, grey vest, and jacket slung over his shoulders. A wide brimmed felt hat shielded his eyes from the sun. One hand held a heavy cane for support, the other a wooden rack that was resting on his shoulders on which, covered by canvas, was a Fontina cheese. They exchanged greetings.

Finally, after an ascent of ninety minutes, the young couple came to a level area, a balcony from which they looked upon a sweeping vista of the Valpelline.

To the east, the high peaks that formed the frontier with Switzerland, were hidden in clouds. Across the river were the hanging glaciers that flowed down from the Dome di Cian, and to the west, pointing towards the Grand St. Bernard Pass, was the Valpelline, gouged deeply among the mountains by the immense strength of the glaciers. This superlative view was reward enough for the hard work of the *Valdôtaines* who spent their summers on the *alpage*.

Twenty meters above, outlined against the blue sky, was a cowherd, his animals, and two dogs keeping watch over the moody creatures. A barn and a small hut for the family, constructed out of stone and weathered timber, occupied a section of the balcony. Because of the concentration of animal urine, the alpine grass around the barn was smothered by high weeds. On one side of the crude structure half a dozen pigs were feeding from a metal trough on the morning's whey.

"Look Andy!" Angela cried.

He followed her arm and saw a gigantic eagle, soaring effortlessly on invisible updrafts high above the mountain slopes. To and fro, the eagle swept the skies looking for food, perhaps a marmot, far below. Mimicking its subtle movements were six black choucas, alpine crows that were flapping their wings madly to keep up with the powerful predator whose wingspan was at least two meters.

120

"We are lucky today, there are not many of those majestic birds left. We have shot them all in Italy. Perhaps that one strayed from Switzerland. Their hunting takes them over many square kilometers."

She looked at the sky. "Why does modern life destroy nature and living creatures? Outside of a few reserves, there are hardly any large animals left in Italy. I have read enough to know that the Natives in North America took what they needed and left the rest to continually provide themselves with food and clothing. You told me that they inhabited the land for thousands of years, yet when the Europeans explored North America they wrote that a 'wilderness' had been discovered. At least the Natives worshipped the wind, rain and sun gods, dieties that provided them with life giving substances. What do our gods give us? The right to kill each other?"

They continued upward past the munching cows, whose muted bells provided a fitting musical accompaniment to the alpine tableau. Their tails swished to and fro, dislodging the persistent flies perched on their bony rumps.

The soft grass and flowers gave way to hard fragmented brown rock. The precipitous profile of the mountain changed to a series of barren shelves. To the right, the stark scene was broken by a waterfall that splayed down the mountainside. Patches of snow became more frequent. They were at 2600 meters. At this altitude, another climatic realm began.

The couple slogged through a snow field, past Lac Long, still partially hidden by melting ice. Ahead lay the talus that was dropping down the eroded walls of the cirque. One more pitch and they arrived at the lake. It didn't take them long to understand why it had been named Lac Mort. Enclosed on three sides by an amphitheatre of mountains that rose 600 meters, it was completely frozen and covered with snow.

The sky was perfectly blue, the wind, a cold blast from the north, was blowing fiercely. They fixed the collars of their parkas around their necks, gazed at the Arctic-like landscape, and beat a hasty retreat to some sheltered outcrops below the level of the lake. Here, they opened their rucksacks and feasted on cold veal, *prosciútto*, a chunk of *Fontina*, and an apple. Angela unwrapped a bar of Swiss chocolate that she had been saving for the occasion.

While they ate and took sips from the wineskin, Andy inspected the immediate surroundings. All about them were small angular fragments of rock, that had come to rest on the larger slabs, There was no evidence of human activity. They were the first summer visitors to the lake.

After eating, both relaxed, using the rucksacks as pillows. Angela, arms around her head, talked towards the heavens.

"We humans are such complex creatures. Eagles are born, leave their nest, fly and search for food, mate and raise their young. That is about all they do. Humans never seem to be satisfied. In some ways we are like the gliding eagle searching constantly, not for food but for new stimuli and sensations. We make a mess of our surroundings and rather than improve them we search for new territory to conquer. At times we cannot control our feelings," she laughed, "and we are driven by our sexual urges. In all of us there are male and female components. I guess it is healthy to recognize them and allow them to emerge from within. But how many of us do that?"

She reached for Andy's hand and stroked his fingers. He touched her hair, moved closer to her reclining body, and began to kiss her neck and cheeks....

A violent cracking filled the air as he fell through the upper crusty layers. Instinctively, the lone skier lunged forward away from the widening fissure and struggled to maintain his equilibrium as the large chunks below gathered speed and cascaded down the mountainside in a cataclysmic roar. Andy was nearly a victim of a massive slab avalanche that had created an extensive ragged tear across the fabric of the snow. Still trembling, he placed his pole at the break-off point and saw it almost went down to the leather grip of the handle.

He inched his way forward, stopped and assessed the situation. If the snow had broken off a foot higher, he would have been swept down the mountain and buried under tons of white crystals. For the moment anyway, fate was on his side.

Anxiously, the American again started to climb. He could tell from his laboured breathing that the Col was near. The slope had become much steeper, in fact, he could extend his arm horizontally and touch the snow. Rocks poked through the white layers as he edged up to the crête. An increase in wind velocity announced the divide. He was over 3000 meters. The snow had stopped and the sky was a slate grey, obscuring the top of the Cervin. Shielding his face from the force of the *föhn*, he looked below through an opening in the swirling clouds and saw a large frozen cirque lake. He also noticed that the lee side of the mountain was not as steep as the slope that he had just come up.

Andy's heart was pounding, his muscles quivering as he began the descent towards the head of the Val Tournanche. He leaned back slightly on his skis in order to compensate for the fresh snow. Turning in a regular rhythm, the American was soon floating through the powder, snow streaming up above his hips.

After stopping to catch his wind, he began again, this time pointing his skis closer to the falline. Before he realized what was happening, he had misjudged the steepness in the flat light, and picked up too much speed. Trying to control the descent, he watched out of the corner of his eyes as the ski tips submerged beneath the snow. He struggled to maintain balance, but they dug in. His momentum flipped him through the air in a whirl of skis and poles and he came crashing to the ground, ploughing to a stop.

Stunned, Andy was totally covered with snow. It had funnelled down his neck and up the sleeves of the anorak. His face was stinging from the cold as he wiped a blob of white powder off of his sunglasses. One of his cane poles had snapped and was useless. Luckily, other than having been shaken up and frightened, he was not injured.

Struggling to stand up on the skis, the aviator took off his fogging glasses and, though there was no sun, shielded his eyes from the intense glare. A wave of fatigue overcame his body. After a restless night, he had been up since four and had been skiing and climbing almost without pause for over six hours.

Looking back at the tracks, he saw that he had come down about 200 meters from the Col to a small lake, beyond which was the larger frozen lake that was visible from above. Because the way directly ahead was blocked by mountains, he could only turn to the right and continue his descent. Moving slowly with his single pole, he came to a small stone hut, no doubt the one that Angela had mentioned.

Realizing that he had eaten and drunk hardly at all since the morning, he headed towards the door, took off his skis, and entered into the dimly lit interior. It was sparsely furnished but there was a bunk and blankets. He took off his boots and removed his rucksack, collapsed onto the bed, and fell into a deep sleep.

Thinking that he was dreaming, Andy didn't immediately comprehend that the two men that he was seeing were actually in the hut. They were dressed in partisan uniforms and were eating some bread and cheese.

When they saw that he was awake, one said,

"Cóme sta signóre?"

Andy replied in French but the men only spoke Italian. He then said,

"Americano, Americano, Cervinia,"

"Ah, lèi vuole andàre a Cervinia ?"

"Va béne. Va béne."
The American repeated,
"Carlo, Carlo"
One of the soldiers turned to him quizzically and said,
"Ah Carlo, Levi, Carlo, va béne..."
He nodded affirmatively, "Cervinia, Cervinia."
After eating some of the food that Angela had packed, Andy went back to sleep. When he awoke, the men were gone. He felt for his boots in the dark and found his rucksack by the side of the bed. The aviator had been warm enough under the covers but was aware that the cabin was freezing. He made his way out of doors and saw that the sky had cleared and the air was still. As he urinated against the side of the cabin, he was reminded of the two German soldiers in one of Remarque's books saying as they went to pee under the full moon, "We piss silver".

He went back inside and waited another hour until there was enough light to begin the descent. The peaks were aglow with tones of yellow and orange that gradually faded as the sun came up. To the south, the valleys were obscured by a sea of fog; however, visibility in the direction of Breuil-Cervinia was clear. He headed for a gap in the rocks and came out in a small enclosed basin.

Looking about, the American decided to climb a low ridge so that he could get a better view of the distant mountains. He put on his skins and traversed a short section, skiing for a break in the crête. As he neared the top, an impressive pyramid of snow and ice emerged to the north. There was the Matterhorn! Though it didn't resemble the photos that he had seen taken from the Swiss side, the mountain, nevertheless, had a grandeur that was unmistakable. At its base was the tiny cluster of buildings that comprised Breuil.

Two hours later Andy arrived at the small village. It was only nine. He had skied a high traverse and reached the Marmore

River a kilometer before Breuil. Walking the rest of the way, he went into the bar of the Albergo Astoria, a modest hotel near the building that housed the *téléphérique*. Three men were drinking génépy with their *cappuccíni*.

Andy went over to the bartender and asked for Carlo. The man went upstairs and returned in a few minutes and motioned for him to sit down. Was he really with Angela only yesterday? It seemed as if it were a decade ago. He saw her with the cows struggling through the deep snow to get to Oyace...

Fifteen minutes later, the partisan leader walked in the door. He gave the American a warm hug.

"Andy, you've arrived. Welcome to our little outpost, a small part of the Valle d'Aosta that's free from Nazis and Fascists. How did you come over the mountains and how is Angela?"

The aviator recounted the adventure of the last three days. Carlo, amazed at the endurance of the New Englander after his serious injury, told him that the two men he had met in the hut were patrolling to make sure that the partisans were not surprised by the Germans.

Andy thought of the Christmas eve fondue party and asked Carlo, "Did all of your band make it safely to Breuil?"

"Yes, we were blessed with luck. The route over the Glacier des Dames was difficult and treacherous. We kept breaking through the snow bridges and falling into crevasses, but we were roped together. So when one of us fell in, the rest would pull him out. I wouldn't want to drop into one of those traps by myself. You'd freeze to death in a short time. There've been instances where well preserved bodies have been discovered scores of years after the mountaineers disappeared. The moving ice finally gave up its victims."

Carlo looked at the cloud free sky.

"Andy, the weather is ideal, you must go to Zermatt today. We run the *téléphérique* to the Testa Grigia just before lunch. From there it's an easy run down, especially on a beautiful

126

day."

"What's the date?"

The partisan studied the calendar hanging over the bottles on the bar, "Today is the 22nd of February."

Andy grinned.

"Here I am on Washington's birthday skiing to Zermatt. Not bad for a young man from Newport, New Hampshire. I sure didn't bargain for this when I joined the U.S. Air Force."

He became serious.

"How long can you hold off the Germans?"

"We're well supplied with food, arms, and ammunition. If we need anything special, we can get it from Valais. But we know that the Germans will be coming after us as soon as the snow melts enough for them to move up the Val Tournanche in force.

"We'll fight as long as possible; however, we're outnumbered and it will only be a matter of time before they take over Breuil.

"Millennia ago, my ancestors fought against Roman tyranny. I'll do the same against the Nazis."

"What do you mean?"

"I've no choice Andy, I'm Jewish. If the Germans capture me, I'll be put to death."

The American seemed surprised.

"How did you ever come to the Valle d'Aosta?"

"My forbearers arrived as slaves with the Roman Legions that had sacked Solomon's Temple in Jerusalem. You can see pictures of them carrying off booty on a panel of the Arch of Titus in Roma."

"You mean that your family has been living in this country for nearly 2000 years?"

"Yes, Italy has the oldest Jewish community in Europe. We've been here for far longer than those upstart 'Aryans' in Germany. Have you ever seen pictures of their leaders? They're

127

short, dark haired, and ugly. I tell you, that no matter how bad things were under Mussolini, they were insignificant compared to what was going on in Germany and Austria. In Italy, the population would never have allowed such atrocities to be committed against its own citizens."

Carlo saw that Andy was contemplating what he had said. "Have you had any coffee?"

The flyer shrugged and gestured no.

"Due cappuccíni, per favóre."

"Si segnóre."

Andy saw the bartender scurry about grinding the coffee beans and whipping the milk to a white foam with the steam jet on an enormous machine. Five minutes later, he was sipping on a marvelous aromatic brew, that warmed his body as it settled in his stomach.

He turned to the Italian, "What do you want to do after the war is over, Carlo?"

"I've always desired to be a doctor, like my father, and to study surgery at the University of Ferrara."

"Why Ferrara?"

"Ferrara is an enlightened city. It has beautiful buildings and the inhabitants know how to cook. I went there before the war by bicycle from Pont St. Martin with a group of my schoolmates during the Easter vacation. We crossed the Po Valley, travelling long distances along the levee of the river. With the wind at our backs, it only took us five days. We passed through the rice fields near Vercelli. Then we spent the nights at Pavia, Cremona, Mantova, and Ferrara.

"Each city had its distinct character. In Cremona we climbed the highest church tower in Italy and had a 360 degree view of the hazy Po. There were fields of maize, fruit trees and great farmhouses. This level land is the richest agricultural area in our mountainous country. We then went through the apartments of the *Palàzzo Ducale* in Mantova. Have you ever wondered

128

why the architecture of the past was so much more interesting than that of today? Just look at the horrible buildings that the Fascists have constructed."

Carlo stirred his coffee, the deep brown of the liquid mixing with the white foam of the milk.

"Ferrara had a 14th century Lombard cathedral in the centre of town. There was also a museum that housed ancient wooden river boats and wonderful Greek vases and lamps that were discovered at Spina when they were draining the marshes of the Po. My family had Jewish friends there who lived near the *Palàzzo del Diamànti*; they invited me to the first Seder of Passover. Many relatives attended and their little children were laughing and running around the apartment searching for hidden matzoth, the unleavened bread that we eat to symbolize the hasty Jewish Exodus from Egypt.

"The oldest man began to recite the Haggadah. He was asking the four questions. I have known them by heart since I was a child. *Mah nish-ta-noh ha-ly-loh ha-zeh me-cal ha-ley-los?....* Why is this night different from all other nights?.... Afterwards the men began talking about the significance of the Exodus and argued whether the same thing could happen in Italy. We knew that as Jews we were becoming more and more isolated, that our former Christian friends were becoming indifferent to our fate."

He paused and gazed at the glare of the window that illuminated the room.

"I was reminded of what my father had told me a few years before. He had gone to see 'The Threepenny Opera' after it had opened in Munich in 1928. All of Europe was talking about this daring work that had been produced by two Germans Bertolt Brecht and Kurt Weil. Both, fearing imprisonment or death, had to flee the country after Hitler came to power.

"My father rode all night on the train, first from Torino to Milano, then changing trains in Verona, he headed north

129

through the Alps over the Brenner Pass to Innsbruck and Munich. Staying in a small hotel near the station, he befriended a young German couple, Colin and Hildegard, and a Dutch painter Adrian. I have met them at Pont St. Martin. They managed to get tickets to the performance and walked to the Kleine Schauspielhaus near the Opera. Afterwards they had a beer in a small restaurant in the old town discussing the meaning of the production until the sun rose over the ornate tower of the neo-gothic *Rathaus.*

"When my father came home, he told me, an impressionable young boy, the meaning of what he had seen. *"Carlo, he said, I've seen an opera about corruption. Not about the corruption of one or another group of human beings, but about the corruption of everyone in society. The crooks and beggars were corrupt, so were the police and whores; even the English Royal Family was corrupt. For the first time, I became aware that we all have the same weaknesses; that they've been around since humans have inhabited the earth, and they will remain as long as civilization endures. On the slow train ride home, I realized that Brecht forces us to probe the deepest recesses of our minds and to continually evaluate the religions, philosophies, ideas, and 'truths' that have enabled us to survive by sublimating reality."*

The partisan leader looked straight into Andy's eyes.

"Andy, I can never forget my father's words. We're now witnessing what the total corruption of European civilization has wrought. You and I and millions of others are trying to eradicate the Nazi evil. But even though it looks like we'll win the war, we must forever remain on guard, otherwise the corruption will mutate like a virus and reappear in another uniform."

While trying to perceive what Carlo had said, Andy noticed the mountains were closer than ever. They were dangerous but did not trick or take advantage. They possessed a neutral honesty that must be understood and respected, otherwise they would take revenge.

The *Valdôtaine*, realizing that he had digressed, began to talk again about his bicycle trip.

"From Ferrara we went to Pomposa, an abbey that was founded beside the sea in the 6th century. The *campanile* is a famous landmark, rising above the flat lands of the Po Delta. Because of silting, the building is now many kilometers from the Adriatic."

Carlo went to the window and surveyed the barren snowy landscape, one that was totally opposite to that of the inhabited, cultivated Po, and said, "Ah, those were days to remember!"

Finishing their coffee, Carlo and the American went out into the dazzling light of late morning. The sky was a deep azure blue punctuated by enormous white mountains that encircled the few buildings and *mélèzes*. Dominating the scene was the towering obelisk of the Matterhorn, (the Cervino as Carlo called it) whose lower flanks literally came down to the backyard of the hotel. Viewing this extraordinary sight, Andy could well understand how this mystical mass of rock had possessed the men who came to climb it in the 19th century.

They gathered up his skis and walked to the *téléphérique*. Carlo noticed that one pole was missing and while they were waiting for the cable car, he searched for another pair. They were a little longer than the first ones, but would do.

"We'll leave in half an hour for the Plan Maison, change cars and head for the Testa Grigia. Cervinia is just over 2000 meters and the top is 3480, so we'll be climbing 1480 meters in about 40 minutes."

The first ride took nearly fifteen minutes. They moved into the other car and were off for the top. They had to change one more time. Andy looked down at the moving shadow of the cable car on the snow. Except for the noise of the cable, they could have been in a glider spiralling higher and higher above

131

the snow covered slopes.

A slowing of the *téléphérique* signalled their destination. They arrived at the Testa Grigia. What had taken Andy over six hours to climb the day before, was accomplished in under one today. The air at the top lacked oxygen and both men moved cautiously.

Carlo gazed at the vast glaciers of the Plateau Rosa. He turned and put his arm around the American's shoulder.

"In the distance to the west, higher than any other peaks, is the massif of the Monte Bianco. To the left of the Cervino is the Dent d'Hérens. Can you believe that yesterday morning, you were just on the other side in the *Rifúgio Aosta*?"

He dropped his arm and walked a few steps away from the building. Andy followed.

"The way to Zermatt is past the Col de Théodule. For centuries people have walked over this pass between Valais and Valle d'Aosta. Except for a short climb to the Schwarzsee, you can go downhill all the way. The total vertical is almost 2000 meters."

Andy quickly calculated that the longest drop in the Northeast was about 600 meters. He let out a low whistle.

Carlo took him by the arm and pointed out the route.

"We're close to the border between Italy and Switzerland. There's the *Rifúgio del Teodulo* just below. It's still in Italy but we'ved asked the Swiss Glacier Patrol to stay there with us. They may stop you so tell them that you're an American Air Force pilot seeking asylum in their country. Head past the *rifúgio*, keeping the Cervino on your left and ski down to Furgg. Aim for the tallest mountain; that's the Weisshorn, a giant even higher than the Cervino. I climbed it in two days from the Val d'Anniviers my last year in high school. You'll be on the Théodule Glacier most of the way. At this time of the year you shouldn't have trouble with crevasses but pay attention. If anything looks like it might be a snow bridge, ski around it.

"You can recognize Furgg because from there the slope drops sharply towards Zermatt. The best thing to do is to climb to the hotel at the Schwarszee. There's a T-bar that takes skiers to the base of the Cervino, and if you need something to eat or drink you can get it. Go down the rest of the way on the marked trails."

Carlo reached into his pocket.

"You'll need some good Swiss money."

Smiling, he placed a green 50 franc note in Andy's hand.

"Pay me back when the war is over."

The men embraced and clasped each other's arms. Andy thanked the Italian for all that he had done. Then he said,

"When you're able, please check and see that Angela is safe. I love her very much."

Carlo, his face deeply tanned from the winter sun, looked at the flyer, and said in English, "I will try Andy; goodbye and have a safe trip to America."

Visibly touched, the flyer pushed off in the direction of Furgg. He could never forget what these people had done for him. He would have been in a prison camp or worse. Because of their bravery and love, he was a free man.

The glacier fell away in a shallow steady pitch. At times he had to pole to keep moving. Stopping to look at the Matterhorn, he marveled how the view of the giant peak was modified from every perspective. Between changes in the scenery, the seasons, and the weather, he could never be bored in the mountains.

Two skiers were laboriously making their way up the glacier. When he came abreast, he saw that they were Swiss soldiers walking up to the *rifúgio*. In an accented French, they asked who he was and where he was going. Andy replied as Carlo had told him. Somewhat taken aback, the men suggested that he climb to the Schwarzsee and ski down to Zermatt on the

133

trail marked *Weisse Perle.*

The slope steepened and the American picked up speed making a series of precise parallel turns on the corn snow just before he came off the glacier. Following the soldiers' tracks, he veered to the left and continued to descend. It was a long schuss toward Furgg. Ahead to the left, on a ridge about one hundred meters above the slope, he could see the hotel at the Schwarzsee.

Putting on the skins, he climbed up and saw that it was situated on a belvedere with a splendid view of the surrounding mountains. *Duvets* were hanging out of the third floor windows, airing in the crisp mountain atmosphere. Entering the crowded dining room, he ordered a bowl of pea soup with sausage and went back outside. There were a number of skiers sunning themselves on chaise longues before the glassed-in-porch.

The pilot went over to a panorama that was inscribed on a wide metal tablet fixed in the ground and picked out the main landmarks from the immense summits and long tongues of glacial ice. Directly ahead was the Gornergletscher. Then he identified the Monte Rosa, Castor, Pollux, and Breithorn. All were over 4000 meters, with the Dufourspitze on the Monte Rosa at 4633, the highest.

Andy went back inside, found an empty table near a window, sat down, and faced the warm rays of the afternoon sun. Beyond the top of the T-bar, was the Matterhorn, its sculptured flanks and chiseled peak familiar from this angle. Turbulent clouds were building up around the mountaintop, casting a grey curtain over its western wall. One moment their white shapes appeared to form an immense whale, the next a long undulating banner, and finally a gigantic airship that was hovering over the aquiline summit.

While looking at this hypnotic spectacle he finished the soup. Then the American left the dining room, put on his skis and started for Zermatt. The *Weisse Perle*, an easy narrow trail down the north slope of the mountain, took him close to the T-bar and through a series of glades to a snow covered path. He kept going until he came out near signs marked **Furri-Luftseilbahn Schwarzsee** and **Zermatt**. Following the latter, he skirted a gorge cut by the river that flowed from the Gornergletscher, skied past some barns, their smells reminding him of the cheese making at the Tête Blanche, and arrived at the outskirts of the famous village.

Removing the skis, he slung them over his shoulder and walked down the narrow road that led to Zermatt. The snow had been packed hard to provide a solid surface for the horse drawn sleighs that skimmed to and fro. He passed by some dark wooden apartment houses with slate roofs that lined the road, came out in an open square and continued past the church to the Hotel Monte Rosa. Affixed to the street side of the hotel was a bronze commemorative tablet that paid hommage to Edward Whymper, the Englishman who first conquered the Matterhorn on the 14th of July, 1865.

A nearby kiosk featured the latest editions of **La Suisse, Tribune de Genève** and the **Neue Zürcher Zeitung**. Their headlines boldly announced the meeting of Churchill, Roosevelt, and Stalin at Yalta. Andy realized that he hadn't read a newspaper since before the ill-fated bombing mission.

Across the street a blue coach pulled by two proud horses, one grey and the other white, rolled into the Zermatterhof. The coachman jumped from his seat and began unloading luggage and skis that belonged to the arriving guests.

The stores had opened for the afternoon and the townspeople were walking about tending to their errands. Every few moments animated groups of skiers passed him. There were dark-faced ski instructors wearing red jackets with a distinguishing white band across the upper chest and 13 stars, the emblem of Valais on their right shoulder.

People, obviously rather well dressed and well fed, were

135

smiling and talking to one another in a strange German dialect. He walked past a shoestore and stopped by a ski shop to admire the display of clothing and equipment. The bakery window on the corner was overflowing with breads and enticing pastries.

Andy halted for a few minutes to observe this picture of life without war. The battles being fought in the next valley could have been taking place on another continent. Switzerland, the only central European country not under Nazi or Fascist rule, was an island of sanity in a Europe gone mad.

He continued past the post office and the Walliserkanne, stopped in front of the Hotel Walliserhof, placed his skis on the rack by the terrace and walked into the *Stubli*. Sitting down at one of the rustic wooden tables, he was aware of his thirst. A young woman dressed in a black dress, over which was a red embroidered apron, handed him a menu.

"Was Wünschen Sie?"

When he replied in French, she easily switched languages and repeated her question.

He studied the menu and told her that he would like to have a bottle of white wine and an *Assiette Valaisanne*. She suggested a Heida, one from the Nikolaital at Visperterminen, not far from Zermatt.

"The vineyards there are the highest in Europe, and the wine from the village is very special," she said with pride.

Andy nodded, and a few minutes later she returned with a small round glass and a brown bottle. She showed him the label, expertly uncorked the tapered neck, poured the glass half full, and stepped back.

He savoured the taste, looked up at the waitress, and said as his eyes filled with tears, *"Ca va."*

Breuil-Cervinia, Valle d'Aosta

Valpelline and "Tête Blanche"

Epilogue

"We are, in fact, living through a period of general de-sanctification of the Holocaust. In West Germany, historians are explaining away Hitler's crimes by lumping them in with Stalin's; Chancellor Helmut Kohl's official spokesman recently said that Germans have had enough of feeling guilty and that the Waffen S.S. of Bitburg were only good German soldiers. In France, a man called Le Pen considers the Holocaust 'a detail.' Anti-Israeli propagandists compare Israeli soldiers to Nazis, and in France as in the United States, and everywhere else, for that matter, shameless 'revisionists' go so far as to deny the very existence of the death camps."

"As for philosophers and psychiatrists, some of them have long been intrigued by simplistic theories that attribute to the victim a death wish or a secret need to dominate, to victimize, to oppress - in other words. to resemble the executioner. In the course of scholarly colloquia, one sometimes hears more about the guilt of the victims and the psychological problems of the survivors than about the crimes of the killers. Didn't an American novelist recently suggest that the suicide of my friend Primo Levi was nothing but a bout of depression that good psychoanalytical treatment could have cured? Thus is the tragedy of a great writer, a man who never ceased to battle the black angel of Auschwitz, reduced to a banal nervous breakdown."

WIESEL, "Art and the Holocaust: Trivializing Memory", **The New York Times**, 11-06-89.

Andy spent the rest of the war interned in Switzerland. In July of 1945, he sailed from Genova to New York and joined his family in Newport. In 1948, finishing his graduate work at Clark University in Worcester, Massachusetts, he started to work for the U.S. Quartermaster Corps at Natick.

After she left the Tête Blanche with her four cows, Angela walked to Oyace. Some months later, she gave birth to a girl, and waited for her husband to return from North Africa. He did not come home and was listed as missing in action by the Italian army. In 1948, she went back to the hotel with her young child and stayed until the early '60s when an enormous dam was built at Place Moulin, creating a reservoir that reached almost to the doors of the Tête Blanche. The Valpelline, as she had know it, was destroyed. She now lives in Nus, a few kilometers east of the city of Aosta.

Aosta was liberated by the partisans in the spring of 1945. French patrols entered the Valley but were resisted by the *Valdôtaines*. If France could have annexed Aosta, she would have controlled both St. Bernard Passes and dominated an area of 3260 kilometers east of the Alpine crests, providing a springboard into northern Italy. The French attempted to bribe the populace with money and salt, a scarce commodity and an Italian state monopoly, into first agitating for a plebiscite and then voting for annexation. This disruptive action was dealt with by President Truman, who notified General de Gaulle that unless French troops were immediately withdrawn from Aosta, all supplies of munitions and equipment would be cut off.

To blunt any further pressure from the French, the Italian government quickly acted after the war to grant special status to the Valle d'Aosta. Among the more important provisions of the new decrees were that Aosta was separated from the Italian speaking province of Ivrea and became a *regióne* of Italy with its own local government. French was restored as an official language, revenue was divided between the *regióne* and the central government in Roma, and control of such sectors as agriculture, industry, and tourism was handed over to the local government.

Because of the opening of the Grand St. Bernard and Mont Blanc Tunnels in the early 1960s, and the *autostrada*

140

connection from the Po Valley, the Valle d'Aosta has been annually besieged by millions of tourists. Automobiles bearing license plates from all over Europe clog the villages. Giant international trucks hinder the movement of the cars, and the fumes and noise from both foul the clean Alpine air. New motels, petrol stations, restaurants, and auto agencies compete for space along the valley's roads. ESSO, AGIP, and FIAT blot out the vineyards, Roman ruins, and glaciated peaks. In the towns, jukeboxes blare forth the latest banal tunes fabricated in Napoli or Roma. The splendid side valleys and the main valley of the Dora Baltea, which before the war were fresh beautiful places, have been transformed by the local population and the *nouveau riche* of Torino and Milan into vast garbage dumps strewn with tin cans, wine bottles, and human waste. And the haphazardous expansion of Cervinia has desecrated the terrain at the base of the Matterhorn. Though the Valle d'Aosta has become the most prosperous of the Italian *regióne*, the environment has been irreparably damaged.

Thirty years after the war, Andy returned to the Valle d'Aosta with some of the crew members from the "Suicide Six". They had been captured by the Germans and held as prisoners until the end of hostilities. The small group of boisterous middle-aged men took in the Roman ruins of Aosta and had *cappuccini* in one of the cafés that border Place Emile Chanoux. They stayed at the Hotel Bus in the old city and ate an exceptional meal of sautéed veal and linguini at the Brasserie Valdôtaine. The following day they skied at Courmayeur and then went to Cervinia. Late in the afternoon, driving up the Val Tournanche within sight of the jagged south face of the Matterhorn, they stopped their Volkswagen van by the side of the road to inspect a carefully tended small monument. Engraved in the grey stone was the following:

141

CADUTI
DELLA
VALTOURNANCHE
BRIGATA AUTONOMA
"MARMORE"

Among the names of the thirty-four men was,

LEVI CARLO	8-4-45

FIN

GLOSSARY

Abyssinia. The African country now known as Ethiopia that was invaded by Italy in 1935.

AGIP. *Agenzia Generàle Italia Petrolio*, the Italian state oil company.

Ah, lèi vuole andàre a Cervinia? Oh, so you want to go to Cervinia?

Algeria. A North African country, formerly a colony of France that was invaded by allied forces in 1942 during World War II.

alpage. A summer grazing area in the high Alps.

alpine glow. The period at twilight and dawn when the high snow covered peaks of the Alps turn an orange or pink colour.

Alpini. Italian soldiers, specially trained for fighting in the mountains.

Alsace-Lorraine. An area of northeast France that at various times during history has been occupied by the Germans or the French.

Anschluß. The annexation of Austria in 1938 by Nazi Germany.

anthracite. A form of coal containing up to 95 percent carbon used in the manufacture of steel.

Aosta. The Roman city of Augusta Praetoria, now the capital of the *regióne* in the Valle d'Aosta, situated at the junction of the Grand and Petit St. Bernard Passes at 581 meters.

aperitif. A small alcoholic drink, such as vermouth, taken before a meal to stimulate the appetite.

Aprilia. A four door model of a Lancia automobile.

Arch of Augustus. The triumphal arch erected by Augustus Ceasar in 11 B.C. at the eastern entrance of Aosta to commemorate the conquest of the Salassi.

Arch of Titus. Built in Roma in 81 A.D., between the Coliseum and the Roman Forum, the arch is adorned with scenes from the life of Titus.

arête. A sharp mountain ridge formed by alpine glaciation.

armoire. A free standing closet usually made out of wood.

Arrivederci. Goodbye.

Aryan. In Nazi doctrine an Aryan was a non-Jewish Caucasian of Nordic stock.

Assiette Valaisan. A typical cold plate served in Valais with cheese, dried beef, bacon, pickles, and pickled onions.

Auberge de la Jeunesse. Youth Hostel.

Auf wiedersehn. Goodbye, until we see each other again.

Augúri. Best wishes.

Austrian and Bavarian immigrants. Men such as Otto Schniebs, Hannes Schneider, and Sepp Ruschp who brought skiing to New England.

Austro-Hungarian Army. An army comprised of men from the Austro-Hungarian Empire that numbered 2,700,000 troops by the end of World War I. About 75 percent of the officers were of Germanic origin, while only some 25 percent of the soldiers understood German.

Austro-Hungarian Empire. Known as the Dual Monarchy, the Empire was created in 1866 by the Austrian Emperor Franz Joseph. The main ethnic groups were Germans and Magyars. Minorities included Czechs, Poles, and Romanians.

autostràda. Four lane divided highways that criss-cross Italy, toll in the north and centre and free in the south.

avalanche. A mass of snow, often mixed with ice, trees, and rock that descends from mountain slopes. It may start from a single point on the slope or a vast slab of snow may break away and move at varying speeds from a few kilometers per hour to over 200 kilometers per hour.

B-24. A four engine, high wing, split tail bomber used by Allied forces during the Second World War.

bagel. A leavened doughnut-shaped crusty roll made from flour and water that was eaten by Jewish immigrants to North America.

balaclava. A close fitting knitted wool hat that covers the head and neck.

Balkans. The mountainous peninsula in southeast Europe that comprises Greece, European Turkey, Bulgaria, Albania and much of Yugoslavia.

Bard. A narrows at the entrance to the Valle d'Aosta, guarded by an enormous fort that almost stopped Napoleon's army on the way to Marengo.

Bardolino. A red wine that comes from the region of Verona.

Basin of Tzan. The high mountain basin situated between Valle di St. Barthélemy and Val Tournanche

Bayern. The southern German *Land* that includes the Alps.

Bienvenue au Chalet des Chutes, Famille Arsenault. Welcome to the Chalet des Chutes, Arsenault Family.

blue wax. A hard wax used on the bottoms of skis during very cold weather.

Bohemia. The western region of Czechoslovakia, bounded by a rim of mountains that form the border with Germany.

Bonjour messieurs. Good day men.

Bonne Année. Happy New Year.

Bonne nuite. Good night.

Bonsoir. Good evening.

Bourg St. Maurice. A small village in France at 840 meters, located at the southern terminus of the Petit St. Bernard Pass.

Breithorn. One of the mountains to the south of Zermatt, 4160 meters, that forms the frontier between Valle d'Aosta and Valais.

Breuil. The French name for the village at the south base of the Matterhorn at the head of the Val Tournanche in the Valle d'Aosta.

Buona fortúna. Good luck.

Buon giórno Americano, cóme sta? Good day American, how are you doing?

Buon giórno dottore. Good day doctor.

Burgundians. A barbarian tribe that settled in the area between the Rhône and Saône Rivers after the downfall of the Roman Empire. They ruled the Valle d'Aosta intermittently from 443 to 1032 A.D.

Burlington. A city in northwest Vermont on Lake Champlain.

Buthier. A tributary of the Dora Baltea that rises in the Valpelline.

cabane. Cabin or small hut.

CADUTI DELLA VALTOURNANCHE BRIGATA AUTONOMA "MARMORE". Fallen in the Val Tournanche the Autonomous Brigade of the "Marmore".

café au lait. A large cup of coffee to which hot milk is added.

Calabria. The mountainous Italian *regióne* at the southern tip of the country from which many emmigrants left for northern Italy.

campaníle. The bell tower of a church.

cappuccíno. A cup of coffee that is made by forcing steam through the grounds to which steam-whipped milk is added. It is topped with powdered cocoa or chocolate.

Celsius. The Swedish astronomer who devised the centigrade scale of temperature.

Celtic. Groups of people from central Europe who were dominant in the Alpine Valleys before the Romans.

Central Powers. The Alliance of Austro-Hungary, Germany, Bulgaria and Turkey that opposed the Allied during World War I.

Cervin. The French name for the Matterhorn, the mountain at 4477 meters that forms the border between Valle d'Aosta and Valais.

Cervinia. The Italian name for the village at the head of the Val Tournanche at 2006 meters that lies at the south-facing base of the Matterhorn.

Cervíno. The Italian name for the Matterhorn.

Chamberlain. The British Conservative prime minister who came to office in 1937. He and Daladier sacrificed the Sudeten regions of Czechoslovakia to Germany in the mistaken believe that this would appease Hitler.

Chamonix. The French village, 1037 meters, in the Arve Valley at the base of the Mont Blanc.

Channel. The body of water between England and France, known as the English Channel by the British and la Manche by the French.

Chin chin. Cheers.

Christian Democrat. An Italian political party backed by the Catholic church.

Ciào. Goodbye.

cirque. A natural amphitheatre surrounded by mountains that has been formed by Alpine glaciation. The bottom of the cirque is often filled in by water forming a small lake.

Ci védiamo. Until we see each other again.

Clark University. A small liberal arts university in Worcester, Massachusetts well know for its Geography Department.

climber's register. The book that is found in mountain cabins in which the climbers sign out and sign in so that the guardian can keep track of where they are going.

climbing skins. Sealskins strapped to the bottom of the skis that permit the ski to slide forward but not to slip back.

closed gate. Two slalom poles set perpendicular to the fall line through which the racer must pass.

Cogne. A village, 1534 meters, in the Val di Cogne above which was an important iron mine.

Col de la Division. A pass above the Rifúgio Aosta at 3314 meters that leads over the glacier to the Col de Valpelline.

Col de Théodule. The pass between Breuil and Zermatt at 3468 meters that has been used by pilgrims, traders, and skiers between Valle d'Aosta and Valais.

Col di Valcournera. A pass at 3066 meters leading from Prarayer in the Valpelline to the Val Tournanche.

Col du Créton. The pass at 3406 meters over the Glaciers des Dames in the Valpelline to the Val Tournanche.

Cóme sta signóre? How goes it mister?

Communists. An outlawed political party in Italy under the Fascists, that played a major role in the partisan movement.

Connecticut River. Delineates the border between the states of Vermont and New Hampshire.

Connecticut Valley. The valley through which the Connecticut River flows that lies between the White Mountains of New Hampshire and the Green Mountains of Vermont.

cornice. An overhang of snow and ice built up by wind on the tops and crêtes of mountains.

couchette. A communal bunk that is common in the hotels and cabins in the Alps.

couloir. A steep gorge or gully on the side of a mountain that is often the only route up during a climb and can be an avalanche trap.

Courmayeur. A well known mountaineering center on the east slope of the Mont Blanc in Valle d'Aosta at 1226 meters.

Cremona. An agricultural centre in the *regióne* of Lombardia, sited near the Po River, that was noted for its violin makers such as Stradivarius, and its 13th century *campaníle*.

crevasse. A deep vertical crack, many meters deep, in a glacier that is often hidden by a snow bridge during the winter.

Daladier. The French prime minister, who along with Chamberlain, sacrificed the Sudeten regions of Czechoslovakia to Germany.

Davos. A famous Swiss ski resort in the canton of Graubünden in the eastern part of the country at 1560 meters.

Dents des Bouquetins. Mountain peaks, 3838 and 3668 meters in the upper Valpelline that form the border between Valle d'Aosta and Valais.

Dents d'Hérens. The peak to the west of the Matterhorn, 4171 meters that forms the border between Valle d'Aosta and Valais.

divertiménto. Amusement.

Doire. The French name for gold and the Dora Baltea. The river for centuries was mined for gold.

Dome di Cian. A mountain, 3351 meters, between the Valpelline and the Val Tournanche.

Donnaz. A small village north of Pont St. Martin in the Valle d'Aosta.

Dora Baltea. The main river of the Valle d'Aosta whose source are the glaciers of Mont Blanc. It flows into the Po east of Torino.

Due cappuccíni per favóre. Two cappuccíni please.

Dufourspitze. Part of the massif of the Monte Rosa, it is the highest point in Switzerland, 4634 meters, and forms the border between Valais and Piemonte.

duvet. A down comforter.

East Prussia. A former province of Germany that was separated from the rest of the country by the Polish Corridor during the years 1918 to 1939.

edge. A ski technique that uses the edge of the ski to climb sideways or to brake.

Edward Whymper. The English climber, who after many years of attempts, was the first man to climb the Matterhorn. During the descent four members of the party fell to their deaths when the rope broke.

Einsatzkommando. Men who were part of the *Einsatzgruppen* or Special Action Groups whose task was to exterminate Jews, gypsies, and Soviet political commissars by execution. At first all victims were shot and usually buried in a ditch. Later women and children were asphyxiated in specially designed "gas vans". Statistics vary, but at least 700,000 Jews were killed in this manner on the Russian front.

Emile Chanoux. The notary and resistance leader from Aosta who helped to found *la jeune vallée d'Aoste*, an organization pledged to defend *Valdôtaine* culture. He was tortured to death by the Nazis on May 8, 1944.

enfilade. An arrangement of slalom poles set in such a manner that the skier must pass through with out making a complete turn.

ESSO. The acronym used by Standard Oil on its former petrol stations in Italy.

Export. A type of ale brewed by Molson's of Montreal.

Fair of Saint Orso. An annual fair of artisanal objects that has been held on January 31st in Aosta for over 2000 years.

falline. The most direct way down a slope.

Fascists. Individuals who followed the authoritarian philosophy of Mussolini. They held power in Italy from 1922 to 1943, then collabrated with the Nazis (Republic of Salo) until the end of World War II.

Fendant. White wine produced in Valais.

Fenêtre de Tzan. A pass at 2734 meters between the Valle di St. Barthélemy and the Basin of Tzan.

Fenis. Site east of Aosta of a medieval castle erected in 1340.

Ferrara. A city in the *regióne* of Emilia-Romagna sited just west of the Po Delta.

FIAT. *Fàbbrica Italia Automobila Torino*, a company that manufactures a range of industrial products and best know for its automobiles.

First World War. Began on July 28, 1914 and ended on November 17, 1918. It pitted England, France, Russia and the U.S. against Austria-Hungary, Germany, and Turkey. The War was the first to involve the total resources of the combatants and to cover such a large part of the globe. At least 8.6 million men in uniform were killed and over 21 million wounded. The chaotic conditions created by the conflict (four empires, Habsburg, Ottoman, Imperial Russian, and Imperial German, collapsed), led directly to the rise of Hitler and the outbreak of World War II in 1939.

Flanders. A low-lying flat region in northern France and southern Belgium that suffered enormous damage during the First World War.

Fleur-des-lis. The distinctive blue and white flag of the province of Québec.

flush. An arrangement of slalom gates that force the racer to ski a series of tight turns down the falline.

föhn. A strong adiabatic wind that develops over the Alps during cyclonic storms, that is cooled dynamically as it passes over the mountain crests, precipitating either rain or snow. This releases heat, thereby retarding the rate of cooling. When the wind descends on the lee side, it is warmed at a constant rate and therefore is drier and has a higher temperature than at the same altitude that it began its upwards flow.

Fontina. The typical hard cheese that is made in the Aosta Valley.

forerunner. Skiers who test the course before the race begins. By skiing through the gates they set a track that the racers can follow.

Franks. Ancient Germanic peoples that lived in the region of the Rhine. They gave their name to France.

fraternity. A social organization for men at colleges or universities in the United States.

Furgg. An alp at 2431 meters above Zermatt.

Furi-Luftseilbahn Schwarzsee. The cable car that connects Furri 1886 above Zermatt with the Schwarzsee, 2582 meters, at the base of the Matterhorn.

General Cadorna. The chief of the Italian General Staff during World War I. He was relieved of his command after the disasterous defeat at the Battle of Caporetto.

General de Gaulle. The French General who emerged from the French defeat in World War II, to lead French forces in the final period of the War.

Génèpy. a liqueur made by distilling the essence of Alpine flowers.

Genova. The main port of Italy sited at the base of the Ligurian Alps. Because of the mountains, the city has had to expand east and west along the Ligurian Sea.

glaciated massifs. A range of mountains that have been eroded into distinctive forms by Alpine glaciers.

glaciated valley. A valley that has been eroded by the effects of glaciation. It is often of a U-shaped nature.

Glacier des Dames. A hanging glacier that is located on the east side of the upper Valpelline.

Glacier Patrol. The organization of the Swiss Army that patrolled the high mountain borders of the country during World War II.

Glühwein. Heated wine drink made with red wine and spices.

Gordze. The site of small barns in the upper Valpelline.

Gornergletcher. The 14 kilometer long glacier above Zermatt that feeds from the Monte Rosa and surrounding massifs.

Graien Alps. A chain of mountains northwest of Torino.

Grand Isle. A large island in the northern part of Lake Champlain in the state of New York.

Grand St. Bernard Pass. Connects Valais with Valle d'Aosta at 2469 meters. Before the tunnel under the pass was built in 1964, the pass was closed for upwards of six months each year because of the winter snows.

Grand St. Bernard Tunnel. A 5.8 kilometer toll tunnel under the Grand St. Bernard Pass that has covered access highways in both Valais and Valle d'Aosta to insure that the route is unaffected by snow.

grappa. An unaged brandy distilled from the pulpy residue of the wine press.

grolla. An ornate goblet carved out of wood that is used for wine.

Gruß Gott. Greeting from God.

Guardà! Guardà! Look! Look!

"H" gate. Slalom pole arrangement that gives an option for the racer to ski through the gate in either direction.

Haggadah. A book containing the liturgy for the Seder service on the Jewish festival of Passover.

hairpin. A close arrangement of slalom gates that force the racer to turn rather abruptly from one direction to another.

Hall of Mirrors. The large hall at Versailles in which the Treaty was signed on June 28, 1919.

hanging glacier. A glacier that comes down the mountainside but does not reach the valley floor.

Hillman's Highway. A steep trail above the tree line on Mount Washington in New Hampshire that is often skied in the spring. time. It is on the way to Tuckerman's Ravine.

Hindenburg. The German Field Marshall and commander in East Prussia who was revered for his victory over the Russians at Tannenberg in 1914. He was elected president of the Reich in 1925 and, no longer in full possession of his faculties, appointed Hitler chancellor in January 1933.

Hitler. German dictator, founder and leader of National Socialism. He was born in Upper Austria in 1889, fought in World War I, was virulently anti-semitic, and was responsible for the outbreak of World War II and the subsequent death of fifty million soldiers and civilians. Throughout his adult life he miraculously escaped death and assassination attempts, finally committing suicide in 1945, a few days before the end of World War II in Europe.

Hotel Monte Rosa. The hotel in Zermatt where Edward Whymper, the first person to climb the Matterhorn, stayed.

House of Savoy. A feudal dynasty founded in the late 10th century that controlled strategic regions of the western Alps. It expanded into becoming the Kingdom of Savoy and Sardinia. Members of the dynasty became the first kings of modern Italy.

Imperial Russia. The Tsarist government that broke down during World War I and was overthrown by revolution.

irrigation canals. Small channels used by the peasants to irrigate their fields with water from the glaciers. The system originated during the Middle Ages to insure adequate moisture for the pastures in what otherwise would be an arid climate.

Ivrea. Italian city south of the Valle d'Aosta in the *regióne* of Piemonte. It is the home of Olivetti.

Jacques Cartier Bridge. The bridge across the St. Lawrence River that connects Longueuil with the island of Montréal.

Jupiter. The largest planet in the solar system.

kick turn. Performed on skis while standing still to reverse direction.

kirsch. A colourless brandy distilled from a mash of cherries.

Kitzbühel. The famous Austrian ski resort located in Tirol at 762 meters.

Kleine Schauspielhaus. Small theatre where Threepenney Opera played in München.

Kommandant. Commander.

Kristallnacht. Crystal Night, November 9th, the date of the abortive Munich beer hall *Putsch* became a national holiday in Nazi Germany. On that day in 1938, a Nazi pogrom systematically attacked and destroyed Jewish property throughout the country. A total of 101 synagogues were destroyed by fire, 76 demolished, 7500 shops destroyed, 91 people were killed, and more than 26,000 Jews were carried off the next day to concentration camps.

La jeune valée d'Aoste. The young valley of Aosta. An organization established during Fascist times to defend *Valdôtaine* tradition, preserve the use of French, and revive old customs and folklore.

La Suisse. Newspaper published in Genève.

Lac Long. A small mountain lake in the Valpelline at 2720 meters.

Lac Mort. A cirque lake in the Valpelline at 2843 meters.

Lake Champlain. A large lake that forms the border between the states of New York and Vermont and whose northeast arm extends into the province of Québecé.

La Lechère. A small hamlet in the Valpelline at 1808 meters where the dirt road ends.

la montàgna. The mountain.

Lancia. An Italian automobile.

lateral moraine. Rock and fine material that is deposited at the sides of glaciers.

Laurentians. Low mountains composed of ancient igneous rock found north of Montréal.

lavabo. A small wash basin.

la violètta. The violet.

Lawine. German for avalanche.

les fleurs des Alps. Flowers of the Alps.

Les Murettes. The low walls that are used for terracing the vineyards in Valais. They are on the label of a fine Fendant produced in Sion.

Levy, Primo. A chemist from Torino, who was captured in the mountains by Fascists, imprisoned in Aosta, and then sent to Auschwitz in February 1944. After the war, he wrote incisive and powerful books and poetry describing his experiences that have been translated into many languages. Levy committed suicide in Torino in 1987.

Lignan. A small village at 1633 meters in the Valle di St. Barthélemy.

Ligue Valdôtaine pour la langue Française. The *Valdôtaine* league for the French language.

Ligurian Alps. Mountains found along the Mediterranean coast to the west of Genova.

Lombards. An ancient Germanic tribe that settled in Italy.

long thongs. Leather thongs attached to ski bindings that racers used to wrap around their boots to give them better control.

Lyskamm. A 4527 meter peak south of Zermatt that forms the border between Valais and Valle d'Aosta.

Mackenzie King. Born in Kitchener, Ontario, he was the prime minister of Canada during World War II.

maize. Corn.

Màmma mia! My mother!

Manchester. A city on the Merrimack River in southern New Hampshire.

Mantova. An agricultural center southwest of Verona famed for its Ducal Palace.

maple syrup. A sweet syrup that is made in the springtime from the boiled sap of the sugar maple tree in northeastern North America. It is eaten on waffles and pancakes and is poured over ice cream.

Maquis. Drought resistent vegetation in the Mediterranean region and the name give to French guerrilla bands during World War II.

Marengo. Village in Piemonte where on June 14, 1800, the French army led by Napoleon defeated the Austrians.

Marne. A river in northern France that flows into the Seine at Paris. In September 1914, French troops beat back the advancing Germans in this area, thus preventing the fall of the capital.

Martigny. The former Roman city of Octodurus, located at 467 meters where the Rhône river turns north in Valais. It guards the northern approach to the Grand St. Bernard Pass.

Matterhorn. The distinctive glaciated peak, 4471 meters, that lies between the villages of Zermatt and Breuil-Cervinia.

McGill. A largly English speaking university on the slopes of Mont Royal in central Montrèal.

MCMXXIII. Roman numerals for 1923.

Mein Kampf. "My Struggle", the book written by Hitler when he was in Landsberg prison that outlines his political philosophy and sets forth his plans for the conquest of Europe and the elimination of the Jews.

mélèze. French for larch or tamarack, a coniferous tree that sheds its needles in the late autumn.

metal edges. Segmented edges that were attached to wooden skis. They were mounted flush to the base using small screws.

Milano. Large Italian city on the Po Plain south of the Alps. It is the center of the most significant economic region of the country.

157

miss a gate. Occurs when the skier fails to pass through two slalom poles in the required manner. He or she is then disqualified.

Molson Brewery. The oldest brewery in Canada with headquarters in Montrèal.

Mont Blanc. A mountain of resistant granites, 4807 meters, that seals the border between Haute-Savoie and Valle d'Aosta. It is the highest in Western Europe.

Mont Blanc Tunnel. The 11.5 kilometer-long vehicular tunnel between Entrèves, Valle d'Aosta and Chamonix, Haute-Savoie, that opened in 1965.

Mont Emilius. The dominant peak, 3559 meters, that rises south of the city of Aosta.

Mont Rolland. A small villge in the Laurentian Mountains north of Montrèal.

Mont Tremblant. The highest mountain, 915 meters, in the southern Laurentians, located 140 kilometers north of Montréal. The ski area was opened in 1937.

Monte Bianco. Italian for Mont Blanc.

Monte Rosa. The massive mountain, 4554 meters, southeast of Zermatt, that forms the border between Switzerland and Italy.

Montpelier. The captial city of Vermont that is located in the north-central part of the state.

Morocco. Former North African colony of France, now an independent country, that was invaded by Allied forces in November 1942.

Mount Sunapee. A small ski area to the east of Newport, New Hampshire in the southern part of the state.

Mounties. The Royal Canadian Mounted Police, the federal police force in Canada, noted for their distinctive red tunics.

Munich Beer Hall Putsch. An attempted coup by Hitler that took place on November 9, 1923. As a consequence, he was sent to prison for nine months.

Mussolini. The Italian Fascist leader who was dictator of the country from 1922 to 1943.

Natick. A small Massachusetts town located a few kilometers west of Boston.

Nazis. Individuals belonging to the National Socialist German Workers Party that gained control of the country in 1933.

Nebbia. A location in the Valle di St. Barthélemy, 2389 meters, where one can go either over the Fenêtre de Tzan to the Val Tournanche or over the Col Livournea to the Valpelline.

Nebbiòlo. A red wine that comes from the Alba region of Piemonte.

Neue Züricher Zeitung. A world famous newspaper that is published in Zürich, Switzerland.

New England. A largly mountainous region of six states in the Northeastern United States.

New Hampshire. One of the New England States.

New York. A large state that lies to the west of Vermont and borders on the province of Québec.

Nikolaital. The dry, lateral valley that leads from Visp in the Rhône Valley south to Zermatt that is also know as the Mattertal.

North Africa. Originally the strategic sphere of the Italians, the Germans had to relieve their annihilated allies in August 1940. Commanded by the able General Rommel, the Germans forced the Allied forces to the gates of Egypt. The armies swept back and forth over the Libyan desert like "fleets of warships on the sea", before the Germans were finally broken.

Northeaster. A violent cyclonic storm that moves from south to north up the coast of eastern North America. In the winter it carries copious amounts of moisture from the Atlantic Ocean to the interior that falls as heavy snow against the north-south trending mountains of New Hampshire and Vermont.

nouveau riche. newly rich.

Nuremberg laws. Passed September 15, 1935, deprived the Jews of German citizenship and confined them to the status of "subjects". They also forbade marriage between Jews and Aryans as well as extramarital relations between them, and prohibited Jews from employing female Aryan servants under thirty-five years of age.

open gate. Slalom gates that are set across the falline in a staggered sequence.

Orion. A large constellation, named after a mythical Greek hunter, that is visible in the southern winter sky. It is composed of seven stars, of which the most prominent four, form a huge quadrangle.

Ortler Mountains. A glaciated mountain range near the Swiss-Italian border that before 1918 was part of Austria. It was a region of violent battles between Italian and Austrian mountain troops, that were fought at elevations of up to 3000 meters during the First World War.

Ottoman Turkey. The Empire that was founded about 1300, reached its greatest territorial extent in the 16th century, and collapsed in 1918. Much of the Balkans was controlled by Turkey before the First World War.

Oyace. A village, 1365 meters, in the Valpelline.

Palàzzo del Diamànte. Palace of Diamonds in Ferrara, built in the 14th-15th century, owes its name to the 12,500 blocks of marble on its facade, which are cut in facets like diamonds.

Palàzzo Ducàle. The Ducal Palace in central Mantova that comprises courts, chapels, squares, gardens, and over 450 rooms dating from the 14th and 16th century.

Papal-Nuncio. A permanent diplomatic representative of the pope, he was seen with Hitler on an election poster and quoted as saying; "I have not understood you for a long time. But I have worried for a long time. Today I understand you." On July 20, 1933, the Nazi government concluded a concordat with the Vatican in which it guaranteed the freedom of the Catholic religion and the right of the Church "to regulate her own affairs." Shortly thereafter, the terms of the agreement were broken by the Nazis.

Paris Basin. An area of low-lying sedimentary rocks that covers almost one-quarter of France. Structurally, the Basin can be compared to a nest of broad shallow bowls with jagged edges, each bowl and edge representing a different rock layer and escarpment respectively.

Parmigiano. Parmesan cheese manufactured in the region of Parma in the Po Valley. It is a hard cheese the requires a long aging process and a great deal of skill and care.

Partisans. Guerrilla soldiers who fought against the Nazis and Fascists during World War II.

Passover. Jewish festival that often coincides with Easter and that celebrates the exodus of the Hebrews, led by Moses, from Egypt

pasta. Various flour and egg food preparations of Italian origin, made of thin unleavened dough and served in a variety of forms.

patois. A dialect of French.

patron. proprietor.

Pavia. A city on the Ticino River south of Milano.

Pearl Harbor. The American naval base near Honolulu on the island of Oahu in Hawaii that was bombed without warning by the Japanese early Sunday morning on December 7, 1941, thus bringing the U.S. into World War II.

Petit St. Bernard Pass. At 2188 meters, it connects the Valle d'Aosta with Haut-Savoie and was the route that allowed the House of Savoy to maintain control over the Valle d'Aosta during the Middle Ages.

Piemonte. A wealthy *regióne* of northwest Italy that comprises sections of the Po Valley and the Western Alps.

Place Moulin. A hamlet in Valpelline at 1856 meters that is presently the site of a large storage dam.

Planavilla. A village at 1106 meters, near the mouth of the Valle di St. Barthèlemy.

Plan Maison. A site above Cervinia at 2547 meters, where the *téléphérique* departs for the Testa Grigia.

Po Delta. The low lying area of the Po, built up by deposits of the river, that juts into the Adriatic Sea.

polenta. A traditional peasant dish in the north of Italy, made from ground corn meal.

Pollux. A mountain at 4091 meters, south of Zermatt, that forms the border between Valais and the Valle d'Aosta.

Pomposa. The site of a Benedictine Abbey founded beside the sea in the 6th century.

Pont St. Martin. An industrial city, 345 meters, that is sited at the entrance of the Valle d'Aosta.

Po Valley. The rich industrial and agricultural heartland of northern Italy.

Prarayer. An *alpage* at 2005 meters, in the Valpelline that is the site of the Hotel Tête Blanche.

Praz. A small hamlet, 1756 meters, where the paved road ends in the Valle St. Barthélemy.

President Truman. American president who came to office in the waning days of World War II, after the death of Franklin D. Roosevelt.

Près St. Didier. A village in the valley of the Dora Baltea, 1108 meters, where the railroad from Torino terminated.

prosciútto. A spiced or smoked ham that is cured by drying and served in wafer-thin slices.

Québec. A predominantly French speaking province of Canada, that is over twice as large as France.

racard. A small wooden barn placed on stilts that has a large round stone between the base and the legs to keep out rodents.

Rathaus. City hall.

Red Ensign. The old flag of Canada that had a small union jack in the upper red corner.

Remarque, Erich Maria. German author who wrote anti-war novels such as **All Quiet on the Western Front** and **Three Comrades.**

rifúgio. A cabin or hut in the mountains that provides shelter for hikers, mountaineers, and skiers.

Rifúgio Aosta. A cabin at 2781 meters in the upper Valpelline

Rifúgio Jumeaux. A cabin at 2787 meters, above Cervinia.

Rifúgio Rivolta. A cabin in the Basin of Tzan at 2900 meters.

Rifúgio Théodule. A large cabin at 3317 meters, just below the Testa Grigia near the Col de Théodule on the Swiss-Italian border.

Regióne. The regional political units in Italy.

rennet. The lining membrane of the fourth stomach that is used to curdle milk in the making of cheese.

Rhineland. The region of Germany that bordered the Netherlands, Belgium, and France. It was demilitarized by the Versailles Treaty in order to insure that Germany would remain vulnerable to attack. Hitler ordered German troops to enter the area on March 7, 1936, and when there was no action taken by the French to stop his army, refortification began.

Richelieu Valley. The valley through which the Richelieu River flows north from Lake Champlain to the St. Lawrence River.

Romanesque Campaníle. A style of bell tower that prevailed in Western Europe from the 9th to the 12th century.

Romans. Conquered and controlled the area of the Valle d'Aosta, Valais, and Haute-Savoie, that previously had been inhabited by Celtic tribes.

Rouses Point. A small border crossing station between the state of New York and the province of Québec on the northern shore of Lake Champlain.

rucksack. A special backpack, made out of reinforced cotton or light canvas, that is used in the mountains to carry equipment or clothes.

saddle. A low lying divide between two mountains.

St. Adèle. A small village in the Laurentians north of Montréal.

St. Agathe. A village in the Laurentians north of St. Adèle.

St. George. A Christian saint who is depicted in sculptures and paintings slaying a dragon.

St. Jean. A city in Québec on the Richelieu River east of Montréal.

St. Jovite. A village in the Laurentian Mountains just south of Mont Tremblant.

St. Lawrence River. The outlet of the Great Lakes that begins on the eastern end of Lake Ontario and passes Montréal and Québec City on its way to the sea. Ocean going boats could make their way as far as Montréal before the Seaway was built.

St. Vincent. A small village at 575 meters, in the main valley of the Dora Baltea where it turns south to the Po Valley.

Salassi. A Celtic tribe that lived in the Valle d'Aosta from about 600 B.C. to their conquest by the Romans 600 years later.

164

Salúte Carlo. To you health Carlo.

Salzburg. A baroque Austrian city on the Salzach River, celebrated as the birthplace of Mozart.

Sarajevo. A city in Bosnia in central Yugoslavia where the Austrian Archduke Ferdinand and his wife were assassinated on June 28, 1914. This was the final event that precipitated World War I.

schuss. A ski run that requires no turning.

Schwarzsee. A small mountain lake, 2552 meters above Zermatt at the base of the Matterhorn.

Seagrams. The world's largest manufacturer and seller of whiskeys, wines, and spirits. Its original distillery is in Waterloo, Ontario.

sérac. A large block mass or pinnacle of ice on a glacier.

Serbia. An ancient Slav Kingdom, later part of Yugoslavia, that became independent in 1878. After the assassination of Archduke Ferdinand as a result of a Serbian plot, Austria's demand for control of Serbia precipitated the First World War.

Shawbridge. A small village north of Montréal in the foothills of the Laurentian Mountains.

Shuhplattler. A traditional circle dance of the Tirol performed by men who keep time by slapping their thighs.

Sicilia. The island of Sicily, a *regióne* of Italy.

sideslip. To slide down a steep slope by controlling the angle of the edges of the skis.

Sion. The capital of the canton of Valais located at 491 meters in the Rhône Valley.

skate. To move along flat areas on skis by a skating motion.

slalom. A timed ski race in which slalom poles are arranged down the slope to control the turns of the participants.

slalom poles. Bamboo poles that were used to set the course of the slalom.

snow bridge. Drifting snow that forms over a glacial crevasse. It is extremely dangerous because mountaineers or skiers cannot tell if there is a crevasse below the bridge. Often, they fall through.

Socialists. A political party that was outlawed by Mussolini.

sorority. A social organization for women at colleges and universities in the United States.

Soviet-German Non-Agression Pact. Signed on August 23, 1939, it divided Eastern Europe into a Soviet and German sphere and paved the way for Hitler's invasion of Poland on September 1st. The Soviet Union took over Estonia, Latvia, Lithuania, and eastern Poland. Germany took over western Poland.

steel mill. The mill built in the 1920s in Aosta that utilized iron ore from Cogne and anthracite from La Thuile. At its peak during World War II, the complex employed 8,000 persons.

Stelvio Pass. A high pass in the Ortler Mountains of Italy at 2757 meters, that links the upper Adige Valley with the valley of the Adda. It was the scene of heavy fighting in World War I.

stem christie. A ski turn by which an edge change is made by shifting the weight from one downhill ski to the other during the time that the skis are placed in a snowplow position.

Stowe. A small village in the Green Mountains of northern Vermont that is the gateway to the ski runs of Mount Mansfield.

Stubaital. A long lateral valley in the Tirol, southwest of Innsbruck, that is famous as a mountaineering centre.

stubli. A small cozy informal room that is part of a restaurant or hotel.

Suicide Six. One of the original ski areas in southern Vermont.

Switzerland. The neutral democratic, mountainous country in west-central Europe that was not occupied by the Nazis. It controls key north-south passes through the Alps, is composed of independent cantons, and has three major official languages, French, German, and Italian.

téléphérique. A cable car that connects the valleys with the higher areas of the mountains.

Testa Grigia. Terminus on the Italian-Swiss border at 3480 meters, of the *télélépherique* that starts from Cervinia.

Third Reich. The Reich of Nazi Germany that was to last 1000 years. It collapsed in twelve.

Threepenney Opera. *Die Dreigrosschenoper*, written by Kurt Weill and Bertold Brecht and first performed in Germany in 1928, was banned by the Nazis in 1933.

Tirol. An Austrian *Land* in the mountainous western part of the country that embraces the watershed of the Inn River.

tonneau. A wooden cask used for the storage of wine.

Torino. A large industrial city on the Po River that is the capital of Peimonte.

Tribune de Genève. A newspaper published in Genève.

Tuckerman's Ravine. An enormous cirque on Mt. Washington in northern New Hampshire that fills in with snow during the winter and is skied in the spring.

un po piú lúngo. A little bit longer.

U-shaped velley. The shape of an alpine valley that has been glaciated. This contrasts to the V-shaped valleys that have not been glaciated and have been eroded by running water.

Va béne. O.K.

Valais. The Swiss bilingual canton bordering on France and Italy that embraces the watershed of the upper Rhône Valley.

Val d'Anniviers. Valley in the canton of Valais in Switzerland, known for transhumance, the movement of whole families who went with their cows from the shelter of the valley bottom in winter to the alpage on the mountain sides in summer.

Val di Cogne. A lateral valley not far from the city of Aosta that is south of the valley of the Dora Baltea.

Valle d'Aosta. A bilingual *regióne* in northwest Italy that borders on France and Switzerland.

Valle di St. Barthélemy. A sparsely populated lateral valley near Nus that leads north from the Dora Baltea.

Valpelline. A remote northeast-southwest trending tributary valley of the Dora Baltea.

Val Tournanche. A north-south trending lateral valley that leads from Châtillon in the main Aosta Valley to Breuil-Cervinia at the base of the Matterhorn.

Vercelli. An agricultural center in the Po Valley in the heart of the rice growing district of Piemonte.

Vermont. The New England state that is located to the west of New Hampshire.

vermouth. An aromatized wine in which herbs, roots, bitters and other flavourings have been steeped.

Verrès. A village in the main Aostan Valley north of Pont St. Martin.

Versailles Peace Conference. Conference after World War I that led to the Versailles Treaty signed on June 28, 1919. Among its many resolutions were the demilitarization of Germany territory west of the Rhine; limitations placed on German armaments; and the imposition of heavy reparations (though never completely collected). In addition, Poland, Czechoslovakia, and Yugoslavia were reconsitituted from territory detached from Germany, Russia, and Austria.

Via de Tillier. Leads west from the main Piazza of Aosta toward the Petit St. Bernard.

Via Saint Anselme. The east-west street in Aosta that leads from the Arch of Augusta through the Roman gates.

Villefranche. A crossing point of the Dora Baltea between Aosta and Nus.

Visperterminen. A small village at 1336 meters above Visp in the Vispertal noted for its fine wines.

Vosges. A mountain range in France located in the southwest corner of the Rhine Valley across from the Schwarzwald.

Washington's birthday. February 22nd, traditionally celebrated as a ski holiday in the Northeastern United States.

Was Wünschen Sie?. What would you like?

Wehrmacht. The German army.

Weimar Republic. The name by which the first German federal republic was known from the city in which its constitution was adopted. It lasted from 1919 to 1933.

Weisse Perle. The white pearl, a ski trail that leads from the bottom of the T-bar at the Schwarzsee to Furi and Zermatt.

Westmount. An autonomous residential area in Montrèal on the southwestern slopes of Mont Royal that was inhabited mainly by English speaking Québecois.

White River Junction. A small city in central Vermont on the Connecticut River.

Yalta. Seaport in the Crimea where a wartime conference with Roosevelt, Churchill, and Stalin took place between February 4th and 12th, 1945.

Yugoslavia. A country of diverse physical regions and ethnic groups extending from the Adriatic Sea to the Danube Plain. It was attacked by Germany in the spring of 1941 and Yugoslavian resistance forced Hitler to postpone his invasion of the Soviet Union by up to four weeks. This proved to be a fortuitous event for the Russians and the Allied cause when the German armies became bogged down in an especially severe winter at the gates of Moscow.

Zermatt. World famous ski and mountaineering village in Valais, 1616 meters, on the north side of the Matterhorn.

Station, Mont Blanc Massif, Près St. Didier,
Valle d'Aosta

Enrico's War

by Enrico Loewenthal

The true story of a Partisan war hero

translated by Vera Auretto

Published by Media International, Waterloo, Ontario, Canada

Enrico, October 1945

ENRICO'S WAR
THE TRUE STORY OF A PARTISAN HERO

By Enrico Loewenthal
Translated by Vera Auretto

Summer, Gastaldi Shelter Before the War

Forward
By Vera Auretto

When my parents settled in Pittsburg in 1949, nine years had passed since they arrived in the United States and the war had been over for five. Although most of their assessments of life in the U.S. were far from being positive, they always marvelled at the ease with which people entertained in this country. They frequently took advantage of these easy-going attitudes to invite guests to our home for dinner, usually professors who had presented an afternoon colloquium at Carnegie Tech where my father taught physics. These illustrious visitors (I wouldn't be surprised if some had Nobel Prizes) were treated to a home-cooked meal as only my mother could make.

At the beginning of the meal, when the steaming bowl of pasta was first set at our honoured visitor's elbow, my father, who was not a man of great tact, generally deemed it prudent to announce that we were about to embark on an Italian-style dinner. If this required further explanation, which was usually the case with Americans, my father condescended to explain how in (civilized) Italy, meals consisted of three or more courses, of which pasta was only the first. After our guest helped himself to an appropriately scaled portion, the dinner would proceed uneventfully with the men indulging in talk of mu mesons, gamma rays and bubble chambers, and other equally unintelligible fare, while my mother bounced from kitchen to dining room graciously serving each course with the help of us children.

As the meal wound down, after the fruit was put out, or perhaps as the adults lingered over their espresso, talk would turn to more personal topics. Our guest might innocently ask when we came to the States, since my parents' accents were unmistakable and their affection for Italian customs unquestionable. Or he might ask why they had come, or if they had known Enrico Fermi, or any of a number of questions which were meant to bring the conversation to a friendly conclusion.

As the conversation peeled back the years, we children held our collective breath. Maybe tonight my father would go all the way. Maybe he would tell the whole story of how he left Fascist Italy after earning his doctorate in Florence, how he got an appointment to the Curie Labs in Paris, how he fled on a bicycle as the Germans approached the city, how he finally arrived in the U.S. after waiting months in Portugal for his papers to arrive.

My mother's story, if it was told at all, was generally subsumed under my father's, for she was only a teenager when the war broke out. But she had her share of adventures. Mother had been sent to a Swiss boarding school at sixteen, after the Italian public schools were closed to Jews, and then was stranded in that country with her eight-year old brother when the Germans invaded Poland. Meanwhile, my grandparents had been forced to leave Italy, where life had become more and more difficult for Jewish citizens. After several months of anxious waiting, the family was finally reunited in the French capital, but they hardly had a chance to settle down when the Germans began their lightening march toward the city. Guessing at the unpublished schedules of the Channel ferries, they were able to escape on one of the last boats to England, arriving on the day that Italy declared war on the French. Once in England, they barely avoided internment as enemy aliens by booking passage on the next ship to New York.

To our guest, the most remarkable aspect of these war stories generally lay in our family's Jewish origins. But if the poor man was naive enough to admit that he had never heard of a Jewish Italian, he earned the immediate scorn of my father, who became especially disdainful if the listener was of Jewish background himself. In either case, he was quickly put out of his miserable ignorance by my father's observation that the Jewish community in Rome was "older than the Pope", and that a Jewish temple, which can still be seen among the ruins at Ostia, had been built centuries before St. Peter's.

As my father delivered the facts, we children basked in the glow of being the only living representatives of Jewish Italians which this person was likely ever to encounter. The story of the creation of our family seemed to us so improbable as to be miraculous; boy meets girl on an epic scale, and each retelling helped to explain why we were sitting at this particular dinner table in this Catholic neighbourhood in this Appalachian factory town, drinking espresso out of tiny gold-rimmed cups with tiny matching spoons.

Although we revelled in the adventure, uniqueness and triumph of my parents' exodus, we could also have told the stories of greater hardship and equally miraculous survival. They were the stories of friends and relatives who had remained in their native Italy. Of these, none was more fascinating than that of my mother's cousin Enrico, who as a teenager, had joined the partisans in the mountains around Torino. At the end of the war, he had written his memoirs and sent them to my grandfather in New York. Although I did not read them until much later, it was the dangers of battle, not those of escape, that captured my imagination as I was growing up.

If I had been suffered to speak at the dinner table, to reveal the fantasies which I had woven around those years, parents and guest would have been entertained with adventures of guerrilla warfare in the hills of Pittsburg. On this New World battleground, every train tunnel and alleyway, every shortcut, every landmark had a significance which transcended its obviously day-to-day functions and artifact of a living city, as I led my partisan band to victory against an unknown enemy.

If I had any heroes at all, my cousin was the one, the one

who had stayed and fought and brought glory to himself and his nation. I wanted to be like Enrico, strong, smart, self-sufficient, unbowed by enemy invasion, unfazed by the unimaginable cruelties of war. In Pittsburg, the songs of the partisans and those of the mountain people, who sustained the resistance against fascism, were my spiritual nourishment. When we sang, our small chorus of voices filled me with passion and pride and nostalgia for the land my parents had left behind. Far from our true home, exiled in this barbarian outpost, I was keenly aware that our family was but a tiny offshoot of two family trees which had deep roots in Italian soil.

As I struggled to put down roots in this new American soil, I tried to find a patch of ground where I could naturalize my experience. Because my father was against the bomb (the Big One which he had helped to build), in high school I found refuge with the Quakers. But their Christian piety was incomprehensible to me, so in college I switched my allegiances to the political left, which espoused anti-war politics from another angle. I nonetheless despised them for their glib references to the coming revolution. (The only thing I knew with total certainty, was that the revolution was not going to be pretty.) After dropping out of college in 1968, I vaguely understood that the left was being redefined by Israel's occupation of the West Bank and that if I was going to have an authentic political opinion, I was going to have to sort out the tangled web of Jewish, Italian and American roots that was my inheritance.

During a period of utter distraction in the years after college, I embarked on my career as a translator. Armed with a degree in history and passable writing skills, I undertook the challenge of translating Enrico's memoirs, synchronizing dates and agonizing over the turn of a phrase. This was a labour of desperation, designed to give me a grasp on my life through the lives of others. I must have succeeded for I survived. But the fruits of my labours lay buried for years in college notebooks until the information age dawned in my consciousness.

Having sorted out my complicated inheritance in the intervening twenty years, I realized that the memoirs were an important part of the legacy. Reviving them electronically, I took many liberties with the original text. I have tried to keep the vividness of his narrative and in the attempt have kept some sentences which were addressed directly to my grandfather ("You have already heard of the bombing of Cavoretto..."). Enrico has assured me that the story is faithful to his original except for some details of weaponry. He has also promised to send an introduction, an epilogue and possibly a few more incidents of those years which he had left out of his original letters.

In the meantime, imagine yourself to be the visitor in our dining room. You watch in dismay as my father peels an apple with his knife, insisting that this is the only civilized way to eat fruit. You hesitate between selecting bananas or grapes, but he has already moved on to *"la stòria d'Enrico,"* the story of another survivor, now himself a grandfather, still living in Italy, a successful entrepreneur, rumoured among other things, to have sold arms in the Middle East.

This is Enrico's story.

Partisans and Destroyed Village,
Valle d'Aosta

CONTENTS

MAPS

Historical Background

In the forty years since this story was written, Enrico's account has entered the realm of history. Thus, the general knowledge that Enrico assumed his readers knew, has been all but forgotten. In fact, Italy's wartime role was confusing, to say the least, and some historical background will help to illuminate the events.

The story begins with the fall of Mussolini in July 1943. His position in the Italian political scene was curious. He was universally considered to be an entrenched dictator; however, *"Il Duce"* actually ruled with the consent of the King. He was the King's Prime Minister. When the King realized that Mussolini was no longer in control of the nation, which was long after many of the Italian people had grown sick of dictatorship, his intention was to replace the man and a few of his more corrupt followers. Fascism in one form or another still found favour in royal eyes, for the system had given the royal family a measure of peace and stability which no previous parliamentary coalition had been able to produce. Obviously, freedom and justice were not a priority on the King's agenda.

The underground parties, however, had been agitating for freedom and justice for years with little apparent success. The communist party structure of disciplined clandestine cells was well suited for survival in an oppressive political environment and many endured intact through the years of fascism. The more democratic forces were directed from Paris through the exile-based part of *Giustizia e Libertà* which limited its activities to the dissemination of subversive literature in the peninsula. Their efforts finally came to fruition with the strike by Fiat workers in Torino in March 1943. Spreading rapidly throughout all of northern Italy, this strike was a direct challenge to a government that had come to power on a pledge to ban all strikes. For the first time in twenty years, the people

1

openly demonstrated their opposition to the government.

The success of the opposition forces was based on the Italian people's disillusionment with the war, which by this time had been in progress for three long years. The country had entered the war with the "stab in the back" against France at the time that German armies were marching unopposed toward Paris. Unprepared for a war that Hitler seemed to be conducting with little regard for the needs of its purported ally, Italy's involvement never earned the glory that Mussolini had promised. Furthermore, most Italians were never terribly keen on having the Germans as allies. As recently as 1918, the Austrian Germans were "Public Enemy Number One".

With the American entry into the war and the subsequent bombardment of Italian cities, the tide turned quickly against Mussolini. Peace, therefore, was the most immediate goal of the King's new government, which was headed by Marshall Badoglio, one of Fascism's most honoured military heroes. Peace meant switching sides, a delicate assignment under any circumstances, and with the Germans at their doorstep, one that had to be executed without delay. Although the Badoglio government attempted to throw a smoke screen over their intentions by announcing that "the war goes on", no one was deceived, least of all the Germans, who immediately began sending additional troops into Italy. By the time the Italians signed the Armistice with the Allies, forty-five days had elapsed, giving the Germans enough time to consolidate their position on the peninsula.

Those forty-five days resulted in two more years of ruinous war, that was all the more devastating because it pitted brother against brother, neo-Fascists against pro-liberationists, in a classic, brutal civil war, fought without mercy. The neo-Fascists were led by Mussolini, who had been snatched from his mountain prison, where the King had confined him, by a daring German glider raid. Mussolini presided over the

Republic of Salo, which despite its democratic name, was nothing more than Hitler's puppet regime in Italy. It attracted to its banner the worst elements of Italian society. These were the people, disparagingly known as *"Republichini"*, that Hitler used to keep the partisans in check.

The organization of the liberation forces is fairly well covered by Enrico. During the time that Italy was cut in two, northern Italy saw the mobilization of an estimated 200,000 people in the armed resistance. Many more gave aid in one form or another to the partisans, who like all guerilla forces, had to rely to a great extent on the assistance of the general population, among whom they lived. The jockeying for power that Enrico describes, especially on his mission to make contact with the Allies, was a preliminary to the inevitable struggle among the parties who wished to shape the political and social character of the Italian nation in the post-war period.

If the reader would like to consult an excellent history of Italy during this period from which much of the above information comes, I would recommend **The United States and Italy**, by H. Stuart Hughes, published in 1965 by Harvard University Press.

Partisans, Valle d'Aosta

The Game is Up

Except for the heat, which was really extraordinary, the night of July 26, 1943 began no differently for me than many other summer nights that I had spent in Cavoretto. Besides providing a degree of security from the bombardments which had become a regular occurrence in Torino, the summer house was supposed to be cool. But on this night, there was not even a breeze and I tossed sleeplessly in my little bed until sunrise, when a farmer's familiar dialect reached me through the open window. "Mussolini's a dirty bastard," he said, and this surprised me because people rarely expressed such opinions out loud any more. Then he continued, "He's through; it's about time." And that was how I found out, from a passing farmer, at five o'clock in the morning, that the game was up for Mussolini. General Badoglio had replaced *Il Duce* "by order of His Majesty the King and Emperor."

Those who had been lucky enough to hear the broadcast on the radio the previous evening were making the most of the good news. In the city there were disturbances at the Fascist Party headquarters. Black shirts were stripped of their guns. Trucks smashed through prison gates and all prisoners were released, including criminals. The German Consulate and Cultural Academies were ransacked by people armed with nothing more than sticks, fists, courage and good will. Sporadic attempts at resistance were stopped short by the people or the carbinieri. People paraded down the streets dragging busts of the ex-divine *Duce*, while others covered the detested objects with gobs of spit. In other streets, mobs destroyed portraits of Mussolini and looted the apartments of former top-level bureaucrats.

After three days, things returned to normal. The Fascists went into hiding but the anti-Fascists didn't dare come out. It was clear from the start when Badoglio announced that "the war goes on," that the military were in control and it was in the military that the Fascist corruption had penetrated most deeply. In fact, this announcement caused a furore among the people.

In my opinion, what Italy needed now was a man with some guts, someone who would legally or illegally eliminate all the top officers who were known to be Fascists; someone who would order the army to dissolve the already weak groups of German sympathizers. Instead, Badoglio contented himself (and the royal family) with dealing in appearances. All outward signs of the old order disappeared such as the *fascii*, the badges, and the insignia. But he outlawed all political parties and generally followed a policy of overt repression which put Mussolini to shame.

In Torino, Badoglio gave full power to General Adami Rossi, who later moved on to the neo-Fascist army. The general installed himself in the city in all his military splendour. Machine guns lined the streets at regular intervals while the Italian army's most powerful 20-ton armoured cars cruised around the city brandishing 45mm cannon and shooting long volleys into the air. Furthermore, Rossi always seemed to find some excuse to have patrols in the streets, armed to the teeth. These deadly clowns would occasionally club down a passer-by just to make it quite clear that not all Fascists had gone the way of Mussolini, whose whereabouts were still unknown.

In Cavoretto, though we were not treated to this military spectacle, we could feel the tension in the air. During the Badoglio days, everybody tried to keep abreast of events, but everywhere rumour seemed to spread faster than news. At one point, word got around that Hitler had committed suicide and the workers in the city poured into the streets to demonstrate their joy. Rossi immediately responded with an impressive display of machine guns, armoured cars and cannons. Another more sinister rumour was making the rounds in those days. It was said that the Germans were concentrating more divisions in Italy in preparation for a complete military take-over. But though this hearsay proved to be only too true, the Italian military took no measures to defend the country. In fact, the Germans had the cooperation of almost all of Italy's top brass. As soon as news of the armistice reached them, it was easy for the Italian officers to disarm the troops. In some cases, the soldiers were actually locked into their barracks, forced to wait for the Germans, who disarmed and deported them.

Though these details were not known to us at the time, when the armistice was finally announced on September 8th, there was no jubilation in Cavoretto. In the square there were long faces and gloomy stares. Everyone sensed that the worst was yet to come. The next day we heard that the Germans had occupied one village and then another. There was talk of the treaty of Brandizzo by which Rossi sold Torino to the enemy. And nobody ventured out of doors. Here and there you could hear a single rifle shot or the staccato of machine gun fire coming from God knows where and aimed at God knows whom. The air was stormy and everyone was busy hiding valuables. And thousands of ears listened at all hours to Radio London, Milano, Torino, and Fascist Monaco.

Then on the day of September 11, the first German tanks entered the city, firing at every living soul in sight. Any able-bodied man was in danger of being stopped on the spot and deported to Germany. These were the days of the Terror.

Into the Mountains

At our house the Terror struck doubly hard. Besides the fact that we were Jewish with a name which was unmistakable to the Germans, the life of every young male was endangered by the merciless hunt for men of fighting age.

Dad buried himself in an armchair tugging at his beard, wondering what was to be done; mother knitted away nervously, ruminating over countless unspoken thoughts. And I, who had been confined to the house for three days, paced the floor like a caged lion, biting vigorously at my fingernails. Finally we decided to go to the mountains to wait until the storm blew over. Each with one suitcase, taking a thousand precautions, we boarded the train for Cirie-Lanzo. From there we took another train to Ceres and then a bus into the Stura valley to the town of Ala, where we took a room in a little hotel.

At the time, we were expecting the Liberation from week to week, but in the meantime we were forced to cope with the realities of enemy occupation. The Germans would frequently send small units into our valley, either in search of Italian deserters or to find ex-officers who had already begun organizing the armed resistance, or sometimes just for recreation. But if they happened across any young man during these forays, his fate was sealed. So as soon as the Germans appeared in Ceres at the entrance to the valley, the telephone operator quickly relayed the news to all the other operators in the upper villages. Each time, the entire male population of Ala would take to the woods until the danger had passed--usually not more than a day. During these periods, my parents usually stayed back at the hotel in relative calm, or they'd go hunting for chestnuts in the nearby woods. I of course, joined the other men on the higher paths for greater security.

Other than these disturbances, our life in Ala was fairly

peaceful. My parents made frequent trips to Torino to look after the business which was now being managed by our employees. I left the valley only once, in November to go to Cavoretto to buy a radio, the one which was to be our only source of hope and comfort during the worst hours of the war.

"You have already heard of the bombing of Cavoretto and how seven people who had taken shelter in the garden of your house were killed. The bombing was completely off target, even though it was broad daylight, and in many places houses were destroyed and people were killed. Mother and Father happened to be in Cavoretto that day and like everyone else, they spent the day running around in a state of shock, despairing that they couldn't fix the unfixable and bring the dead back to life. It wasn't until, after all that chaos, everyone was convinced that the bombing was over, that your house was hit. An explosion, and that was it..."

By the time they were able to return to Ala, I had lost hope of ever seeing my parents again. But the reunion was hardly a happy affair. They had survived the bombing but they were crazed with fear, for on that very day, the Germans had issued a decree by which all Jews would be sent to concentration camps. Convinced that the *carabinièri* would be at our door that night, Dad insisted on leaving the inn immediately. The only safe place we could reach on such short notice was an empty barn outside the next village. It was the beginning of December and the first winter snow had begun to fall the night before. It crunched under our feet as we trudged up the mountain with our little suitcases. We must have been a very sad sight to behold; I felt like I was going to a funeral.

We found out later that, in a show of pure formality, the *carabinièri* did come and ask the inn-keeper if we were still boarding there. But they were satisfied with a negative answer and didn't pursue it any further. In any event, we could not return to Ala, where we hadn't taken the precaution of hiding our identities, and Dad was under the impression that we were still being actively sought. He therefore resolved to ask for help from an acquaintance of ours, Miglietti, who had a beautiful villa above Ala. Mr. Miglietti very kindly consented to let us stay in absolute secrecy and we were there for about a month and a half.

As soon as they knew we were safe, Mom and Dad calmed down and began looking more relaxed. In moments of tension both of them became nervous and pale and hardly had the energy to eat. Their eyes would shift involuntarily toward the door as if fully expecting the *carabinièri* or the Germans to walk in at any time of day or night and take them away. I handled things with a great deal more calm and courage, though there were many times that I was convinced that sooner or later during that winter, we would fall in the hands of our enemies.

In the middle of January we decided that it would be safe enough to move out of Miglietti's home and into an "apartment" we had rented in Martassina. This smoky, dirty little hovel consisted of three tiny rooms; the two on the ground floor were directly interconnected and the third, my own room, could be reached by a little staircase rising steeply out of the living room. Our life was totally centred in the one room where we had the heater, the radio, the kitchen and the table where we ate and played cards. It was during this time that I learned how to play bridge. This was a moment of absolute tranquillity during which we hardly ever left the house. Our only source of comfort and hope was the voice of the broadcaster from Radio London which travelled over the airwaves like the messenger of Faith in Victory. We also heard broadcasts of special messages, which you must have also picked up, bringing the happy news of the next supply drop.

10

As the war dragged on and the Germans tightened their hold on the country, events forced us to set aside, at least temporarily, our optimistic expectations for a speedy liberation. Life grew steadily more dangerous for us, and the day neared when I would share the partisan struggle which was to culminate in the glorious insurrection of April 1945.

I Join the Resistance

I had been involved in some underground activities the year before, between bombardments and classes. At that time the political movement was still very small, about one activist for every 3,000 people, and with police harassment its effectiveness was reduced to organizing new cells and distributing leaflets. The latter was a clandestine affair which had to be conducted with the greatest caution.

I received political literature from a man who always talked in a whisper and constantly looked around to make sure that no one was watching or listening. He would then pass me leaflets put out by the organization called *Giustizia e Libertà*. I knew no one but him and those people to whom I passed the literature. They in turn knew no one but me and their four or five contacts, so that the leaflets passed from hand to hand down the line.

Despite the fact that we took great pains during these transactions not to be seen or heard, the Fascists somehow got wind of my unorthodox political activities and in the reprisals after the famous strike in March 1943, I was twice summoned by the police and interrogated briefly, but in both cases I was released unharmed.

When we were forced to take to the mountains, we were well aware that all around us, bands of partisans were being organized to resist the enemy on his own territory. Most of these men were either already trained for war or completely dedicated to the resistance. Many were ex-soldiers who, during the Terror, had managed to escape to the mountains rather than surrender, and were then unable to return to their homes. There were also many officers (only the low-ranking ones, the rest were all traitors) who surreptitiously transported military stores and ammunition into the mountains or who had deserted with their entire regiments. In our valley, the Germans were particularly anxious to find a Colonel Fino who, as commander of the Lanzo garrison, had gone over to the *Màcchia* with all his men. Finally there were the political bands, groups of veteran anti-Fascists who joined together in the mountains to continue the underground political struggle with guns and blood.

The original partisan bands were organized embryonically. They did not communicate with one another, and what was worse, they often disagreed on strategy. Each band was organized on the principles of its leader. Above Chiaves, there were little bands of ex-soldiers and officials from the Lanzo garrison. There were communist units at Monti and Bogliano and military units at Brachiello and in the Viù Valley. The caches of arms and ammunition were either exhausted or had fallen into the hands of the enemy. There had not been a great deal of fighting, but whenever any action was taken it was inevitably followed by German round-up operations which decimated the bands and often destroyed their supplies.

The pattern of round-up operations began in early January after the band from the mountains above Bracchiello disarmed some innocuous Fascist soldiers who manned a reconnaissance post on the Mussa Plateau. After several days, fifty soldiers arrived in two German trucks to withdraw all that was left at the outpost. As they returned across the Bausan Plateau below Pessinetto, they were ambushed and almost all were killed or wounded. After two weeks, the area around Chiaves-Bogliano-Monti underwent its first round-up involving hundreds of soldiers, cannon and a special hunting device. The Germans singled out the town of Traves for a special reprisal and, as a warning to the people, it was ransacked and burned to the ground.

At the end of February there was another round-up with even greater forces. Like the earlier one, this one failed to destroy the partisans, but it did weaken them considerably. However, in the middle of March, the Germans launched an intensified operation with combined forces which left all but the communist bands in complete disarray. After this disaster, realizing that they needed some kind of centralized organization to provide supplies and assistance and to maintain an effective communication network, the surviving partisans came into the valley and formed an alliance.

In Torino, a Committee for National Liberation (CLN) was created on the model of the central Roman CLN which directed partisan activity in the southern part of the peninsula. The CLNs functioned through the collaboration of the six parties which had survived the Fascist repression. The partisan chiefs aligned themselves with one of the parties according to their own political ideals and those of their men. The *Giustizia e Libertà* allied themselves with the *Partito d'Azióne*; the Communist party supported the Garibaldi brigades, and the independents, who were apolitical, aligned themselves with the Liberal party. But only about 50 percent of the men in the various formations shared the politics of the sponsoring party.

The political commissars of the Garibaldi brigade in the Lanzo Valley for example, were Liberals or Action Party people as well as Communists. And there wasn't one partisan formation that asked about your political beliefs before accepting you in the band. As long as you were anti-Fascist, you were OK. At least that's how it was when I joined in the spring of 1944.

I first worked at the brigade headquarters and then in the police force. In that period we didn't have much work. We spent most of our time searching for arms and ammunition, most of which turned out to be defective beyond repair. We were lucky if we could get fifty rounds from a gun; combat or offensive attacks were out of the question. As for Allied assistance, the Lanzo Valley had a single small supply drop and all of the equipment was either used or defective.

Meanwhile, the Nazi *razzias* continued. Every month, with a half hour's notice we had to hide everything and "cut the cord." While we stayed hidden in caves for a day or more, often without food, the Germans searched for our supply dumps and caches in the valleys. They threatened people and ransacked their houses if they refused to inform on the "rebels". At the slightest provocation, they burned houses, making sure there was no way of salvaging anything.

During these operations, Mom and Dad would shut themselves in the apartment and pray that no one would get the bright idea of knocking at their door, as if anything but their own fear would have betrayed them. Maybe because you had to twist around several turns and then go up a small flight of stairs to reach the apartment, the Germans never came to visit. But as time passed, the Germans would stop more and more frequently in the little villages of Martassina and Ala to find rebels and Jews. The people, and especially the local authorities, always responded negatively to the Germans' insistent questions, and they are the ones to be thanked for the fact that Mom and Dad are alive today.

Partisan Summer

The summer of 1944 has been called the golden age of the partisans, and in our valley the facts certainly sustained this conclusion. During the entire summer, there were no more round-ups (I don't know why this was so), and everything operated as in normally liberated territory. We organized a rudimentary administration for the valley with our own taxes, police force and criminal courts to try theft and homicide cases. Our newspapers could be found on the newsstands alongside the Fascist papers, except that ours were given away free. Of course we could never forget that our enemies were close at hand and one incident in June served as a particularly brutal reminder of their presence.

Our combat unit, which was stationed in the lower valley, seized ten artillery pieces in a surprise attack. They were transported by railroad to the upper valley. There were 75/27s and 149s with ammunition, but we just had time enough to set up one 75mm on the road, when the enemy troops arrived with seven Tiger tanks armed with 88mm guns. Against this formidable opponent, our 75mm was virtually useless. Two shots fired at the turret of a tank failed to even damage it, and of the three partisans manning the weapon, two were killed almost immediately. Naturally, we also lost the weapons we had captured and one of the houses at Balme was burned. But most incomprehensible of all, three captured partisans were tortured and killed on the bridge between Balme and Cornetti. When we returned to recover their bodies, we could see that their legs had been broken, their eyes had been gouged out and their backs had been punctured by German bayonets. Civilization...?

In Ala Valley, I had been assigned to do police work which, besides maintaining order, meant searching for Fascist spies. From time to time, Torino would send out descriptions of persons who were known to be spies but I was most successful by just keeping my eyes open for suspicious-looking people. I had the luck of turning up three spies. One time, at the railroad station at Ceres, I met a woman carrying a suitcase. When I asked her to open it, she started to cry, so I opened it myself and found a neatly folded military uniform of the Republican National Guard. Under questioning, she confessed that her husband belonged to the Fascist garrison at Lanzo and he had sent her into our valley to collect information. She was later tried by a military tribunal and shot.

During this summer, the partisans were deluged by a record number of new recruits. The influx began when the "republicans" began drafting certain classes for military service. Whenever a new class was announced, these men would flood into the valley. By coming to us, they were not hoping to avoid work or danger; rather, they were motivated by a spirit of patriotism, preferring to do their stint with the partisans than with the so-called republicans. The great problem of the partisans was to provide arms for all these men. In the Ala Valley, we had 800 men and 100 guns; in Viù Valley, 1,700 men and 700 guns. And still there were no supply drops.

The Fascists were aware of this state of affairs but they did not attack. They had more pressing problems to worry about. In June, Roma was liberated and shortly afterwards the Allies landed in southern France. The new front provided opportunities for us in the strategically located Val di Stura. From the heights on the border between Italy and France, we could observe the German retreat. Our assignment was to determine whether the troops would be withdrawn over the Moncenisio where a good road provided passage for military vehicles, or whether, if the Allies were able to block this route, they would be forced to retreat through the Val di Viù just south of us. At the end of June, I was assigned to a detachment of relatively well-armed partisans whose principle duty was to

17

report on these troop movements. The mission was carried out regularly three times a week. A patrol unit would leave from the Gastaldi Shelter where the 20-man detachment was stationed and climb to a hut on the vertical face above Bessans in France. There we would make our observations through binoculars and wait for further communication from the *Maquisards* who were to meet at the hut if there were any new developments.

I don't know how many times that summer I travelled from the apartment in Martassina to the Gastaldi shelter and, on my assigned day, from there to La Buffe in France. But I'm sure that there's not a stone in that area that I don't know. The hike took many hours and we carried food, ammunition and often a machine gun. The conditioning was to prove vital during the next winter, when crossing the border, on more than one occasion, became a matter of life and death.

Retreat into France

In early September, the Allied troops were already in Grenoble and Modane, and the maquis occupied the Iseran Valley just across the border from us. But on on our side of the frontier, the troubles were just beginning. Already in August, the Germans had attacked the 4th Garibaldi Brigade in Corio Canavese (that's where my brother's friend Sergio Piazza was killed). Corio fell for lack of ammunition after ferocious combat. At that time, the Fascists imposed a blockade on the Lanzo Valleys which affected Val di Viù, Val di Stura and Val Grande. The blockade lasted a full month, exhausting our food provisions and reducing us, both partisans and peasants, to near starvation.

Then came the attack. We had never seen such forces but we resisted with all we had. After several hours of fighting, inflicting significant damage on the enemy, the first line of defense at Traves surrendered, having exhausted its ammunition. The second line of defense was improvised from the weak armed forces available at Ceres, the remains of contingents from other valleys who had taken refuge with us. These men held tight during all the following morning. There were losses on both sides, but soon our ammunition turned into piles of empty shells and the Fascist forces shattered our resistance. Now they were free to stalk us like hounds with their mortars and self-propelled guns and armoured cars.

We were completely routed. The Nazi-Fascists had promised to spare the life of anyone who surrendered within two days and the starving men, hunted and defenceless, gave themselves up in droves. Many others were captured and according to their partisan rank, either shot or sent to Germany.

The day of September 8, 1944, the final remnant of the 11th Garibaldi Brigade climbed to the Gastaldi Shelter in a torrential rainstorm. As we reached the higher ground, the rain turned to

19

snow. Never had the simple stone walls and sloping roof of the shelter looked so inviting. We all crowded inside and that night we held a meeting. There were about 100 of us equipped with the best weapons of the brigade. In addition, we had two pack mules and two calves as a final reserve of provisions. We decided that 20 men would stay behind at the shelter while the rest retreated over the border into the Iseran Valley. The political commissar and I and another partisan were to march ahead to the *Maquis* headquarters to find food and ammunition for the brigade.

Luck was with us for the 9th of September was a beautiful day. We were ready to leave at daybreak and, according to plan, the three of us went on ahead. From high above, we could see the long column of the brigade slowly winding along the path that we had marked over the glacier. As we walked on I thought how remarkable it was that, despite the defeat, we had still been able to lead a hundred men across the border to safety.

The men performed miracles. They had barely eaten for several days. The day before, they had only a fist-sized portion of polenta and a half a slice of cheese. And now they were crossing the mountains, with fresh snow up to their knees, rucksacs on their backs and leading mules and calves through the maze of deadly crevasses. Some of the men from the cities had never even seen a glacier!

Of course we were not exempt from the hunger. We trudged down the French side of the mountain trying to forget the painful cramps in our stomachs. The hamlets of Averole, Vincendieres, Bessans and Villaron disappeared behind us. At each village people greeted us cordially but when we mentioned food, it was "sorry." The Germans had plundered everything before retreating to the Moncenisio and in Bessans Fascist bullets still rained down, splattering the chalets and barns as a reminder of the enemy.

Finally, we arrived at Bonneval. In normal times this town counted a population of about 100. With the war, a garrison of *Maquisards* had been stationed there but after the rakings across the border, the town had been literally invaded by two thousand Italian partisans from the Val Grande and the Canavese area. There had been nothing to eat for three days. Men took turns sleeping in a stable which was the only vacant space in all of Bonneval. Their weapons lay idly in heaps on the floor of a warehouse which was locked and guarded by a French and an Italian sentry.

When we arrived, as negotiators for the 11th Brigade, we were immediately received by Captain Chebert, commander of the local *Maquis*, as well as an old general who, from what I heard, was the commander of the *Maquis* in the entire upper valley of Isère and of Arc. Introductions were given. Finally, we got down to business, but we were already prepared for the worst.

That evening, as usual, we had nothing to eat. But when it came to sleeping, our status as officers and negotiators earned us an attic room with a mattress on the floor but no blankets. This was at an altitude of 2000 meters. The penetrating cold kept us awake the whole night. Nevertheless, at six in the morning we were again on the road with bellies and hands empty. Dejectedly, we turned our backs on the village, the cramps in our stomachs gradually giving way to weakness in our legs.

We struggled to arrive at Averole by noon. There we found that while we were gone, in the certainty that we had found provisions, the men of the brigade had eaten the two calves and were waiting for our orders to continue down into the valley toward France. My two companions fell on the ground, overcome by hunger and fatigue and unable to speak. I was left to tell the expectant men the outcome of our mission. When I finished by saying that we had no choice but to turn back to

Italy, my words were greeted with shouts and curses from the group, as no one had the energy to go back over that same trail again.

By late afternoon, twenty-five of the men had decided to turn back. The rest of the brigade headed on into France where they were later interned by the French in concentration camps. Our small band left Averole with two mules laden with all the weapons. The path we chose was unfamiliar, but led to the Viù Valley which we knew had not yet been occupied by the Germans. We dragged ourselves slowly up the mountain, chewing on twigs in an attempt to alleviate our hunger. With the last rays of the sun, we arrived at the top of the pass and found a nice mule trail on the Italian side. Hoping to find some kind of shelter, we kept walking after nightfall. At last, at midnight we fell exhausted among the rocks, groping blindly for a space dry enough to sleep on. With a blanket for every two men, we spent an interminable night at 2800 meters.

The next day we started walking in the faint light before dawn. The village of Malciansia seemed infinitely far away, in direct proportion to the weakness in our legs. I was walking at the head of the column when on the trail I found a beet, probably discarded by a local shepherd. The first rays of the sun caught us hunkered down in a circle, each man munching solemnly on his portion.

When we finally got to the Viù Valley, there was still no food, and the Germans had picked that day to attack the partisan defenses. At midnight we managed to scrape together a hunk of horrible polenta and we slept for a few voluptuous hours in a barn full of hay. But the Fascists attacked again at dawn. The partisans resisted till midday and then the order came to retreat.

The men withdrew into different valleys. A large group headed south over the Pass of the Iron Cross to the Susa Valley, which had been subjected to round-ups only one month earlier and was thus considered relatively safe. The majority of the men decided to go to the Asti region in a series of night marches. Myself and seven others were determined to go back to the Ala Valley.

With half a kilo of apples stuffed into our pockets, we headed toward the Paschiet Pass. From halfway up the mountain we looked back to see the first Fascist troops enter the deserted village of Usseglio and heard the sound of their uninterrupted, ferocious machine gun and mortar fire. Then we faced the mountain again and headed toward the shelter at the pass. As we climbed we were blanketed by a heavy fog and lost our way several times. We finally arrived at the shelter in the dying light. There we found a dozen men who had never left the valley.

By this time, as you may well imagine, my hunger was tremendous. The next morning, I hid my weapon, got myself a false ID and headed for home. Abandoning all precautions, I ate everything in sight. But the Fascists were everywhere, having set up garrisons in the larger villages.

When I arrived at my parent's apartment, a Jewish family had just been found and arrested in a nearby village. Reasoning that they would be safer staying in Torino, my father had a doctor draw up a statement saying that he needed an emergency operation. With the document and their false IDs in hand, they went to Fascist headquarters and asked for safe passage to Torino. The next day they left and they stayed in Torino in Mr. Buffa's house.

This state of affairs continued until the middle of October when the Fascists felt certain that there were no more partisans left anywhere. To the joy and relief of everyone, they withdrew from the valley. Within a few hours the various groups of partisans, who had remained hidden here and there, congregated at the bottom of the valley. The headquarters were reorganized and the detachments were reformed. Out of eight hundred men, there were only one hundred left.

Partisans, Valle d'Aosta

Meeting with the Allies

In early November, I left the 11th Garibaldi Brigade and joined a *Giustizia e Libertà* Brigade named "R. Giua". We were about thirty men, all non-communists who disapproved of the new sectarian spirit of the Garibaldi detachments. As I carried out successive assignments, my association with the G.L. Brigade was to have unexpected consequences. But in mid-November I was busy preparing for my mission to make the first partisan contact of the war with the Allied forces in France.

I set about coordinating my activities with the partisan command in the Locana Valley. This required a day-long hike over the Puglia Pass (2900 m) and then an immediate return to our valley so I could make my rendez-vous in France. Though I started the trip with a friend, he sprained his ankle and I had to leave him behind.

The first night I slept in Chiambelle in a putrid barn where the pigs promenaded across my body and the goats didn't have the manners to warn me before doing their business. Waking up the next morning, I noticed that the light filtering through the solitary, filthy window seemed unusually bright. I got up, stuck my nose out the barn door and saw 20 centimetres of fresh snow on the ground with more flakes falling at an alarming rate.

I decided to leave immediately. With 100 lira I hired a man from the valley to show me the way through the snow. My guide took me to the foot of the pass and then refused to go any farther. It was only 200 meters to the top, but it meant climbing a spur of ice covered with 40 centimetres of new snow. Anyone who's done any climbing knows what this means when you're carrying only a walking stick and no ice axe.

The wind whistled fiercely around my ears; the snow didn't let up for a minute and every once in a while a fog would settle on me as I fell and picked myself up, dragging myself forward in frustrating slow motion. I felt my way up with the toe of my boot and the end of my stick, scared of falling and not being able to get up, which would have meant certain death on the mountain, alone in the blizzard. Just before reaching the top, I took a wrong turn and found myself standing in front of a wall of snow and ice. Over an hour and a half went by. Finally, at three in the afternoon, after a seven hour struggle, gasping and panting, I reached the summit.

Compared to the climb, the descent was a joke. At about five in waning light I stopped in a hut in Vonzo to get a little rest. In the middle of the night, I finally got back to my unit where I got a tremendous welcome from the men.

According to the plan worked out between Bruno Toscano, my commander, and Enrico, the officer representing the G.L. formations in the Susa Valley, we would leave for Grenoble as soon as we received letters of introduction from the Torino CLN. By the time the letters and money for travel expenses arrived, it was mid-December. According to plan, I headed through the Lanzo Valley and Enrico went through the Susa Valley, each of us with a local guide. We were all dressed in the uniform of the Alpine troops. I now held the rank of sub-lieutenant.

On the road, the sky was dark grey and the temperature had fallen to minus 15C. At the pass it was sleeting but the descent of ten kilometers brought us quickly to Averoles. There we heard that French soldiers (from the regular troops) had just arrived at Bonneval and that the area around Bessans was still under fire from German weapons. Soon we started down the same road I had taken in the ill-fated fall of the previous year, the difference being that we were greeted with great respect by the French patrols, since we now could almost be considered officers of Allied forces.

At Bonneval we got a warm welcome from the French officials. (The French would send a delegation to our valley shortly after our return to Italy.) That evening we started toward the Iseran Pass, staying overnight at the Maison Cantonière, which had already been headquarters for the *Maquis*. We crossed the pass (2800 m) the next morning under overcast skies, and went down 16 kilometers to Val d'Isère, a nice little resort town, kind of like Sestriere, with lots of fancy hotels.

At Val d'Isère, we learned that in the village there was an American mission charged with making contact with the Italian partisans. We also found a group of partisans from the Aosta Valley, who had taken refuge here following German round-ups. At this point there was no reason to go on to Grenoble as we had originally planned. We again were welcomed cordially by the French officers, some of whom I had already met (Bonneval 44). The partisan commanders from Val d'Aosta introduced us to two American lieutenants and Major Adam from the Italian army who was authorized by the Italian government to provide assistance to the partisans.

We discussed the various problems regarding provisions, weapons, ammunition and uniforms for the formations in the Lanzo Valleys. Since airlifts were impossible, it was decided to organize a march across the passes to carry the needed supplies into our valleys. We also agreed on intelligence protocols. Meanwhile, we drank round after round of hot chocolate and real coffee and had other delicacies, that I had long since forgotten existed.

The Americans also put us on guard against the French and their annexationist aims. In fact, the next day a French officer from the *Deuxième Bureau* buttonholed us. We were not fooled by his broad smiles and offers of assistance, and we politely let him know that we would have nothing to do with him. He withdrew without further ado.

On the third day another *Deuxième Bureau* officer, a major approached us, and once again we became the recipients of broad smiles and interminable courtesies. And again we let him know that we were not interested.

On the fourth day, the Americans gave us the latest model automatic weapons (9 caliber Thompsons). They loaded up new backpacks with woollen underwear and enough dried food for four days. I signed the invoice with my real name and we started back to Italy in a cable car which deposited us high up the mountainside.

Bonneval, Averole, Col d'Arnaz, the weather was mixed with sun, wind, and freezing cold. The temperature on the pass was minus 30C and our heavy backpacks slowed us down. A few times, the wind was so strong that we stopped and laid down on the ground until it subsided. But as soon as we reached the Italian side, the wind was calm and I had to stop and rub my feet to keep from getting frostbite. Enrico, who had fallen into a small crevice on the glacier, had frostbite on two toes of his right foot.

After a day's rest at Balme, I reported back to headquarters on the results of the mission. We had travelled five days on foot or skis, and covered about 140 kilometers, going up and down four times between altitudes of 1800 and 3000 meters. Our mission had been fruitful, inasmuch as we had been able to establish a basis for collaboration between us and the Allies, and as a result the Allies now held us in high regard.

My arrival at the detachment was triumphant and my weapon was the object of admiration and envy on the part of all the partisans in the valley. While I was gone, a Fascist garrison had been set up at Lanzo by paratroopers from the Folgore battalion. They were terrible bastards, frequently sounding out our defenses which were practically non-existent. They were already preparing for the round-up which was to result in the most complete rout ever of the bands in the valley.

The Convoy

Given our desperate lack of weapons and ammunition, a decision was taken that I would leave in January to go into France and get the supplies promised by the Allies. In this period, I spent all my time working on coordinating the expedition. I had to find about 25 volunteers among the partisans and G.L. auxiliaries who were willing to make the long trek over the mountains.

On the 14th, everything was ready, including the money, which I already had exchanged for French francs. My expedition was made up of myself as commander, 20 auxiliaries from the Val Grande, who were to cross the Sea Pass with a sergeant, and a representative from the Torino CLN. With five men, all of them auxiliaries from the Ala Valley, I was to cross the Arnaz Pass and meet the others at Bonneval.

The crossing was excellent, but the weather was frigid. At Bonneval, I didn't see the others because a change in their plans had forced them to delay their trip until the next day, which was even colder. That morning at Bonneval the mercury read minus 32C in the shade. The upshot was that eleven men had developed frostbite, including the CLN representative, who had 2nd degree frostbite in one foot, and the sergeant, who had 3rd degree frostbite on all ten fingers. (Eventually, three of them were amputated).

The men were tired and demoralized from the terrible crossing and refused to go any farther. That night I tried to boost their morale and the next morning we left at nine in the morning, those who were frostbitten remaining in the care of a French nurse.

Iseran is a relatively long pass, but because it was the only supply route to the Bonneval headquarters, the snow was packed into a nice path and there were two places along the way where we could stop to rest. One was at the mid-way point and the other was at a hostel at the top of the pass. But the blizzard and cold were with us the whole way. Some of the men were wearing snowshoes; others, myself among them, were on skis, but during the descent, the snow was so terrible that the skiers made no better progress than the men with snowshoes.

When we arrived in Val d'Isère, tension and hostility were evident. The commanders of the Garibaldi Brigade were furious because they had been upstaged by the G.L.. In my absence, they had been able to turn the American Lieutenant, a Mexican-American named Jime, against me. He was a communist and was supposed to deliver the war material to me; however, he was the one who called the shots in the little American PC in the Val d'Isère.

So we had a three-way discussion among the Garibaldi soldiers, myself, and Jime. Although I never completely won him over, I was at least able to defuse some of the accusations made against me by the Garibaldi men. Eventually, I convinced him to give me the material and I began making plans to leave within a few days. Hearing this, the Garibaldi's were enraged once more, leading to many more heated discussions with them and Jime.

Everyone who hung around the command at Val d'Isère, including Lieutenant Singer, Major Adam, Derege, (who was the secretary of the CAI acting as a courier with the Torino CLN), Gasperl, and Pirovano, soon was aware of what was going on and almost all lined up on my side. I was indebted to them for their support which helped me win this frustrating skirmish of words.

The men were in a hurry to start back and we finally began packing in preparation for the return trip. We had the latest model caliber Thompson automatic weapons, bombs, plastic explosives, ammunition, guns, clothing, shoes and dried food.

The return trip was bestial, not so much because of the weather, which was frigid but tolerable, but because of the packs which inhibited any turning or maneuvering. I had to ski in a straight line, then stop and make a kick turn to change direction. Out of sheer generosity, Gasperl accompanied me up to the Iseran Pass, carrying part of my load, which all together weighed over 20 kilos.

Starting the descent, I slid on a sheet of ice about 150 meters below the summit. I threw myself onto the ground and rolled, backpack and all for about 70 meters. When I finally managed to stop, the men helped pull me out of a tangle of arms, poles, skis, and legs. I felt myself carefully to see if I was seriously injured. Twelve more meters and I would have slid through the couloir onto rocks and ice. There must truly be a God of skiers. The excited men congratulated me on my luck and we continued down the mountainside.

The next day at Bonneval, the expedition split; part of the men heading for the Val Grande and I, with six companions, crossing the Arnaz Pass. On the French side we had to struggle against a piercing wind. When we crossed into Italy there was a meter of fresh snow plus the usual frigid temperatures.

As we started across the Mussa Plateau we saw in the distance a little red flag poking out of the snow. We skied over to it and found a scribbled note with the following news: "Fascist round-up. Have occupied Ceres and are coming up the valley." If the seven of us were caught on a field of fresh snow by several hundred Fascists, we wouldn't have a chance.

Without leaving a trace, we hid the weapons and cargo in the snow under the hay in a nearby hut. My six men, who all had proper identification papers, simply put on civilian clothes and went home. I kept my uniform and my weapon and went to Balme where Aunt Rita was in hiding. There, seated in front of the heater, with warm food in my stomach, I heard the latest news.

31

Who, Me?

The Fascists had attacked the valley two nights before with about 2,000 troops, many of whom were dressed in camouflage and travelled on skis. The attack had taken place at one o'clock at night only a few hours after a snowfall and under a full moon. The first patrols had moved up along the mountainside, spaced out over a hundred meters. These were followed by heavily armed units which moved along the floor of the valley.

My G.L. unit had taken refuge in the Cantoira mine, but their tracks had given them away and they were attacked by the Fascists. The other partisan bands had also been discovered, but Ala di Stura had been taken just that day and the Fascists were not expected to reach Balme until the next day.

I left Aunt Rita's place at nine o'clock at night, warm, dry and well-fed. Over my Alpine uniform I was wearing an American overcoat and over that, I wore white camouflaging. With my backpack and the loaded Thompson in my hand, I would have mowed down in the blink of an eye any suspicious shadow that crossed my path.

There was no one in the street. Everyone, especially my parents, was staying behind closed doors, expecting the worst. When I pushed open the door to my parent's apartment they let out a little cry. I saw them turn pale with fright as they sat at the table in the middle of the room. With a command post located no more than two kilometers away, they fully expected the Fascists to be at their door at any moment, and here instead was their son, dressed from head to toe in "Made in U.S.A." or rather, "U.S. Army, complete with weapon, ammunition, and supplies."

With the help of the landlord, we hid everything-in the beehives, in the gutters, and in the eaves. By midnight I had transformed myself from a Jewish partisan communications officer into Lamberto Enrico, baptized at birth, draft-exempt,

32

vacationing high school student. With escape impossible, only sheer gall could save me.

Next morning at nine, I was in the stable by the house when I saw the Fascist troops coming up the road. As they passed in front of the house, I saw four of them leave the group and run up the steps which lead to our apartment. "This is it," I thought. "This time I'm screwed." I went to the woodcutter's block and took a couple of swings at a piece of wood. I heard the Fascists enter the building, two pairs of boots quickly approached the door of the stable. A sharp kick opened the door and there, perfectly framed in the doorway, appeared two Fascist paratroopers in full combat gear, with various insignia and their Mausers, with safeties off, levelled at my head.

"You're a partisan."

"Not me."

"Come out."

"O.K."

"Put your hands up."

"O.K."

My guardian searched me to see if I was carrying a weapon. Of course he found nothing. Meanwhile, the other guy who was checking out the cellar, yelled up, "Massi, what's happening?"

"I got one, " he said.

As you can imagine, I was not in the best frame of mind at this time.

"Lower your hands and show us your papers."

I showed them my false papers. He read them. He reread them and looked at the documents in the light. The soldier asked me what I did, where I went to school and why I was at Martassina.

I lied through my teeth but with a certain candour. Eventually, he gave me back my papers and said "Stay cool", and then they all left.

The valley was completely occupied by the Fascists. The only partisans left were me and three or four others. That day, the Fascists issued an order for all able-bodied men to appear in the square the next morning to help shovel snow from the road to allow their vehicles to pass. The only way to hide in these circumstances was to show up.

Like a good Fascist, I obeyed the order and punctually at eight the next morning, I went to the square with a shovel over my shoulder. I hardly worked at all since there was no supervision; during the whole day, I shovelled maybe thirty times. But I had the satisfaction of having a German captain and Fascist major, with their entire retinue of course, walk within one meter of where I stood. This did not scare me nearly as much as it did the other workers, all of whom not only knew my true identity, but also that I was a partisan.

Several days passed in this manner. Our apartment was searched, God willing not very thoroughly. They came very close to finding my American equipment and if they had, you can be sure I wouldn't be writing these memoirs.

Meanwhile, we got news of the other partisans. My band, trapped and under siege in the mine, surrendered after seven days. The Fascists had been able to find all the entrances and despite the defense, they had been able to penetrate to some distance into some of the shafts. The food stores and many blankets had fallen into enemy hands. The men surrendered (I learned this after the Liberation) after having lived for seven days on two spoonfuls of raw rice per day, in utter darkness, after some of the men had developed frostbite and others were beginning to show signs of mental breakdown.

My commander, Bruno Tuscano, and two others known to me only by their combat names, were shot immediately. Others were taken to Rivoli and shot after several months for reprisals. The rest were supposed to be shipped to concentration camps in Germany and were spared only because the Brenner Pass was closed. They were still in Bolzano when they were liberated in the Victorious Insurrection.

As for the Garibaldi units, many were captured; many were able to turn back to France and others were able to break through the Fascist armour and go into the Asti area.

The Fascists also got wind of a certain young Lieutenant Ico of the G.L. formation who was bringing supplies from France. They tried to locate me by interrogating the men who had made the trek over the mountains. Thank God nobody knew my real name, but the Fascists had been able to find a photograph of some partisans in which I appeared in civilian clothes in the second row. They showed it to the prisoners who had been in my unit, but they naturally did not admit to knowing me.

Plebiscite Sign and Partisan
Valle d'Aosta

An Officer with no Men

Given the search that was being made, I kept myself locked up in the apartment day and night. During one of those days a little Fiat 500 with plates from Torino pulled up at the house, the passengers wanting to buy some firewood. A friend of mine called for me and after breaking the ice, the "tourist" pulled his G.L. membership card and a letter from the CLN out of his sock. It appeared that my new assignment was to go to the American headquarters in France with another letter, still closed and sealed, containing information on supply drops.

The Fascists of the Folgore division were leaving the village on that day, to be replaced a few days later by another group from the so-called Alpine Brigade (the Green Flames) of the Monterosa Division, trained in Germany and equipped with German weapons. I took advantage of the lapse and left that night, without much hassle, for Aunt Rita's place in Balme.

The next night we were warned that the Fascists were about to enter Balme. Finally dressed again in my alpine officer uniform, I left with two friends and spent the night at Comba, two barns about an hour and a half outside of Balme. That morning we realized that we couldn't go by the usual route (Canalone d'Arnaz) because the Fascists would be able to see us from the Pian della Mussa and kill us like sitting ducks. We were forced to go by a much longer way: Col delle Serene, Passo delle Mangioire, and an overnight stop at Rossa Lake.

At the lake we found a few remnants of the Garibaldi band from the Viù Valley who were heading toward France. According to them, the Fascists would reach the lake by morning, but we were too tired to move that night. We decided instead to leave early the next morning, and at dawn we were on the road. I was on skis and the other two on snowshoes. (One of my companions was old Vulpot from Balme whom you know well. He was wanted by the Fascists because, in addition to having two sons with the partisans, he had helped us greatly.)

We had the usual long climb and then the descent and finally many interminable kilometers over flat country. When evening fell we arrived, dead tired, at Bonneval. There I found the many men whom I had left behind on the previous expedition to be treated for frostbite. None of them showed much sign of improvement, in fact two of them faced the prospect of amputation. They were housed in a French infirmary and were being extremely well cared for by a friendly, young French medical officer.

The next day, Lieutenant Walter A...arrived in Bonneval by way of the Sea Pass from the Val Grande. An officer of the G.L., he was passing through the Val Grande when he got caught in a round-up. We decided to leave together the next day for Val d'Isère. Tired and demoralized, the Iseran Pass seemed longer than ever to our weary bodies. As we were coming down the French side, one of my toes began to freeze, so at 2800 meters, in the middle of a blizzard, I had to take off my boot and warm my foot. After fifteen minutes of rubbing, the blood began circulating again and we started off. Finally, just before arriving, I fell badly and sprained my foot. I was limping for the next week.

In Val d'Isère I delivered my letter and, speaking for both myself and Walter, I explained our situation to the American officers. Basically we were two partisan officers without any men. With American help we could have organized and armed some partisans who had been interned after taking refuge in France following the September round-ups. This however was not possible because the French Deuxième Bureau (I'm sure you can guess what it is) wanted to keep the partisans as weak as possible, obviously for reasons of possible annexation after the war was over.

The days dragged by monotonously. The Americans had requisitioned three big hotels in Val d'Isère for the partisans who, having come to France to get weapons, had been blocked in by enemy round-ups. Only the Rhêmes Pass, which led down a valley by the same name into the Aosta Valley, was not occupied by the Fascists. There were numerous convoys of partisans from those valleys going back and forth for provisions, weapons, and clothing.

A little villa served as headquarters for the American PC which consisted of two lieutenants, supply officers and cooks and other American or English officers who spoke Italian perfectly. These people were rather mysterious, sometimes appearing in uniform and sometimes in civilian clothes. You will surely understand who they were.

Then there was a little English PC, staffed by a certain Lieutenant Fernandez, who was always drunk, violently anti-Italian, and really hateful. Two of the hotels belonged to the French, who had installed their garrison, command post and headquarters for their secret service. Some secessionists from Val d'Aosta were working with them. All of this took place under three meters of snow and the constant sound of shooting from every direction. The partisans, who had come to get arms made a practice of testing them before leaving. They tested rifles, machine guns, Thompsons, mortars and Bazookas.

Val d'Isère was a horrible place. There was continual Anglo-Franco-American partisan conflict. In this period Walter and I were offered various rather delicate missions (which I can't specify for now) which we didn't accept because they couldn't guarantee we would be demobilized after the war. The French, with few exceptions, tried to screw us in any way possible. They put pressure on the Americans to turn us over to their concentration camps and it was only by a hair that they didn't succeed in carrying through with their intentions.

Getting to Aosta

Shortly after arriving at Val d'Isère, I made the acquaintance of a certain Captain Jorioz from the Aosta Valley. He returned to Italy at the end of February and from there he wrote me a letter in which he invited me, if I was still free from other commitments, to take command of a battalion in the Aosta Valley. Given the uncertain situation in Val d'Isère, I decided to accept.

In his letter, Jorioz had arranged for a guide to accompany me across the Rhêmes Pass to Charvensod, in the vicinity of Aosta, where the headquarters for the Valley was located. On Sunday, February 28th (I'm using a little diary that I kept at that time) at six in the morning, my guide and I left Val d'Isère in favourable weather. The crossing was very easy. We spent the night at the Benevolo Shelter which was still standing but completely gutted inside. At seven that evening we arrived at Rhêmes.

The Germans had occupied the valley just that day. If we had arrived an hour earlier we would have run smack into them at Rhêmes. They had already set up garrisons in the valley just below. We didn't think it was wise to stay in the village that night, and in any case, nobody would have been willing to put us up. So we decided to head back to the shelter and return to France the next day. By midnight we were at Benevolo, totally exhausted, and after a few hours sleep we were already on the road back.

By now, Val d'Isère was surrounded on all sides. The Lanzo valleys were garrisoned. The only escape route would have been through the Galisia Pass above the Locana Valley. There were hundreds of partisans who needed to get back into the valley but couldn't.

I'll skip over the negotiations I had with a major from HM's forces...negotiations which went nowhere. Finally, we decided the only way to get through was by a series of night hikes. On

Saturday, March 3rd, at eight-thirty at night, we left in three groups. The first group, 30 men, was equipped with automatic weapons and carried relatively light loads. The second, 33 men, had standard equipment and heavy loads. I was in command. Group three carried powerful weapons with light loads and was led by the aforementioned British Major. The plan was for the groups to gradually dissolve as the men reached the sites of their respective bands.

Wearing heavy packs, my group crossed the Rhêmes Pass in the most bestial conditions; it was dark, freezing cold and in the middle of a blizzard. Every so often one of the men would fall in the fresh snow and ask in a pitying voice to be left to rest. That was out of the question as stopping would have meant freezing to death.

I don't know how we made it. After hiking for ten hours, we got to the shelter at seven in the morning. There was still no time to rest because a line of defense had to be prepared in case of enemy attack. The human will is incredibly strong and it adapts to the most unfavourable conditions.

Meanwhile, the English major and his men, who were travelling with no packs, arrived at the shelter at about one in the afternoon. The major's instructions were clear. "In case of enemy attack resist until I have time to get back across the border. After that, do what you like." Fortunately, the attack never materialized and I don't know what would have happened to him if it had.

The next night was another night of hiking through the snow. We passed within 100 meters of a German checkpoint at Rhêmes-Notre Dame. Then we took a day to rest in a dilapidated abandoned hut. Then another night was spent hiking. We crossed a ravine and stream near Cogne under difficult conditions. At Aymaville we passed within 150 meters of a very well armed garrison. We passed another day in an abandoned hut and then at night we again skirted within 100 meters of a Fascist blockade at Pont Suaz (Aosta) before finally climbing to Charvensod.

At last, the next day we arrived at our destination, the command post of the first independent division of the Aosta Valley, staffed by Guarini, commander of the division, Jorioz, commander of the 87th brigade, two couriers and a cook.

Ambushed

During the whole summer of 1944, the Aosta Valley and the adjoining valleys had been occupied and administered by the partisans. The Fascists hardly dared to leave Aosta. There was a transmitter at Cogne, Radio *Valdôtaine Libre*, which broadcast every night. Then, as in every other valley, came September and with this autumn month came the round-ups in grand style. All the valleys were occupied by the Fascists and permanently garrisoned. Many partisans surrendered; others found refuge in Switzerland and some in France. Only about 200 men remained in the valley, especially the high side valleys, mainly in the area of Valtournanche.

At the time I arrived, men were coming back and reorganizing for "hunting season" which normally would have opened sometime in April when the snow melted and the trees were budding. Being March, the valley sides were bare and the snow was still deep. We had to move with great care because from Aosta, with an ordinary pair of binoculars, they could have seen the smoke from a pipe. The Fascists were very strong in Aosta and they would often fire into the surrounding mountains with mortars. Every morning like clockwork, 200 men would leave the city for a round-up in the vicinity.

We were stationed on a farm at about 700 meters as the crow flies, from Aosta, in a little house on a hill with few trees nearby. Eighty meters below was the military road which runs between Aosta and Pila.

I allowed myself a week's rest but on the 16th of March a nasty incident happened. We were all inside the house, Guarini, Jorioz and I, and the cook was on guard duty. The couriers were out on assignments. Jorioz left the house to commune with nature when he caught sight of a group of Fascists on the road below. He came back and said, "There are some Fascists down on the road; let's not get excited." What he had not seen were those other Fascists who were right below the house at the bottom of the hill. As luck would have it (I learned this later), they were moving very slowly for fear of ambushes and this was the only thing that saved us.

In a few minutes we had hidden all of our things in the hay. I picked up my weapons (a Thompson and a hand-gun) and I took one last look through the back door into the house. Right through the front window, about 20 meters away, I saw three Fascists from the Black Brigade. Busy as they were looking around, they didn't catch sight of me.

I ran behind another house, alone. The others were already 30 meters ahead. Then I raced up the steep meadow toward Jorioz. We were completely out in the open and had no choice but to keep running up the open pasture toward the few scraggly trees higher up.

Then we heard the first shot. It was aimed at Guarini but missed. By that time we must have been about 70 meters away from them and the mountain was extremely steep. We were out of breath and my heart felt like it was going to explode. Soon the shots were followed by machine gun volleys, but they still didn't hit us. Picture forty men firing for a quarter hour with rifles and submachine guns at two slowly moving targets 70 meters away without hitting them, and tell me if it's true that miracles no longer happen.

Earth and grass danced around us as the bullets hit the ground. Every once in a while, we had to stop and lean against a tree to catch our breath. From where we stood, we could see the men below, on their knees or lying on the ground calmly taking aim at us. We'd hear the explosion and then the hiss of a bullet. We took the opportunity to unload a few rounds on a contingent who was preparing to follow us and I saw three of them fall. I can't be sure, but I think I at least wounded them, if I didn't actually kill them.

As we got to higher ground, we came to a dense forest where we exchanged more fire with another patrol which we could barely see for the trees. Eventually, I lost sight of Jorioz and decided to wait until night fell before trying to hook up with the others again. I waited patiently all day, sitting in the snow, with nothing to eat. I later discovered that the Fascists were convinced that they had hit me in the left arm and that they tried to find me by making all the young men show their left arms on demand.

In the middle of the night, with my weapon in my hand, I headed toward Charvensod along a mule path. All of a sudden, as I was leaning against a wall to rest, I saw a man appear on the path no more than 8 meters away. Then I saw another one and then another. They were wearing helmets; obviously they were Fascists on a night march.

I quickly released the safety on my weapon. Hearing this, they asked me to identify myself. When I didn't answer they repeated the call and soon they were looking for me with their flashlights. There were sixty of them (I found out later) and I was alone. I started to run. They didn't see me. I fell in a strip of snow. I ran and fell again, but this time my weapon hit me hard over the right eye. My face was instantly covered with blood and the Fascists were almost on top of me. I stopped the bleeding and eventually went on my way, ever so cautiously. That night I slept a few hours in the sunroom of a house, on top of a bundle of dried pea plants. I was safe by a miracle which was nothing short of divine.

Partisans, Valle d'Aosta

Raid on Aosta

I rejoined my friends in a little wood below Charvensod, a stone's throw from Aosta. We agreed that I should go to Prarayer (St. Marcel) during the night. I would inspect a battalion which was stationed there and after a few days I would go to Met de Frassy, above Aosta and from there to the Val del Grande with the battalion which had been assigned to my command.

A relatively short night march at the bottom of the valley took me to the headquarters of the II Battalion, that is, to a tent where Lieutenant Garcia (combat name) and eight of his men were living. We were only some 100 meters from a German check point on the main road, hidden only by a patch of trees.

Lieutenant Garcia was preparing a daring attack on Aosta and he asked me to help him refine his strategy. The two of us sat down to talk in a little clearing above the tent, surrounded by five or six men. No sooner did I realize that the line of men at the top of the mountain were wearing helmets, than the first rounds of machine gun fire went over our heads. We responded immediately to their Spitfire (a very rapid fire German machine gun) with our Thompsons and Brens (an English machine gun). Sustained fire from both sides ensued. Soon the rest of our men, who were camped higher up than we were, let loose a heavy barrage of cross-fire on the enemy patrol. Eventually they withdrew carrying their wounded with them. These were normal administrative hazards in the Aosta Valley.

The same night we approached the Fascist checkpoint at Pont Suaz, one of the entrances to the city. We waited for the enemy searchlight to complete one of its rounds and then we raced headlong through a path which had been opened by a friend through a field of barbed wire. There were about forty of us, all carrying the late model Thompson machine guns, three Brens, one Bazooka, and a small mortar. We arranged for the safety of the two Fascists who had helped and then we roused the others from their bunks with the butts of our weapons. They were shot on the spot. There were eight of them. They went down pleading for mercy.

Suddenly, the phone rang. Garcia picked it up,

"This is the Fascist Party Headquarters here! Why all the shooting?"

"This is the Commander of the II Partisan Battalion."

"What's that?"

"The Volunteer Freedom Corps has entered Aosta."

"But, I don't understand."

Maybe when Garcia fired into the phone, and when our men spread out into the city, shooting up a storm according to plan, maybe then he understood.

With one of the groups, I pushed right into the central square of Aosta. But we didn't see a living soul. The Fascists had shut themselves into the barracks and, thinking that the war was over, they didn't react. We shot up the hotel where one of the Fascist commanders was staying, emptying our weapons, but they didn't fire a single shot.

In the western part of the city, our Bazooka and mortar opened fire against the Testafochi barracks and the Fascist headquarters. There, too, the cowardly enemy refused to fight. After walking around Aosta for an hour and a half, we withdrew with our captured weapons. An American incendiary bomb transformed the wooden guard booth at the checkpoint into a flaming torch. We had attacked the enemy just where he thought he was most secure.

Justice, Partisan-Style

I took a few days off to rest. Then one morning with three buddies, I crossed the main road at the bottom of the valley. Our destination was Met de Frassy. Before crossing the road, we waited behind a bush for two trucks to pass, carrying men from the Black Brigade. We passed right under a large sign which said in block letters *"Banden gefahr."* Hiking all day and most of the night we arrived at Met just before dawn. There in a little house hidden from view, about thirty men were living, a detachment of my Battalion. I spent some time getting to know them and after a few days I took my first action with them. It's worth repeating here what took place in all of its detail.

We had found out that the party secretary of Aosta, no less than the commander of the local Black Brigade, had a pig butchered and had given the meat to a butcher to make sausage. This man lived in San Martino in Corleans, fairly near the Fascist checkpoint. That night we came down the mountain and took the sausage at gunpoint without further incident. We were twelve and each of us filled our knapsack with meat. We decided nonetheless to go to a nearby village to buy some wine.

As we were about to enter the tavern, someone alerted us with the news that two Fascists, one "black brigand" (from the Black Brigade) and the notorious Carlo Glarey, nicknamed Charlot, were drinking inside. We sent a civilian in to tell them that they were needed back at the post. When they came out, we ordered them to put their hands up. They didn't respond, but instead readied their weapons. Two of my men jumped on them and took their weapons. They had machine guns and pistols.

I made the "black brigand" sit down and tried to light a match to see his face. He threw his arms around my neck, crying. Two sharp smacks put a stop to that outburst of frightened

49

emotion. He was saying, "I have two brothers, a mother and a sister. Don't kill me. We're Italians, we're all brothers." A shower of blows made him fall to his knees at my feet. He grabbed my legs, screaming and crying and begged me not to injure or kill him. He swore that he had never killed a partisan. He wanted to fight on our side.

I put my pack on his back, and after tying the two prisoners by the wrists, we shoved them up the mountain. He would fall to the ground begging us not to make him run because he had an open wound on his foot. This was a delaying tactic to give the Fascist time to catch up with us. In fact, after half an hour we saw the headlights of the trucks and armoured cars approach the restaurant. That night the Fascists took sixty hostages, and for retaliation they killed the village priest.

With the help of kicks and blows, we managed to get our prisoners to walk to the camp. Then we interrogated them and I summarized the charges: Carlo Glarey, spy for the Political Investigating Office (UPI), torturer (he put steel bands around the heads of captured partisans and then tightened them with screws); he was also guilty of having burned the village of Troisvilles.

He was broken. Glarey knew we would dispense justice. With more slaps and punches we made him talk. He told us everything he knew and I assure you, he knew a lot and the information was put to good use.

The other guy, a Neapolitan called Tropea, had taken part in many round-ups and had been wounded in combat several times. He was involved, among others, in the round-up of Charvensod where I barely got away with my life. I didn't need to know more.

In the presence of all the men, that same night I drew up the official report and I signed the sentence of death. When I read it to the prisoners, they fell to ground, begging for mercy. We took them to the grave we had dug in the woods. I gave them five minutes if they wanted to pray.

At this point I must tell you that my mother has censored a page in which I describe in some detail the execution of two Fascists. She claims that from my writing, I appear to be a blood-thirsty cut-throat, which I most assuredly am not. Even though I maintain that sometimes it is necessary to kill, that is, to eliminate from human society those individuals who have demonstrated themselves unworthy of possessing life, I have never destroyed life irresponsibly, without weighing the deed.

If at times I have passed a sentence of death, I have always acted with full awareness, convinced that those individuals would have been destructive to society for the remainder of their natural lives; convinced that I was carrying out a necessary act of justice toward my friends and companions who died at the hands of the Fascists; convinced that it was necessary to apply the law of retaliation, an inflexible law which governed our relations with the Fascist enemy. There is no doubt that had I myself fallen into the hands of the enemy, I would have suffered a far worse death by torture.

Mother further claims that the story would have doubly upset you, who are far from Italy and, unlike the Italian people, are unaccustomed to the sight of corpses swinging from the trees of the city (an everyday sight during the occupation) and bodies lying in the streets. I am therefore relaying the duly corrected and censored version which has been suggested by mother and follows in brief.

....despite their pleas for mercy and their offers to join our side, justice was carried out at dawn the next day, nor could we have contemplated mercy for those sorry individuals who had terrorized villages and tortured so many of our companions. It was the 29th of March, the day of my 19th birthday, truly a strange way to celebrate a birthday.

51

Waiting and Watching

My battalion consisted of three detachments of about twenty men apiece. The command detachment with whom I resided, was stationed above Allen at a very strategic point. The two other detachments were together at By under the command of my aide an ex-marshall of the *Carabinièri*.

During the day, I lived with my command unit in a barn above Allen, while at night for greater security we slept, first in a tent and then in a log shelter a little bit higher up in the woods. Every evening when we left the barn, we hooked up a trip mechanism to two American anti-tank mines so that if the enemy were to open the door in one of their regular round-ups, they would be blown to bits. Unfortunately, this never happened.

Life was tough in the valley of the Grand St. Bernard. There were frequent skirmishes with the Germans, partly because food was very scarce and in order to survive we were forced to attack their supply convoys. Also, for command purposes, I would often have to move from one place to another with five or six men, and we would frequently have run-ins with German patrols.

During this period, German soldiers began deserting. The village people had received very stringent orders from me to bring all deserters who asked for a guide into Switzerland to my camp for interrogation. I would then take care of getting them to Switzerland, since it was impossible for me to keep them as prisoners. As a result of these interrogations, I had a very good idea of the weaponry and the strength of the German troops in the Val del Grande and in Valpelline

The remains of an *Alpenjaeger* company, which had been defeated in Bologna, made up the presidio of Valpelline, Roisan, Gignod, Étrouble, and the Grand St. Bernard Pass. They were very heavily armed, disproportionate to their numbers; they had three 88mm cannons and one 150mm cannon, two 81mm mortars and a 20mm machine gun. Surprisingly, a relatively small number of men had, besides heavy equipment, individual arms which were also very powerful. From the statements made by the deserters, it appeared that this company had absorbed the weapons from other companies which had been liquidated.

I also found out about enemy ammunition supplies and anything else which might be of help in the future. After the Liberation, I was able to confirm the reports that I had been given.

In this period, I also had an Austrian deserter translate some leaflets into German and into Austrian dialect and then I had them mimeographed and delivered by various means into the enemy camp.

Thus we came to April 24th.

The Bluff

There was a lazy drizzle and the fog was low. I heard the sentry yell "Who goes there?" One of our men, a courier from headquarters had arrived. He had been walking for two days from Valtournanche to Allen to bring me a sealed yellow envelope on which was written "For the Commander's Eyes Only". I opened it with emotion. Inside was nothing but a little note which said, "ACTIVATE PLAN 33. GOOD LUCK." I had waited eighteen months for this day. Finally....

When I had taken command of the battalion, I had received two plans; one to be used for a withdrawal of our troops, and the other in the event of German surrender. The two plans had been given code names. The time had come to effectuate the plan for a German retreat.

I gave the men five minutes to celebrate the news. Then we went to work. We had to arm some seventy civilians who had been recruited and organized as auxiliary forces for this purpose. Couriers ran back and forth. Weapons passed from one hand to another. That night at nine, at my headquarters in the priest's house, my couriers returned with their reports. All the passes leading into Switzerland had been secured. At the Grand St. Bernard Pass, rather than risk a fight, fifteen Germans had preferred to flee into Switzerland. The pass was solidly in the hands of my men.

At eleven, I was still at the priest's house, organizing and arming the auxiliary squads with the few available weapons. In the midst of these preparations, a civilian courier appeared with some interesting information. German soldiers from the garrisons in the surrounding villages were coming up the road with all their equipment. They were probably headed for the border. I decided that I would try and stop them.

I had sent all but twelve of my best men into the upper valleys. Armed with automatic weapons and an American submachine gun, we hurried down to the main road on the other side of the valley. I stationed the men in a semi-circle on both sides of the road. Soon, out of the fog we heard the noise of the half-tracks approaching with their headlights out. When they were close enough to hear the sound of men's voices, I launched into a speech that I had prepared for the purpose, *"Deutsche Soldaten..."*

I was interrupted at this point by a German voice. *"Comaraden, nicht schiessen."*

I moved in a little closer and suddenly I was surrounded by them, alone, in the midst of all those swastikas and iron crosses and enemy weapons. They were pleased that I spoke German and they anxiously asked me what we were going to do. Although they seemed to be very scared of us, they didn't have any intention of giving up their weapons. Instead, they wanted our authorization to pass into Switzerland fully armed, and from there, they hoped to return to Germany, as if the Swiss would let them through the country with their weapons.

Their commander had disappeared so I spoke to their marshall, the Storrer. We decided that we would go down the road to Étroubles and negotiate. I got into their vehicle with two of my men and we drove to Étroubles where we requisitioned a room at the local hotel. I and another partisan and the Storrer and a subordinate, sat down for a session which was to drag on at length. The Storrer was determined to follow his orders to cross into Switzerland the next day, even if it meant combat with my men who were in control of the pass. Taking advantage of the fact that it was a dark night, I decided to bluff.

"Either you surrender within five minutes or I'll have the village attacked by five hundred partisans. The area is surrounded so don't even think of escaping." They considered this information for a few minutes and then with an almost theatrical gesture, the Storrer handed over his pistol and threw his MP (*Machinenpistole*) onto the floor.

In a short time we negotiated the terms for surrender. We would take no lives but every piece of military equipment would be confiscated. Only then would they be allowed to continue their retreat.

Unit by unit, one after the other in an orderly manner, the German troops passed through a room guarded by two partisans with their machine guns levelled. Inside, I made sure that everything was turned over to us, weapons, ammunition, binoculars, compasses and anything else I thought might be useful. They were allowed to keep only their personal belongings.

Convinced that they had fallen into the hands of a large partisan force, the Germans went to get a few hours of rest. I stayed behind with another man to take an approximate inventory of what we now possessed. In addition to individual arms, we had bombs, binoculars, mines, blankets, provisions, canned food, four artillery pieces, two jeeps in perfect condition, two halftracks, a big new Fiat truck, 300 litres of gas, and thirty horses and mules with pack saddles. We had the entire German military telephone system between the Grand St. Bernard and Aosta, a warehouse full of the most diverse assortment of military paraphernalia, from telephone wire to wirecutters to replacement barrels for machine guns, a broken motorcycle, and a broken 20mm cannon, not to mention the piles of gas masks and helmets.

At dawn the next day, we watched the column of over one hundred Germans winding its way up the Grand St. Bernard road. They were escorted by four partisans carrying machine guns at the ready. What a beautiful sight! They walked downhearted and humiliated, without a single weapon, not even a hand grenade. Besides feeling the humiliation of defeat, they were angry because, with the morning light, they realized that they had been fooled. We were only twelve, not five hundred.

Nevertheless, they could congratulate themselves on having gotten away with their skins, because Nazi propaganda was famous for its depictions of partisans as bloodthirsty cut-throats. Perhaps they realized, that despite everything, people still could be generous and true to their word.

Preparations

During the morning, I beefed up the weaponry for my regular units, arming the so-called Auxiliary units (those persons who had helped us without leaving their homes). From them I formed a garrison in every village of any size. I recruited infantrymen from among the auxiliaries and the general populace and sent for a minor infantry officer (who wasn't a partisan) to organize the men and equipment into an effective fighting force. (Unfortunately the same morning, as I was testing a *Panzerfaust* we had captured from the Germans, it accidentally went off right next to me and a piece of metal lodged in my thigh; however the wound did not seem severe.)

Because of the partisans, the village people were ecstatic. Every house was open to us and to me in particular, at any hour of the night or day. Whether we wanted to eat or sleep, they were ready to cater to our every wish. You could say that the whole town of Étroubles was working for us. Some were reconnecting the telephone lines with the hotel at the Grand St. Bernard, whereas other were acting as couriers.

Meanwhile, my detachment in Valpelline had taken control of the passes and had disarmed about twenty Germans. I gave orders to send them on into Switzerland. We couldn't hold so many men prisoner, as they would have diverted necessary manpower for guard duty and they would just be more mouths to feed.

At eleven a messenger arrived from headquarters to ask about our situation and to notify me that the Black Brigade in Aosta had surrendered. The GNR had also surrendered, but six hundred Fascist paratroopers of the Folgore division (the same ones who had been dropped into the Lanzo Valley) were armed to the teeth and resisting fanatically and had no intention of surrendering. Aosta was surrounded on all sides except for mine. They requested that I join the battle for Aosta with all available equipment.

At noon, having attended to the final details, I began the descent into Aosta with five motorized vehicles and 4 artillery pieces. Although at the start, we were no more than a dozen partisans and 15 auxiliaries, as we advanced down the valleys, the men of the villages volunteered to join us with an assortment of weapons. Already people were celebrating. It was a chaos of men and arms. With no vice-commander, I didn't have a moment's peace. I was responsible for everything.

As we marched towards Aosta, according to plan, I effectively took possession of the valleys in the name of the Allied government. Finally we stopped at Seraillon, only a few hundred meters from the Aosta city limits, where I set up a check point. Explosions and gunfire could be heard here and there, but nothing in my area. At dusk the artillery was in position, the three 88mm pieces close by and the 150mm guns somewhat higher up. I informed my headquarters, which was stationed at Veynes (St. Christophe), that at dawn the next day I would be ready to open fire on the barracks and on the Fascist checkpoint. They congratulated me on my coup and informed me that Major Scala, the Fascist commander, had asked for a negotiating meeting at midnight.

I spent the night inspecting equipment and positioning my men, looking out at Aosta below. The usual sounds of gunfire and isolated explosions punctured the air, along with occasional volleys, but otherwise the night was calm. At five in the morning a messenger arrived to inform me that the Fascists had decided to surrender, and that the threat of my cannons had contributed to an early decision. The two sides had agreed that at one o'clock in the afternoon the Folgore division would evacuate the city with their weapons. They would then be disarmed and interned at St. Vincent down the valley. This strategy would avoid incidents in the city which might result in

59

"assistance" from the French, which we hoped to avoid at all costs.

We spent the morning observing Aosta through binoculars and could see that the Fascists in the courtyard of the barracks were making preparations to leave. We too were busy preparing for possible ambushes and for the heavy fighting we expected when we entered the city. Messengers came and went and signal flares went off continuously to coordinate the various battalions. Finally, the II Battalion and its commander Mosquet, who had pulled off the mid-March raid on Aosta, joined us from St. Marcel. At twelve-thirty, half an hour before the Fascists were to complete their evacuation, our patience ran out. Mosquet and I decided to enter Aosta.

Insurrection

I was very disappointed that I could not have all my men with me when we entered the city. Most of them were needed to guard the passes, but even the Valpellina detachment, which I had sent for, did not arrive in time. In contrast, Mosquet had his whole battalion of eighty men. They had taken many prisoners from the Fascist Black Brigade and thus were very well armed. He had a dozen assorted *Panzerfaust*, Bazookas and similar weapons. My twenty partisans were armed with automatic weapons plus three heavy Germany machine guns mounted on the vehicles, two *Panzerfaust*, and three cannon, all of which were manned by teams of auxiliaries. Even without the 15mm piece, which we had to leave behind, we couldn't have had more powerful weapons.

Slowly, with two columns of partisans walking alongside the armoured cars, we began the descent toward Aosta. I stayed in the car because the wound in my thigh had developed an infection and my leg was so swollen that I couldn't straighten it. The town's people were delirious with joy. As we came abreast of each house, the residents hung their flags and came out into the street to greet us. They jumped on top of the car to shake our hands. As we moved forward, we looked over our shoulders to see more and more houses festooned with flags, while in front of us, there was silence except for a few rifle shots, shuttered windows, and deserted streets.

We arrived at the city limits. Beyond a curve in the road, 50 metres away, there was the guard house of the Fascist checkpoint. As a precaution, we fired a Bazooka and a few rounds into it, blowing the structure to pieces. The Fascists had already abandoned the place.

Slowly we walked between rows of houses with the men positioned in a rake pattern, guns loaded, fingers on the triggers. A red thing dropped onto the hood of the jeep from a

61

third floor. I thought it was an Italian bomb, but it turned out to be a red rose.

We fired at two patrols. After a brief exchange of gunfire, we forced the Fascists to flee. At last we were on the offensive. But when I thought that there were six hundred Fascists in the city and no more than four hundred partisans, I got chills down my back. And to think that we had taken the initiative.

Cautiously, we advanced through the city. Ten minutes before one, we decided with Captain Jorioz to take a drive around to see if there were any Fascists left. We turned down Via Croce and Corso Battaglioni at top speed and found no one. Then we burst onto the Piazza Carlo Alberto and by the time the driver realized that the square was still in the hands of the Fascists, we were practically up against the wall of sandbags in front of the hotel. The square was swarming with them, the last contingent to evacuate the city. We faced each other for a moment, with guns drawn and ready to fire, just long enough for the driver to spin the car around and re-enter the partisan zone.

At one o'clock, the partisans filled the joyful city. Flags were everywhere. Flowers rained on our heads. The roads were so crowded with people that our vehicles couldn't move. People jumped onto the cars, sitting on the bumpers and on the hood. They shook our hands and brought food and drink. Personally, I was about to collapse from exhaustion. I was filthy, my hair had not been touched by scissors in six months, my beard was long, and my leg was killing me.

Once the cannons had been positioned at the entrances of Aosta, the men and vehicles arrayed throughout the city, my report delivered to headquarters at the Testafochi barracks, I headed directly for the hospital. By mistake, instead of going to the civilian entrance, I entered on the ground floor, where the Fascist hospital had been authorized to remain. A Fascist doctor removed the metal fragment and a nurse, also Fascist, fed me and showed me to a bed. From there, I received a visit from the four hospital doctors, who begged me to intercede on their behalf at my headquarters. They told me what they thought of the *Duce*, of Italy, Hitler, the Allies and pledged loyalty.

The next morning, despite the polite insistence of my doctors, I got ready to leave. After a hot bath, which was nothing short of divine, and with clean Fascist underwear, I left the hospital feeling like a new man.

Military Governor

I went from the hospital directly to Étrouble where I had to take care of all kinds of business. As military governor, my jurisdiction extended from the Valley of the Grand St. Bernard, up to Arpouilles, to Valpelline and Oyace. I established my headquarters at Étroubles in a room from which I could communicate by phone with all my detachments in the various valleys to arrest unaffiliated Fascists or Germans. We captured many, who were then sent to internment camps. During this time, we were always well armed and we didn't even hear about the Americans.

In my valleys, everything functioned very smoothly (as was true in every valley). We set up a kind of military administration, with my headquarters or myself issuing orders asking the people to do one thing or another. I immediately made arrangements to purge the Fascist mayors and have them replaced. A week after the liberation, elections were held in every town to vote for new municipal officials. But my job also was to decide whether the butcher should sell meat, whether dances should be held, and other details of day-to-day living.

I was also responsible for authorizing the entry of all ex-refugees who crossed the border from Switzerland. Among others, I authorized the return of Count Maroni (Ditta Cinzano) and Mr. Elter. But my most noble visitor was the Crown Princess of Piedmont, who arrived in early May. After being contacted by my partisans at the border, I received orders from Aosta to have her wait at the pass for two days. A few nights later she arrived at St. Oyen accompanied by two partisans. She stayed overnight at the priest's house and the next day, I went out to greet her. We had a nice chat and then I had her chauffeured to Aosta in my car.

On the whole, the time was marvellous for me. Not only did I have two cars, with gas, I had a white horse with a German saddle, which I actually rode twice. As you can well imagine, the partisans were the idol of the girls. And I got great satisfaction, seeing official notices posted on the town walls, which opened with, "The Commander of the Fourth Battalion orders...Signed Ico." Fortunately nobody knew my true age or they never would have obeyed me. But both the partisans and the people respected me and I had no trouble. In fact, twice I even served as a judge.

Nonetheless, I missed my parents. I didn't know if they had returned to Torino and it was still impossible to travel because of the fighting in the region. But within a few weeks, the Americans arrived and the demobilization quickly followed.

Demobilization

Late in May, I received a call from Gignod that an American armoured column had arrived and was coming up the Grand St. Bernard Pass. They had been able to contact my divisional headquarters, which had directed them to me. I must say that my first meeting with the Americans was very cordial.

Lieutenant Dussel was the commander of a force which consisted of about thirty jeeps and fifteen armoured cars. He and sub-Lieutenant Fregny shook my hand vigorously and expressed their admiration for the partisans, citing our excellent work. You, who know Americans, can imagine how the evening ended with lots of eating and drinking. Afterwards, Dussel wanted to discuss serious business. He told me that they had orders not to touch the partisan formations and to leave things as they found them. They had come solely to prevent French troops from entering Italy and for this they were counting on our help.

Relations between me and the American officers were always very friendly, partly because I was the only partisan officer in the area who spoke any English. I had an open invitation to eat at the American mess in Aosta whenever I went down to the city on business. In this way I tightened my friendships with them and got to know other American and Brazilian officers. I was really sorry that because of bad timing we never exchanged addresses. I'm sure we would have remained very close friends.

At the end of May, a high ranking American officer arrived in Aosta. As the new governor of the city, he gave orders to completely demobilize the partisan troops within a few days. Having no more work to do, I decided to go to Torino to see my parents. We met in the square at Cavoretto. My father barely recognized me in my khaki uniform.

After a week, I returned to Aosta to complete the demobilization of my Battalion. I was sad to see the warehouse piled high with weapons which had cost us so much blood and sweat, which for so many months we had considered more precious than anything in the world, which for us had become Life.

With 5000 Lire and our discharge slips, we were sent home. We went back to our cities and villages, while all around us, the johnny-come-latelies, who had been home or with the Republic until yesterday, were proclaiming themselves superfighters and partisan heroes. If at times there had been inevitable friction between us, everything now is forgotten. Because partisans, the true ones, are all brothers, always ready, whenever circumstances require, to fight for a weapon with which to defend our threatened freedom.

"But their is no rationality in the Nazi hatred: it is a hate that is not in us; it is outside man, it is a poison fruit sprung from the deadly trunk of Fascism, but it is outside and beyond Fascism itself. We cannot understand it, but we can and must be on our guard. If understanding is impossible, knowing is imperative, because what happened could happen again. Conscience can be seduced and obscured again-even our consciences.

LEVI, **Survival in Auschitz and The Reawakening.**

Enrico (far right),
Head of the Second Detachment
Entering Aosta April 25, 1945

Enrico Riding Through Aosta's Main Square
in Captured German Car, April 25th.